ABOUT ELIZABETH HOLLAND

Elizabeth Holland is a writer of romance novels. She enjoys the escapism of picking up a book and losing herself in a new world. Elizabeth is a keen advocate for mental health and often speaks out about her own struggles. She writes to escape her own thoughts. When Elizabeth isn't writing, she's usually outside walking the dog. Her favourite walks are when it's cold and rainy, so she can work on her next plot.

The Cornish Vintage Dress Shop

ELIZABETH HOLLAND

THANK YOU

Thank you to everyone who's been on this crazy writing journey with me, and to Twitter's Writing Community for always providing feedback and for sometimes feeling like my colleagues in what can be a lonely journey.

A special thank you to Deborah and John.

Thank you to my family for all of your input and support.

CHAPTER ONE

Rosie unlocked the door to The Cornish Vintage Dress Shop after popping out to grab a sandwich for lunch. It was like stepping into the arms of a loved one. Rosie immediately felt her body relax as she breathed in the familiar scent of roses. The smell transported her back to her grandmother's bedroom. Granny Maeve's perfume bottle was always on the dressing table and when Rosie was little, she would sneak in and cover herself with the delicious scent. Rosie unwound the scarf from her neck and hung it on the hook in the backroom. She pulled out her sandwich from her pocket and took a bite.

"Hello? Rosemary, are you there?"

Rosie jumped at the interruption. She hadn't heard the bell as the front door opened. She placed her cheese and chutney sandwich back on the counter. The voice was familiar. It was Wendy from the charity shop up the road. The old post office had closed down a few years ago and so Wendy had converted the building into a treasure trove filled with household items. Thankfully, Wendy didn't sell clothes. There was no competition between Ives-On-Sea's Bits "N" Bobs and Rosie's Cornish Vintage Dress Shop.

"Coming!" she called back. Rosie flicked the few crumbs from her jumper and walked towards the voice. Standing in the middle of her shop was the older lady with three black bin bags at her feet.

"There you are. I have to be quick as I've turned the sign on the door to 'closed'. These just came in with a house clearance. I'll see you soon, bye!"

"Thanks Wendy!" Rosie called after her, but it was too late. The door had already shut behind her. Wendy often dropped off clothes that came in with a house clearance, and in return, Rosie would give her any unexpected household items that appeared in her auction purchases. They supported each other.

All thoughts of her lunch disappeared as Rosie's eyes settled on the bags in front of her, each one filled to the brim with strangers' treasures. She was itching to dive in and look at them. Without pause for thought, Rosie emptied the contents of the first bag onto the floor and gasped. It was beautiful. She ran her fingers over the pile of clothes and sighed in contentment as she picked up a beautiful 1920s beaded dress. It was in exquisite condition, given its age. The blush pink beads sparkled in the overhead light and they let out a soft jingle as they brushed against each other. A handful of them showed signs of wear, but Rosie loved that. It showed that the dress had lived a life. It saddened Rosie to think she would never know the history behind it. Who had worn it? What parties had it been worn to? Rosie forced herself to put the dress back down and return her attention to the other items of clothing. Each piece was special in its own way; the black leather driving gloves to the fur stole. Although Rosie could appreciate the beauty of vintage furs, she refused to sell them in her shop. She would contact her buyer and they would collect them shortly.

After moving the bags of clothes to the storeroom, Rosie picked up the rest of her sandwich and took it onto the shop floor with her, sitting behind the till to eat. Her mind was still thinking about the clothes in the bags. Some items would need altering, others needed mending, and they all needed steaming before she could put them out for sale. Rosie finished her sandwich and took the empty plate back out to the kitchen area. As she walked past the mirror, she caught a glance of herself. She was smiling. Her red curly hair framed her face in a wild mess from the sea breeze, and her freckles were proudly speckled across her face. This Rosie was worlds apart from the woman she was only six months ago, but she was finally feeling happy and confident again. She was free, and there was nobody telling her how she should live her life. Rosie intended to keep it that way. At least she did until her phone bleeped.

There was a message from her mum asking her how the shop was going and if they could come up in a few weeks. A message from her friend in London saying she missed her and asked when she was coming home from her little quarter-life crisis. Rosie chuckled darkly at the message. Her friends all thought she would soon come running to London. The last message sent a chill down Rosie's spine as she saw who it was from. It was Oliver. Her hands shook as she opened it.

I got a letter from my solicitor today. Do you really want me to sign the papers? I've bought a little flat. It will always be your home, too. I love you and miss you. Your Oli xxx.

Rosie felt her heart constrict as she read the words over and over. He could be so charming. When Rosie had met Oliver at a University dance, she had thought she was the luckiest girl in the world. They loved each other dearly, and they worked hard to create their perfect life together. Their friends all aspired to relationships like theirs. How silly they had been to think things were perfect. How silly Rosie had been to think everything had been perfect. She stuffed her phone into the drawer underneath the till and forced herself to concentrate on the shop.

It was early afternoon and she would soon have a few stray tourists peering through the window and wandering into her treasure trove of history. The welcoming warmth of Rosie's shop drew in lots people, and few left without purchasing a piece of history. The brass bell above the door chimed as a few stragglers walked in. They rubbed their hands, warming themselves up. Rosie watched as they took in the interior; their eyes lit up. The Cornish Vintage Dress Shop was a feast for the senses.

"Good afternoon!" Rosie called, greeting them with a big smile. The two women smiled back at her and wandered over to the display of jewellery that was scattered over the up-cycled sideboard. The jewellery ranged from costume earrings to antique diamond rings, some of which were on loan to the shop, as Rosie couldn't afford to purchase them. Many of the locals had donated items to help Rosie launch. They knew the shop would benefit their little seaside village and wanted to do everything they could to support it. Their generosity and good nature had overwhelmed Rosie.

Rosie's heart swelled with pride. She had poured her heart, her soul, and her life savings into this venture. Rosie had spent hours painstakingly deliberating over every inch of the shop. Her past life as an interior designer meant she knew just how to make the shop into the welcoming time capsule that made her heart soar every time she stepped inside. There was the herringbone floor, finished with a walnut stain, which was complimented by the dark wallpaper adorning the walls, covered with floral blooms in muted pinks, blues, yellows, oranges, and whites. It was dramatic - the perfect backdrop to selling snippets of people's lives. Velvet pink lampshades with tassels hanging from the ceiling flooded the shop with light. Rosie had displayed the vintage clothes, jewellery, shoes, bags, and accessories in several ways. From shelves made of driftwood, an up-cycled antique sideboard, and brass clothes rails. Each allowed the items to take centre stage. The up-cycled furniture had come from a lovely workshop in North Wales. Rosie had bonded with the owner, Alexis, over their love for vintage items. Alexis had helped Rosie find the perfect pieces for both practicality and prettiness.

"How much is this?" The woman dressed in a beautiful fur coat held up a costume brooch in the shape of a flower and scattered with faux pearls. Rosie checked her price list and informed the woman, who immediately decided she had to have it.

As Rosie took the brooch from the woman so she could wrap in some tissue paper, she glanced at the paper tag which was tied to it with a dusky pink ribbon. Each piece in the shop had a note attached detailing as much of its history as possible. Rosie had bought this brooch at an auction in London. There was a little number in the corner showing that there was an accompanying photograph. Rosie pulled out the leather book from below the till.

"Are you here on holiday?" Rosie made small talk as she flicked through the book, looking for the corresponding photograph.

"Yes, we are. Cornwall is so beautiful but we hate the crowds in summer, so we prefer coming in the winter. Ives-On-Sea is stunning all year round and the friendly welcome from the villagers makes up for the bitter cold." Rosie recognised the smile on the woman's face. It mirrored how she felt about the place she now called home.

"Here it is." Photograph number eighty was of a young woman, wrapped in a black coat with the brooch pinned to the front of it. Rosie remembered the story behind this piece. She had been lucky enough to meet a family member at the auction. The picture dated back to 1939 and showed the woman waving her husband off to war. The woman's great-granddaughter had told her that the brooch had been a present from her husband before he left for war. Tragically, he had died and never returned. The poignancy of the photo never failed to bring tears to Rosie's eyes.

"What a heartbreaking story," the woman commented. "Thank you. It means a lot to know the history behind it." The woman was ecstatic with her purchase and promised to return whenever she was holidaying in the area.

As the door shut, Rosie wiped a stray tear that was slowly making its way down her cheek. She knew all too well the sadness of losing a husband. The feeling of having your heart torn out and trampled upon. Rosie swallowed hard to stop the memories from overcoming her. All the pain and heartbreak had been worth it. Without it, she wouldn't be here. Now she had her own little slice of heaven on the Cornish coast.

CHAPTER TWO

"Over here!" The shout came as soon as Rosie stepped foot into the pub. It was Aisha. Owner of The Scrumptious Sweetshop By The Harbour. Rosie waved over to where she sat alongside Chloe, Milo, and Milo's husband, Craig. She walked over to the bar and ordered herself a large glass of red wine. The story behind the brooch had brought back memories for Rosie, memories she had hoped to never have to confront again. Like the lady whose brooch it was, she had suffered the loss of a husband. However, unlike the poor woman, her husband hadn't lost his life in battle. Her husband was sleeping with his secretary. A much less heroic exit from her life.

At twenty-nine, Rosie hadn't expected to be almost-divorced. Her entire world had come crashing down when she discovered the affair. She had been planning a surprise trip away for their wedding anniversary and so Rosie had grabbed Oliver's laptop to check his calendar. The last thing she had expected to see were the sordid iMessages between him and his secretary. Growing up, Rosie had always been self-conscious of her looks. Her red curly hair, bright green eyes, and freckles had always made her look different. What had hurt the most about Oliver's affair was that his secretary was a blonde-haired, blue-eyed beauty. The polar opposite of her. It had shattered Rosie's confidence, broken her heart, and left her not knowing what to do with her life. She'd packed a bag, told Oliver to put their house on the market, and moved in with her parents. Living in their spare bedroom had only added to Rosie's heartbreak. The affair had stolen her life, her independence, and her confidence. Although her parents were wonderful, Rosie knew they wanted their space back and their daughter to fly the nest... again.

"You've been staring at that glass for the last five minutes." Aisha, who had wandered over to see what the delay was, interrupted Rosie from her musings.

"Sorry, just lost in thought." She sighed and took a big gulp of wine. Rosie wanted to keep drinking, to dull the memories of heartbreak and pain. Oliver's text had dragged up a multitude of emotions.

"Care to share?" asked Aisha, climbing onto the bar stool beside her.

"I sold a brooch today and the story behind it

got me thinking about husbands."

"Ahh." Aisha knew all about Rosie's cheating ex-husband.

"The brooch belonged to a woman whose husband died in war. I was thinking about her sorrow and how heartbroken she must have been. Then it got me thinking about how I lost my husband. Physically, he might still be alive, but I lost the man I married the second he started flirting with his secretary. Sometimes I wonder if I acted too fast, giving up my life in London and moving here. I was grieving in my own way and I made such a huge decision. He was planning a whole new life with her, but that didn't mean I had to overhaul my life. I could have kept my job, my friends, and my life. Instead, I threw it all away and moved here. Utterly blinded by heartbreak."

"He was planning a whole new life with her?" Aisha asked, her brow furrowed.

"I assume so. Why else would he have thrown away our marriage?"

"Oh, Rosie. It's all 'what ifs?'. Maybe he was planning a whole new life with her. Maybe he wasn't. What matters is you left him. I think you followed your heart to Ives-On-Sea. You're happy here, aren't you?"

Rosie thought about the question for a moment. Was she happy? On the day she married Oliver, she thought she would never feel happiness like it again. Yet, the day she picked up the keys to The Cornish Vintage Dress Shop and stepped inside, she felt that same happiness envelop her.

"I am. Sometimes it just amazes me that this is my life. It's nothing like the plans I once had." After graduating university, Rosie had joined a London based interior design agency. She had enjoyed waltzing around expensive properties in London and telling their owners how they should spend their money and decorate.

"Rosie, you put too much value on plans. This is life. Let's be honest, our plans would never have happened. Now, come and join us. It sounds like you need a good laugh tonight." Aisha picked up Rosie's glass of wine and led her to the table where their friends were sitting.

"Rosie's had a bad day, so she needs cheering up!" Aisha announced as they took their seats.

"Rosie, dear, your day cannot have been anywhere near as bad as mine." Milo sighed dramatically. He owned the surf school down at the beach, aptly named The Surf Shack, and often had hilarious stories of holiday makers attempting to learn a new skill.

"What tales do you have for us today?" asked Rosie. She took another sip of wine and settled into her seat. She'd only been living in Ives-On-Sea for six months and yet she felt she'd always been here. Rosie felt as though she belonged.

"I had a man turn up in an actual suit! He read the leaflet and took 'wet suit' a little too literally." The table erupted into a fit of laughter.

Later that evening, Rosie wandered down the

hill to her little shop. She paused outside and felt her heart burst with pride. The shop had only been open for a month, but so far it was going wonderfully. When Rosie bought the premises, it surprised her when she discover her budget stretched to the flat above. It was small but cosy and the sea view made up for the dated kitchen. Ives-On-Sea was a pretty beachside village that Rosie had visited as a child with her parents and brother. As she spent her evenings in her parents' spare room, she had felt a pull towards the quaint village by the sea.

Closing the door behind her, Rosie threw her jacket over the coat rack and let out a sigh of relief. Sometimes socialising was exhausting. Rosie much preferred being surrounded by clothes and the ghosts of their owners rather than real-life people. Her heart hammered in her chest as she placed her keys on the hall table. Beside the keys sat the letter from the solicitors. All she needed to do was sign it, send it back, and her divorce would be complete once Oliver had done the same. It had been Rosie who had instigated the divorce proceedings. In the light of discovering her husband's infidelity, the rage had masked the sadness. Eventually, the rage had dampened, leaving her with the raw heartbreak. The future she had once wished for was firmly out of reach. Perhaps it had never really been within her reach.

With a cup of tea in hand, Rosie went into the bedroom to take off her makeup. She had positioned her vanity table in front of the window so she could look out to sea. It was dark, but she could still see the lighthouse flashing in the distance and hear the gentle crash of waves down below. She enjoyed the few brief moments of tranquillity before taking her phone out of her pocket. With a sigh, Rosie pulled up Oliver's text. She felt her heart constrict as she re-read the words. After a quick glance at the clock, Rosie gave her mum a call. She needed a distraction from the thoughts and emotions whirling around inside of her.

"Hello?" Rosie's mother, Alice, answered on the second ring.

"Hello, mum. Sorry it's so late." Rosie was almost whispering down the phone, scared that if she spoke any louder, her emotions would get the better of her.

"Rosemary, how lovely. Did you get my text?"

"I did. Sorry I didn't reply sooner, but I was at the pub with some friends."

"It's lovely to hear how well you're settling in. Dad and I will come up soon if that's okay? I'll have a look at dates tomorrow and message you. Dad says the bus is due an MOT soon, so he wants to have a quick look at it." The bus was an extension of The Vintage Dress Shop, allowing Rosie to travel to local markets to sell her clothes. Originally, The Vintage Dress Shop was to be on wheels, until Rosie discovered the shop for sale within her budget.

"That sounds perfect, mum."

"Now, Rosie, tell me what's wrong."

Rosie's breath caught in her throat. She had

thought she was doing a good job of fooling her mother.

"The divorce papers have arrived and Oliver texted me." It all came out in a jumble, and it took Rosie's mother a few seconds to decipher it.

"Rosie, dear, he's not worth your tears. Look how well you've done for yourself. I know you two were together for a very long time and you loved him. Things will feel strange for a long while, but you're doing amazingly. We're so incredibly proud of you, darling. Oliver was a stupid man to have lost you and he's realised that. Don't underestimate your worth, Rosie. You don't need him. You've already proven that."

"You don't think I've made a mistake moving here? It's not what I had planned for my life."

"Rosie, your eyes lit up the second you stepped inside your shop. I don't think this was ever in your plans, but I think it was in your dreams. Leaving Oliver allowed you to follow your dreams. Forget those plans you once had."

As the words sunk in, Rosie knew her mother was right. But that didn't stop the pain and the grief for a life she would never have.

"Thank you, mum. Send me those dates tomorrow. Love you."

"Love you, Rosie. Dad sends his love, too."

Rosie put the phone down and glanced back out to sea. The darkness was foreboding, and yet there was something magical about it. Rosie had her whole life ahead of her. She could choose her future, not just settle for the one life had dealt her the day she met Oliver Barnett. No, she could do anything she wanted. She already had her shop and could indulge in her love of the past. Oliver had hated her love for old things. Every time she came home from an auction with a new piece, he would roll his eyes and tell her she better put it somewhere out of his sight. Looking back, he had never supported her.

CHAPTER THREE

Rosie strolled along the beachfront with her croissant in hand and the shrill squawks of seagulls flying above her. She knew to shield her food or else the birds would swoop down and take it from her hands. It was a crisp October morning and Rosie was having her breakfast alfresco before opening the shop. Truthfully, she'd drunk a little too much at the pub last night and needed the fresh air to blow away her residual hangover. She wished it would also blow away the memories of Oliver's text. Before Rosie had even switched the kettle on to make her cup of coffee, she had signed the divorce papers and posted them on her way down to the beach. It was too late now; they were sitting inside the little red postbox waiting to be collected. She had ignored Oliver's message. After all, he didn't deserve a reply from her.

"Morning!" Milo called from the Surf Shack, where he was opening up for the day. Despite the freezing cold temperatures, there was still a demand for winter surfing.

"Good morning!" replied Rosie, forcing a smile across her face. She glanced out at the cold choppy sea and wondered who would choose to go for a swim in this weather.

"You look like you carried on drinking last night," Milo commented, taking in Rosie's appearance. Despite the concealer, Rosie's face was still red and puffy from crying herself to sleep. Her outfit was plain, a simple pair of navy waist high trousers and a cropped black jumper. It was very understated compared to the flamboyant outfits she had taken to wearing since opening her shop. Rosie had woken that morning wanting to be invisible.

"Just the ghost of my almost-ex-husband haunting me last night." Rosie's attempts at jesting fell flat. Milo saw right through them.

"I'm sorry. Would you like to come in for a coffee?" Rosie glanced at her watch. She really wanted to chat to Milo, but she had an appointment for a dress fitting in half an hour and she really ought to get ready for it.

"Another time?" she called back, pulling apart the last piece of croissant and throwing it onto the sand for the ravenous birds.

"Sounds good. Have a good day!" With a wave of his hand, Milo returned to the Surf Shack and Rosie climbed the cobbled hill up to The Cornish

Vintage Dress Shop.

Rosie flicked the light switch as she stepped into the shop and smiled as the shop lit up before her eyes. This little haven never failed to put a smile on her face. Rosie switched on the coffee machine and wandered over to the accessories display. Now her mood had lifted, she was regretting the plain outfit. Perched on top of the antique cabinet in the corner was a beautiful hair clip. It had once been a brooch, but someone had since repurposed it into a hair clip. It was a beautiful bronze bee with ruby eyes. Rosie swept back her curls and used the accessory to style her hair into a low bun just as the coffee machine beeped.

With a strong black coffee in hand, Rosie was feeling ready to welcome the day. She had swept all thoughts of Oliver from her mind, and she was excited about her first appointment. Alongside selling vintage clothes, Rosie offered a dressmaking and tailoring service. Today, a woman was coming in with her sixteen-year-old daughter. The woman had explained to Rosie that she was renewing her vows with her husband. They wanted the ceremony to celebrate the family they had created, which was why she had chosen Rosie to make her daughter's bridesmaid dress. She wanted the girl to feel special in a dress that suited her style. Rosie couldn't wait to meet the girl and discover what style would suit her. There was a fizz of excitement in the air as Rosie considered all the possibilities that she could create. Teenagers made for the best clients as they often knew their own minds- at least they thought they did- and so it was a challenge, but made all the more successful when the right style was chosen.

The grandfather clock behind the counter chimed as the front door to the shop opened and in walked mother and daughter.

"Hello, lovely to meet you!" Rosie called as she walked around the counter.

"Rosie, hello. I'm Audrey and this is my daughter, Grace." The mother proudly pushed her daughter forward to greet Rosie. The girl was wearing a black roll neck jumper and checked black and white cigarette trousers which perfectly cinched in her waist. She had a classic elegance about her that Rosie knew would be fun to work with.

"Grace, lovely to meet you. Come through to the dressing room and let's chat about what you would both like. Can I get you a drink?" Both women declined the offer and Rosie led them through to the dressing room. The retro theme continued with 80s pink carpet and walls adorned with shimmering flamingo wallpaper. They took their seats on the pale pink velvet scalloped chairs and Rosie grabbed her notepad.

"So, Audrey, what are you looking for in a bridesmaid's dress?" Rosie had learned to always start with the bride. No matter how fussy the teenagers could be, the bride always knew what she did and didn't want.

"I'm quite flexible. As long as the dress is a

pastel colour and not too revealing, I don't mind." Audrey smiled over at her daughter. It was clear she was eager to please her.

"Okay. Grace, what do you want?" The girl shifted in her seat and glanced towards her mother, who gave her an encouraging look.

"I don't want pink and pretty. Mum came to you because I like vintage fashion. The 50s are my favourite." The girl took a deep breath at the end. She had come alive for those few seconds as she spoke about fashion, but she had since retreated into her shell.

Rosie pulled out her fabric swatches and flicked through them. As she appraised the girl, a dress was forming in her mind. She had just the idea.

"What do you think of this colour?" Rosie held up a pale blue swatch of fabric. It was pretty, but reserved.

"That's beautiful." Grace gasped. Her eyes glazed over as she stared at the swatch.

"I'm thinking a 50s style bardot dress, perhaps with a petticoat beneath to accentuate the style?"

The girl's eyes lit up as she listened to Rosie and built the dress in her own mind.

"That sounds perfect. What do you think, mum?" Audrey looked so happy to see her daughter so enthusiastic about the dress.

"I also think that sounds perfect." Audrey smiled over towards Rosie, a silent thank you in her eyes.

"Let me just get some measurements and I'll order the fabrics in so I can get started straight away."

As Rosie said goodbye to Audrey and Grace, she couldn't help but feel wrapped up in their excitement. There was something so magical about the way a dress could make you feel. The shopping experience could bring people together and the right piece could boost somebody's confidence.

The rest of the morning, Rosie sat sketching her plans for the bridesmaid's dress. She was excited for the fabric to come so she could start cutting and sewing. There was nothing quite like watching a dress materialise in front of your eyes. A few people popped in and out of the shop. Around lunchtime, Rosie's mum texted her to say they had booked an Air BnB for in a month's time. As she read the message, Rosie realised how excited she was at the prospect of seeing her parents. They had helped her move her belongings to Ives-On-Sea and settle her in. However, they had only spent a couple of days with her before having to return home to their commitments, and so hadn't had the chance to see the shop open. After living with them for so long after the break-up, she missed their company.

Lunchtime soon came around and Rosie turned the sign on the door to 'closed'. Often, she would make herself a sandwich in the morning, but today she wanted a treat. She meandered along the winding street up to Ives Tearoom, which was nestled in a quaint little cottage just a few doors up from the dress shop. Rosie's friend Chloe owned it and made the most delicious sandwiches. As Rosie stepped inside, the smell of freshly baked scones hit her. She immediately spotted Chloe behind the counter and walked over.

"You look awful!" her friend exclaimed.

"Thanks, Chloe. Your customer service is wonderful today." Rosie rolled her eyes. Despite having only been friends for a short while, Chloe was one of the best friends she could wish for. She was honest and had Rosie's best interests at heart.

"What's wrong?" Chloe asked. She was already making Rosie's sandwich. Her usual of mature cheese and chutney on freshly made thick granary bread. The cheese was from a local dairy and it was so creamy and delicious that Rosie could sit and just eat a chunk on its own.

"I had a text from Oliver yesterday." Rosie pulled her thoughts away from the yummy cheese.

"The home-wrecking husband?"

"That's the one."

"Do you want to talk about it?" Rosie thought about it for a moment. This morning she had wanted to talk to Milo about it, but now her mood had lifted and she didn't want to spare a second thinking about her old life.

"Not right now. Are you busy tonight?" Rosie asked.

"I've got no plans. Pub?"

"I'll see you there after work!" Rosie handed over the money and took her sandwich, wrapped in a brown paper.

"I've put in extra cheese!" Chloe called. Rosie really couldn't have asked for a better friend.

As Rosie returned to the shop, she saw someone stood on the doorstep surrounded by suitcases. She squinted to make out the figure. It was a man. He was tall, perhaps almost six feet. His dark hair blew in the sea breeze and the stubble on his face only emphasised his chiselled jaw. Rosie stood still as she continued to take in his appearance. He was very good looking.

"Hello? Do you know when the dress shop will be open again?" His voice was smooth and enticing. Rosie had to stop herself from staring. She shook her head, closed her mouth, and continued the last few steps up to the shop. He was just as handsome up close.

"Hello?" he asked again.

"Sorry, you caught me by surprise. I'd just popped out for lunch and am about to open again. Can I help you?"

"I wanted to donate some items to you." His answer was short as he gestured to the three suitcases surrounding him. Rosie couldn't help but notice the sheen of sweat on his forehead. He wore a very expensive-looking suit and must have carried all three suitcases on his own.

"Come in, let me just put this down and I'll help you with the suitcases." Rosie gestured to her sandwich, which was still grasped in her hands.

"I can manage. After you."

Rosie stepped into her shop, allowing the stranger to follow her. This man was obviously used to getting his own way and being in charge.

"Where shall I leave these?" he asked, carrying all three suitcases into the shop in one go. Rosie had to force herself to stop staring again. It wasn't often she had a handsome man in an expensive suit standing in the middle of her shop.

"If you could just place them close to the counter and I'll sort through them. Would you mind telling me a little about the owner? I like to include the history of each piece." As the words tumbled out of Rosie's mouth, she felt stupid as she read his facial expression.

"Oh, I haven't got time for that. They're a combination of my mother's, my grandmother's, and even my great-grandmother's. I have to go." He glanced down at the phone that was buzzing in his hand. Rosie felt her cheeks burn at the embarrassment. Of course, he didn't have time to talk to her about the clothes. It was another of her silly little ways of romanticising life. Hadn't she already learned that there was nothing remotely romantic about life?

CHAPTER FOUR

The afternoon had passed in a blur as a coachload of tourists descended upon Ives-On-Sea. Despite the awful weather, the beauty of the Cornish coast continued to attract people all year round. The customers, many of whom also wanted to take advantage of Rosie's bespoke tailoring services, filled the Cornish Vintage Dress Shop. She had many orders to fulfil, which she would then post off. There were orders ranging from velvet red cocktail dresses for Christmas Day to a one-off 60s inspired mohair jumper. It was great for business, but Rosie couldn't help but be a little disappointed she hadn't had time to go through the suitcases of clothes. She would have stayed late in the shop, however, she had agreed to meet Chloe at the pub that evening.

Rosie nipped upstairs to the flat to add a little more concealer to her face. Usually she wouldn't have bothered, but it had been a long day, especially given the previous evening. After swapping her plain jumper for a bright red fitted cardigan, Rosie glanced in the mirror at herself. She hardly recognised the woman staring back at her in her vintage attire. Her eyes were puffy, and they had lost their sparkle. It was strange for Rosie to feel so happy and so at home in Ives-On-Sea, and yet there was a hole inside of her. Oliver's infidelity had turned her life upside down. It still felt as though half of her was missing. Despite knowing Oliver could never fill that half again, it hurt to know she was on her own.

The walk to the pub was icy. Rosie wished she had grabbed the faux fur coat her brother had bought her as a moving gift when she bought the shop. Despite the chilly night, Chloe stood outside the pub waiting for her. Aisha was busy with a stock take this evening, and Milo and Craig had date night, so it was just the two of them.

"Shall we treat ourselves to dinner tonight? I cannot face going home to cook." Chloe asked. She linked arms with Rosie as they walked through the door.

"That sounds perfect." Rosie had been planning on making beans on toast, so dinner at the pub sounded like a wonderful idea. They walked together to the bar and ordered their food and drinks before choosing a table close to the open fire. Despite there being a steady trickle of tourists, the pub was relatively quiet. Outsiders often opted for fish and chips by the sea or the fancy seafood restaurant along the seafront. Only the locals and curious tourists ventured up the hill for the delicious pub food.

"So, how was your day after I saw you?" asked Rosie. She wanted to delay having to talk about her own problems.

"Crazy! A whole coachload of tourists arrived wanting cream teas. We ran out of clotted cream. Absolute carnage." Chloe took a big gulp of wine to show just how bad her day had been.

"They popped in to the dress shop. I also had a donation from a man whose mother had died."

"Was he hot?"

"Chloe! I've just told you his mum died, and that's all you have to say!"

"So, was he?"

"He was." The landlord interrupted their conversation as he walked over with their meals. He placed them in front of the women and walked away, a smile on his face, pretending he hadn't just heard their conversation.

"Tell me more." Chloe demanded, pouring vinegar over her fish and chips. The smell wafting over was delicious. Fluffy but crispy chips and perfectly battered flaky fish. Rosie's stomach rumbled at the sight of the food.

"There's not much more to tell. He was very good looking, dressed in a very expensive suit and obviously had little time for the dowdy shop girl." Rosie hung her head as she muttered the last few words. It was true. That was how she felt lately. Being cheated on had destroyed her confidence and she was yet to rebuild it.

"Actually, I noticed the dowdy shop girl." A shiver went down Rosie's spine at the sound of the voice. It was just as smooth as it had been earlier in the day. "I thought she was far from dowdy. Her fiery red hair and beautiful green eyes caught my attention." Rosie's cheeks were on fire as she slowly turned to face the man. He was sitting at the table behind them, still in his suit and eating dinner alone.

"I'm so sorry. I didn't mean to…" Rosie paused. What didn't she mean? To put herself down? To tell Chloe how handsome he was? She wanted the ground to swallow her.

"It's my fault. I shouldn't have been eavesdropping. Although it was nice to hear you appreciate my good looks and expensive suit." He winked at her, and Rosie felt her cheeks burn.

"I'm sorry." She didn't know what else to say.

"There's nothing to apologise for. I'm sorry I was so short today. It's just been a tough week." He sighed. His suave-business-man-look briefly melted away to show a vulnerable man who had just lost his mother. The mask quickly went back on and he took a sip of his whisky.

"No, really, *you* have nothing to apologise for. I'm sorry for your loss and I really appreciate your donation. Actually, I forgot to ask you something. When I have clothes donated, I like to donate a portion of the proceeds to a charity of the donor's choice. Is there a particular charity you'd like the money to go to?" It had completely slipped Rosie's mind earlier. She had been far too busy appreciating his good looks.

"I'll have a think about it. Why don't I pop into the shop tomorrow and talk you through the clothes?" He stood up from his table, giving Rosie little time to reply.

"If you have enough time." Rosie hadn't meant for her answer to sound so abrupt.

"I'm so sorry about earlier. I've not taken any time off from work in a very long while and they're struggling without me." He paused and sighed. "My mother admired your little shop. When I spoke to her on the phone a couple of weeks ago, she was eager to visit. Unfortunately, her illness stole her from us before she had the opportunity. But I know she would have wanted the clothes to go to you." Whilst his voice was still smooth, there was a steely edge to it. He was trying to hide his emotions. Rosie felt sorry for the man. His mother had just died and his pride was stopping him from openly grieving.

"Thank you. I'm sorry she never got the chance to visit."

"So am I. Now, if that's all, I need to leave for a conference call." Without giving Rosie the chance to respond, he turned on his heel and left. Leaving Rosie open mouthed and staring after him.

"Oh, he is hot!" Chloe exclaimed once he'd left.

"He can be quite rude." Rosie observed.

"What are you on about? He's hot and he couldn't take his eyes off you! Isn't it about time you moved on from that cheating ex of yours?"

"Perhaps. He texted me yesterday."

"I hope you told him where to stick his messages."

"I ignored it."

"Is that why you look so sad today?"

"Partly, yes. I suppose I'm still grieving for the life I walked away from."

"Rosie, you did not walk away from your life. You realised your worth and stood up for yourself. It might be a long road, but you'll get there. And I suspect Mr-Expensive-Suit might help."

Rosie groaned. She would never hear the end of this. Although a small part of her was enjoying it. She was rather looking forward to tomorrow.

CHAPTER FIVE

Rosie was determined to be positive today. After yesterday, she had been pondering her lack of confidence following her encounter with handsome-suit-man. She missed the confident girl who would walk into a room and command everyone's attention. Today, she was going to pick an outfit that made her feel good about herself. It was for her, but if handsome-suit-man wandered into the shop when she'd made herself look and feel good, then that would be a nice little bonus. She was going to dress as the independent, successful businesswoman she was trying so hard to become. Rosie pulled out a black midi pencil skirt with a fishtail bottom. It was over-the-top, but she owned her own vintage clothes shop. Why couldn't she be over the top? Rosie paired the skirt with a white blouse with an extravagant pussy bow collar. She piled her hair on top of her head and applied some red lipstick. There was nothing 'dowdy shop girl' about her today. She felt every bit as confident as she looked. A smile crept across Rosie's face as she saw herself in the mirror. It felt like her confidence had returned and with that, some happiness. There was a glimmer of the old, confident Rosie.

With her sketchbook in hand, Rosie opened the shop and started working on the abundance of designs she had to create from the previous day's coachload. There was something so soothing about losing herself in a design. There was a thrill that came with an empty page. All the things it could be. The pencil skirt she had chosen was making sitting down quite uncomfortable, but Rosie refused to get changed. This little outfit had given her a boost in confidence and so a minor discomfort was a small price to pay.

Her sketching was interrupted when her phone started buzzing from the shelf underneath the till. Rosie glanced at the screen. It was Sofia, Rosie's best friend from London.

"Hello?" Rosie answered with some trepidation. It had been a while since they had spoken. The women had been friends at school and done everything together, including marrying young. However, their lives had gone in different directions when Rosie's husband cheated on her in the same month that her best friend announced her pregnancy. With their lives going in opposite directions, they had drifted apart. In those dark months following her separation, Rosie had envied her friend who had the perfect life. She watched on social media as her friend's bump grew and eventually turned into a little bundle of joy. Of course, Rosie had sent her friend a card to congratulate her on the birth of her daughter. However, she hadn't been able to bring herself to speak to the woman, nor meet her new baby.

"Rosie, is that you?" Sofia's familiar voice filled her ears. In that moment, Rosie felt a yearning for her friend and the friendship they had shared.

"Sofia." Rosie breathed out her friend's name. The lump in her throat stopped her from saying anymore.

"Oh, Rosie. I've missed you."

Those three words cured Rosie's silence as she felt a rush of emotion run through her. This was her best friend. What had she been thinking being jealous of her? It was yet another relationship she had allowed Oliver to ruin.

"Sofia, I've missed you so much. I'm so sorry for what a terrible friend I've been…"

Rosie was cut off by Sofia, "Rosie, don't be so silly. It's me who's been an awful friend. I got swept up in a baby bubble and didn't think about what an awful time you were going through. Can you ever forgive me?"

"There's nothing to forgive, Sofia. We both had to concentrate on ourselves for a while. I'd love to stay in touch."

"Me, too. Actually, that's why I'm calling. I've

been trying to call your parents to see whether I could come visit you, but I can't get through to them, so I decided to take the plunge and just call you." Rosie's brows knitted together. Why would Sofia have been trying to call her parents? Sofia must have noticed her silence, "I tried calling you a few weeks after the breakup and your mum answered. She told me how terribly you were taking it and that you were staying with them. I should have made more of an effort after that, but I thought you might not like me turning up at the door with my happy life in tow."

"You're right. I probably wouldn't have coped well. I'm sorry, Sofia. I've missed out on such an important part of your life."

"Rosie, stop apologising! We've both been awful friends, but life happened. I'd like to see you soon. Are you still at your parents?"

Rosie took a deep breath before telling Sofia that she was now in Cornwall, running her own vintage dress shop.

"I knew you'd do something like that one day. You always did love rummaging through other people's things."

"It's wonderful. I finally feel like I've found my place. As much as I loved London, I always felt as though I was slightly on the edge of things."

"I know you did. I still want to come see you, even if you're far away! Let me have a chat with Harry and perhaps we can come down for a weekend."

"That would be perfect! Text me some dates and I'll arrange some cover in the shop so I can show you round."

Rosie put the phone down with a huge smile on her face. It finally felt like the missing pieces of her life were slotting back into place. The bell above the door chimed.

"Welcome to The Cornish Vintage Dress Shop!" she called as she placed her phone back under the till. Before Rosie even looked up, she knew who it was standing in front of her. The smell of his expensive aftershave gave him away. It was Mr handsome-suit-man, whose name she was yet to learn, but whose face she enjoyed staring at.

"Good morning! How can I help you?" Rosie placed her sketchbook to the side and looked up to meet his gorgeous blue eyes. Despite their previous encounters, Rosie hadn't realised just how beautiful they were. The piercing colour captured her attention, and as she looked deeper, she could see the pain buried underneath his charming exterior.

"This very good-looking man in an expensive suit has decided on a charity." He was teasing her, and he had dressed in yet another expensive suit. Rosie wondered whether it was for her benefit, or was it how he dressed every day?

"Which charity have you chosen?" Rosie was always interested to hear which charity a person had chosen. It told you a lot about a person.

"I'd like to donate the money to the local charity. Is it called Ives-On-Sea Bits 'N' Bobs?" He sounded unsure of himself.

"Yes. It's run by Wendy, just a few doors away."

"That's the one. We've lived Ives-On-Sea for my entire life, so it feels right to give something back."

"I'll make a note." Rosie grabbed a post-it note and jotted down the charity. Not that she was likely to forget this encounter.

"What's your name?"

"It's Rosie."

"Nice to meet you, Rosie. I'm Matthew Carter." He put his hand out for her to shake. Rosie couldn't help but lose herself in the feel of his hand wrapped around hers.

"Lovely to meet you, Matthew. Do you have a spare few moments? I'd love to go through the clothes with you, see if you can share any memories. If you still want to..." Rosie was afraid she'd overstepped the mark and was asking too much. He was clearly very busy.

"I'm yours all morning." He gave her a dazzling smile. Rosie liked the sound of that. She blushed at her thoughts.

"Let's bring the suitcases into the dressing room so we can make a mess. Would you like a coffee?"

With the suitcases spread out and coffees in hand, they began sorting through the clothes. Rosie left the door to the changing room open so she could hear the bell above the door if any customers wandered in.

"This pile is my mother's, that's my grandmother's, and that's my great-grandmother's." Matthew had sorted the clothes into piles.

"Thank you, Matthew." Rosie was in her element. Generations of vintage clothes.

"Please, call me Matt. Now, what would you like to know?"

Rosie glanced down at the clothes which were spread across the plush pink carpet. A satin wedding dress immediately caught her attention. She picked it up and inspected it. There was a beautiful sweetheart neckline, delicate sleeves, dainty buttons up the back, with a small bow at the top. It was breathtakingly beautiful.

"That was my great-grandmother's. I never met her, but I've seen pictures of her in the dress." Matt smiled fondly as he glanced at the dress.

"It's beautiful, Matt. It reminds me of my wedding dress." The words slipped out of Rosie's mouth before she could think about it. That seemed to happen to her a lot around Matt.

"I didn't realise you're married." Matt looked as shocked as she did.

"I'm not. Well, I am. I'm waiting for my divorce to complete." Rosie wanted the ground to swallow her up. Why had she just told Matt so much about herself? It wasn't even anything good. He now knew what a failure she was. She couldn't even keep her husband happy.

"Oh, I'm sorry." Rosie couldn't be sure, but it

looked as though Matt's eyes lit up as she told him she was getting divorced.

"No, I'm sorry. I shouldn't have let that slip out." Her eyes locked with his and she felt her heart rate increase.

"You must have looked beautiful." Matt's voice was a whisper as he stepped closer to her. The dress dropped from her hands and she stepped forward to meet him. He towered above her five-foot frame. Slowly, she raised her eyes up to meet his as he moved his hand to cup the side of her face. Breathlessly, she waited for him to lean in towards her. However, the moment never came.

"I ought to go." Matt jumped back. He looked ashamed of himself. Rosie felt the distance between them, both physically and emotionally.

"Sorry," she whispered, feeling like an idiot. Matt had lost himself in the moment. He had pitied her and wanted to make her feel better. Then he had realised his mistake and now he wanted to be as far away from her as possible.

"I have a meeting at midday." He pointed to the clock. It was quarter to twelve.

"Sorry, I completely lost track of time."

"Me too. Thank you for taking such good care of my mother's clothes." With a final smile, he left without looking back at her. Rosie felt her heart rate slow as she watched him walk away from the shop. That had been close. She couldn't allow herself to get close to him again. She wouldn't ever allow herself to get close to another man again. It wasn't worth risking losing everything.

CHAPTER SIX

Later that evening, as Rosie waited for her microwave meal to stop rotating, a text came through from Sofia saying they could come down the following week. She'd even found a little beachside cottage for them to stay in. Rosie felt excitement bubble away in the pit of her stomach at the idea of seeing her friend again. It wouldn't be like old times. Things had changed, but it would be nice to see someone who knew her from before her separation.

Finally, the microwave pinged, signalling that the lasagna was cooked. Oliver had done most of the cooking, so it had come as quite a shock to her to discover she had to cook dinner for herself every night. The microwave meals were a treat for when she'd had a long day. Without them, she'd most likely be having toast for dinner. Just as Rosie was about to take her first bite, there was a knock on the door downstairs. It sounded as though someone was knocking on the shop's door. She sighed and put down her fork.

She tiptoed downstairs in the dark. Rosie didn't know who was out there, so she didn't want to turn the light on and alert them to her presence. What if it was Oliver? Her heart hammered in her chest. What would she do if he had found her? Rosie breathed a sigh of relief as she reached the bottom of the stairs. She could see out of her door to the shop next-door. It wasn't Oliver knocking; it was Matt. Her stomach filled with butterflies as she unlocked the door. What could he want at this time of night?

"Can I help you?" she called. He was still peering into the shop and jumped as she appeared from next door.

"Rosie. Hi, sorry, I didn't know if you'd be in." His words tumbled out of his mouth in one continuous stream as he reached up to scratch the back of his neck.

"I don't live in the shop." Rosie raised her eyebrows at him. Had he really expected her to be inside the shop at almost ten o'clock?

"Sorry. I've been working all afternoon. I completely lost track of the time." He glanced down at his watch. Rosie couldn't help but notice he was still wearing the suit from earlier.

"It's okay. So, can I help you?" Rosie's mind wandered back to her dinner that was sitting on her dining table waiting for her.

"Yes, I just wanted to apologise for being rude again. It really isn't me. I'm so sorry."

"You weren't rude. It was my fault for getting caught up in the history of the clothes and keeping you for too long. Please, don't feel bad." Rosie tried to smile reassuringly at him. Had he really come all the way over here to apologise?

"Well, I'd still like to say sorry. I was also wondering whether I could buy you dinner at the pub tomorrow, say seven-ish? I've found some photographs of the clothes I brought in earlier. I thought you might like to go through them."

"I'd like that." Rosie bit her lip after the words had flown out of her mouth. She hadn't meant to accept.

"Brilliant. I'll see you tomorrow. Sorry for disturbing you." He turned on his heel and walked off towards the sea. Rosie quickly closed the door before leaning her head against it. Why had she allowed herself to accept his invitation? Did he think it was a date?

Rosie ran upstairs to the flat. She needed to speak to someone. Rosie grabbed her phone and dialled Chloe's number.

"Hello?" Chloe answered on the third ring.

"He's asked me out for dinner!" The words breathlessly tumbled out of her mouth.

Chloe didn't even need to ask who she was talking about. "Oh, that's so exciting! Are you excited?" Chloe let out a little squeal of delight.

"I don't know, Chloe. I'm sworn off men. I

don't think he meant it as a date."

"Stop trying to convince yourself you don't like him!" Chloe was perceptive.

"I'm so lost in my head, Chloe. He's attractive and surprisingly endearing for a man that swings from rude and cold to bubbling and awkward. Am I just swooning over him because he's one of the first handsome men that's paid me any interest since my separation? He came in to discuss his deceased mother's donation, and yet here I am, acting like a giddy teenager because I'm craving a man in my life."

"Are you craving a man in your life? Rosie, had Matt not walked into the shop, would you have gone looking for him?"

"Well, no. I'm quite happy on my own in my little shop. I told myself I'd never trust another man again. Never allow one back in my life."

"Rosie, not every man is Oliver."

"But I'm supposed to be this new, and better, version of myself. I can't just let some man in a fancy suit waltz in and sweep me off my feet."

"Rosie, you don't need to prove yourself. You've already done that. Look at the life you're building. Having someone standing beside you isn't a sign of weakness. You deserve happiness, Rosie. Whether that's your shop, an enormous chocolate cake, or a handsome man. Don't overthink things. Enjoy your dinner with him and see what happens next."

"Do you think I'm ready for this?" The words

escaped Rosie before she could hold them back.

"I think you're ready for some fun. Don't put too much pressure on yourself. You're not even sure it's a date. Anyway, what are you going to wear?" With that, Chloe had changed the subject.

CHAPTER SEVEN

Rosie tossed and turned in bed all night. She couldn't stop thinking about her dinner with Matt. With a sigh, she threw the duvet off of herself and pulled on an old tracksuit. Some sea air was just what she needed, and the sun was just rising. Rosie grabbed her travel mug from the cupboard and quickly made a coffee. It wouldn't be as good as the ones she could buy from Chloe's cafe, but at least it was caffeine. It was eerily quiet as Rosie made her way down to the seafront. Living in Ives-On-Sea out of season was a real treat. Rosie knew that as soon as the months rolled into spring, these streets would be filled with families heading down to the beach with their buckets and spades, teenagers pausing for their photographs to be taken with a dramatic Cornish seascape in the background, and locals would be flitting around trying to appeal to every whim the tourists might have. Despite the chaos, Rosie was looking forward to it. She'd just caught the end of the tourist season when she opened the shop.

Rosie's phone buzzed. It was a text from her mother. She smiled as she read the message, asking what Rosie thought of some fabric she was planning on working with today. Rosie ignored the message and carried on down to the beach. She walked over to the rocks on the far left and took a sip of her coffee before dialling her mother's number.

"Rosie dear, what's wrong?" Her mother's answer was instant.

"I'm okay. Just fancied a chat." Rosie cursed her voice for wobbling.

"Rosemary Witham, even as a baby, you didn't enjoy conversing before nine in the morning. You can't pull the wool over my eyes. What's wrong?"

"A man asked me out for dinner. It's not a date." Rosie emphasised the fact that it was not a date.

"If it's not a date, then why are you in such a state about it?" Her mum had a point.

"I don't know, mum. He's attractive. Really attractive." Rosie bit her lip to stop herself from saying anymore.

"So you're going to dinner with a very good-looking man?"

"Yes."

"Isn't that a good thing, darling?"

"Yes..No. I don't know."

"Rosie, you're overthinking this. You don't even think it is a date. Why is dinner with this man any different to when you meet your friends at the pub for dinner?"

Rosie wanted to scream down the phone. It was different because she wasn't attracted to any of her friends. She didn't get lost in any of her friends' eyes.

"I can't help overthinking, mum. I promised myself I'd never let another man hurt me like Oliver did."

"I know, but you can't hide away in Cornwall for the rest of your life. You need to live."

"I am living. I've moved across the country and opened my own shop. Is that not enough?"

"Oh darling. You've achieved so much since leaving Oliver. You know this is nothing to do with what you've achieved. Rosie, you deserve to be happy. I know you said you don't want another relationship, but I don't think that's what you want deep down. You'd never be happy being alone."

Rosie rolled her eyes as she looked out to sea. Her mother knew her too well.

"I'm scared, mum. What if I like this man?"

"Rosie, you have to stop overthinking everything. It's just dinner. You don't even know whether it's a date. Have you considered talking to a therapist about how you're feeling? Perhaps you need someone to help you process the trauma of your marriage ending."

Rosie let out a sigh as she considered her

mother's words. Maybe speaking to someone about it was what she needed. Her mother was right. She'd never be truly happy alone, and yet she felt as though she couldn't ever let a man back into her life.

"Okay, I'll have a look at therapists. I better go, mum. I've got to get some items out on the shop floor before I open for the day."

They said their goodbyes and Rosie put her phone back in her pocket. She really needed to get back to the shop, but she couldn't tear her eyes away from the horizon. There was a dull ache in her chest as she remembered the day she promised her life to Oliver. It had been the happiest day of her life. The moment where she knew she had found the one to spend the rest of her life with. Not once had she considered the possibility that they would break-up. It had always been them against the world, and their wedding had only reaffirmed that. Rosie blinked to stop the tears from coming. She forced herself to stand up and start walking back to the shop. It would do no good to drag up those painful memories.

*****

The day passed slowly, with only a few customers popping in. Rosie was grateful for all the tailor-made items she had to focus on. Not only would it keep her busy, but it would also support the costs of running the shop out of season. It was one less thing that Rosie had to worry about. The idea of losing her shop filled Rosie with fear. It was all she had left in the world, and it was truly hers.

During her lunch break, Rosie had turned the sign to 'closed' and nipped up to the flat. She pulled out her ancient laptop and made a coffee while it whirled to life. All morning she had been replaying her conversation with her mother over and over in her head. Maybe therapy was a good idea. Someone to help her cope with all the thoughts and feelings that were threatening to overcome her.

By the time Rosie returned to the shop, she had booked in a session with a therapist for the following evening. After having spoken to her doctor, Rosie decided to find a private therapist. The doctor had warned her that the NHS waiting list could be a couple of years. Thankfully, Rosie still had a small amount of money left over from the sale of the property she shared with Oliver.

The afternoon was quiet, so Rosie continued to go through the pile of clothes in the back that needed mending and putting out on the shop floor. One bag that Wendy had brought in had a handbag in it. Rosie opened it expecting to find the lining needing to be repaired, instead she pulled out a wedge of letters, tied up with what looked like a belt from a dress. There was nobody in the shop, so Rosie undid the belt and started to read the letters. They were love letters, dating back to the First World War. Rosie was surprised to find letters and their replies in the pile. She took them over to the till and sat down to read them, starting with the oldest.

My dearest George,

It's been five minutes since I waved you off on that train and it feels as though my heart has broken into a million pieces. I miss you terribly.

I look forward to receiving your first letter.

Yours,

Florence

Rosie continued to read through the letters. George wrote back to Florence as soon as he received her letter. Rosie learned that the young couple were to be married once George returned from war. They were very much in love. George's letters were heartbreaking as he did his best to hide the reality of being on the frontline from his sweetheart. Rosie read Florence's last letter to George. She detailed the plans she had made for their wedding that would take place as soon as he returned home. Rosie's hand trembled as she picked up the last letter. She immediately noticed the difference in the handwriting. As her eyes travelled to the top of the page, Rosie felt her heart constrict at the mention of the war office. George was dead.

Putting down the letters, Rosie swiped angrily at the tears threatening to spill from her eyes. Poor Florence. She'd planned their lifetime together while waiting for him to return, and yet it never happened. Rosie shook her head to clear it. A tap on the window brought her back to the present.

Chloe was standing outside, staring in at her.

"Why aren't you getting ready for your date?" Chloe pushed opened the door and stood there with her hands on her hips, demanding an answer.

"What?" Rosie glanced up at the clock. It was half six. "Oh, no. I have to cancel."

"You are not cancelling. Come on, let's get you ready."

Rosie felt sick. How could she meet a man for dinner after reading those letters? It was clear to her that love wasn't worth it. It only ever ended in heartbreak.

Before Rosie could even consider how she would get a message to Matt to cancel, Chloe was flicking through the clothes on display, looking for something for Rosie to wear.

"Where's that gorgeous full length dress, with the sweetheart neckline, and little cap sleeves? It was navy, with a gold celestial pattern sewn onto it." Chloe's eyes were shining as she looked round for the dress.

"It's out the back." Rosie's reply was automatic. The dress had been gorgeous, but it hadn't fit in with the shop's vintage aesthetic. Without saying another word, Chloe ran out to the back and came back with the dress.

"Upstairs, come on." She pulled Rosie up from her seat and pushed her towards the door. Rosie knew there was no point in arguing. Chloe always got her own way.

She quickly showered and allowed her hair to

air dry as Chloe applied a small amount of makeup. Rosie insisted on just a smattering of concealer, a dash of blusher, some mascara, and a slick of clear lip gloss. Her hair had dried into a halo of ringlets. Instead of leaving it free and unruly, Chloe platted it into a side fishtail, leaving a few tendrils down to frame her face. She looked in the mirror and had to admit, even she thought she looked pretty. It was casual, but clearly she had still made an effort.

"You look perfect for your date!" Chloe announced. Was it a date? Their almost-kiss suggested it was, and yet Rosie couldn't wipe the memory of the look of regret that had flashed across Matt's face. No, this wasn't a date. He was simply meeting her for dinner to show her the pictures of the clothes he had donated. It was almost a business meeting.

"I'm going to be late." Rosie took a deep breath and forced herself to forget about the letters. This wasn't a date and so she didn't have to worry about getting her heart broken again. It was just dinner with an acquaintance.

Chloe left her as she pulled on a pair of gold pumps and speed walked up to the pub. Her feet were freezing, but she didn't have time to find a pair of boots to match the dress. Time had run away from her and she was now running late. She had forgotten to put a jacket on in her haste to leave and to her surprise, there were gentle flakes of snow falling. An incredulous chuckle escaped her lips. It rarely snowed by the sea. Quickly, she made her way up the hill and through the door to the pub. Instantly, she spotted Matt sitting facing her to the right, a big grin on his face.

"Evening." Matt greeted her and smiled as she wandered over to him. He was now wearing a navy suit that matched her dress. It was obviously tailor made as it fitted him perfectly, hinting at his muscular physique beneath. She was glad she'd taken the time on her own appearance since he looked so dapper.

"Sorry I'm late," Rosie apologised as she took the seat opposite him.

"It's okay. I said seven-ish." He winked at her. Rosie felt a smile spread across her face. She'd only just sat down, and he was already putting her at ease.

"Good, because I'm never on time." A nervous chuckle escaped Rosie's lips.

"I'm always on time, but I don't mind waiting." He winked again. Butterflies fluttered around Rosie's stomach.

Matt cleared his throat to get Rosie's attention. She had missed him speaking.

"Sorry. I'm a little nervous. It's been a while since I've done this." Rosie felt a blush rise on her cheeks. What if Matt saw this as a business meeting and she'd just suggested it was a date?

"It's been a while for me, too. I recently split up with my girlfriend of six months. Well, I say girlfriend. It was quite casual. Anyway, enough about our pasts.

Let's focus on the future. Prosecco?"

"That would be lovely, thank you." It was a relief to move the conversation on from her past. Rosie didn't want to discuss her failed marriage on their first date. If it was a date.

Matt soon returned with the Prosecco, and before Rosie knew it, her first glass had disappeared in a blur of bubbles and conversation. In that time she had learnt a lot about Matt. He lived near Canary Wharf and worked as a stockbroker. By day he was a serious businessman at work, and by night he was a serious businessman at home. He worked hard, but it seemed like work was all he had in his life. Rosie reminded herself that he had just left a relationship and had probably thrown himself at his job. Just like she had done with the shop. He had ambition, and he was kind. Rosie was keen to get to know him better.

"Did you grow up in Ives-On-Sea?" Rosie asked. She was careful how she worded the question to avoid bringing up any painful memories of Matt's mother.

"I did. You can trace many generations of my family back to Ives-On-Sea." There was a glimmer of sadness in Matt's eyes.

"Impressive. We used to come on holiday to Ives-On-Sea every summer. We rented the little blue cottage by the harbour."

"My parents own that little blue cottage! Well, I guess I own it now." He dropped his gaze to the glass on the table in front of him.

"What a small world. Do you think we played together as children?" Rosie was trying to steer the conversation onto happier topics.

"Probably. Even as a child, I enjoyed the company of pretty girls. So, where were you living before you moved here?" He was moving the conversation away from Ives-On-Sea.

"I was living in Greenwich, so not too far from where you are."

"Perhaps it's fate we met. Normally, I'd blame my mother for match-making, but I don't think even she was good enough to play cupid from beyond the grave." Matt let out a little chuckle as his dark humour trickled through. Rosie leaned across the table and placed her hand over his. His hand was soft and warm beneath hers. She squeezed, and he turned his hand so the palm was upwards before interlocking their fingers. They shared a small smile. The hustle and bustle of the surrounding pub disappeared. They were in their own little bubble. Both were grieving for different things, and yet they had found solace in each other's company.

"Did your mum often match make for you?" Rosie asked.

"She tried. Whenever I spoke to her on the phone, she would tell me about another local girl. She was desperate for me to move home."

"You didn't want to?"

"Ives-On-Sea hasn't always been a happy place for me. My mother loved me, but it wasn't the happiest of childhoods." Matt let go of her hand and took a sip from his drink. His eyes appeared to glaze over as his guard went back up.

"So, what do you do for fun in London?" It was time to change the subject.

The food was lovely, but Rosie couldn't remember what she had eaten. Her attention had been solely on Matt. Somehow, she ate, but her eyes barely left his. Small smiles flickered between them as they both felt the anticipation between them growing.

"Shall we go for a walk?" Matt asked. He pushed his card back into his wallet and slid it into his trouser pocket. He had insisted on paying for dinner.

"It's snowing!" Rosie exclaimed, peering out of the window. It was dark outside. The moon shone above the sea, casting a silvery glow. Soft flakes of snow fell from the sky, landing on the cobbles outside. It would be slippery. Rosie breathed a sigh of relief that she hadn't chanced heels.

"Come on. I'm not ready to leave you yet." Matt slipped his jacket around her shoulders and held out his arm for her to take as she navigated the slippery path. As Rosie stepped closer to him, she breathed in his scent. She let out a giggle as she realised he even smelt expensive.

"Care to share your joke?" Matt asked.

"I was just thinking about how you even smell expensive."

"I like the nice things in life. Maybe that's why I like you." He winked at her and turned back to the path. Slowly, they made their way down to the beach. Neither of them wanting to leave the other's side. There was a sense of peace in being together.

"It's beautiful." Rosie sighed as she stared out at the sea.

"It is." Matt was staring straight at her. His breath was raspy. His arms snaked around her waist and pulled her against him. He towered above her, his eyes boring into her. Rosie boldly reached up on her tiptoes to press her lips against his. Her cold lips moulded against his. They were soft and inviting.

"I need to go." Rosie pulled herself away from Matt and, without looking back, she walked away. She could hear him calling after her, but she ignored him. This wasn't supposed to happen.

CHAPTER EIGHT

Rosie winced as the sun shone on her, waking her from a deep slumber. She'd forgot to close the curtains the previous evening. As the seconds passed and Rosie lay in bed, last night's events came back to her. She had dropped her guard and allowed herself to become too close to Matt. Kissing him had been a terrible mistake. Rosie groaned into her pillow. She would have to see him and speak to him. Tell him she wasn't looking for a relationship. Rosie's groans were interrupted by her phone ringing. It was Sofia.

"Hello?" Rosie answered the phone, attempting to keep her tone light.

"Are you okay?" Sofia had known her for too long to be fooled by her false tone.

"No. I kissed a man last night." Rosie sat up in bed, running a hand through her unruly curls.

"Oooh, tell me." Rosie could hear Sofia pulling out a chair to sit on. She could imagine her sitting in her sunlit kitchen with a coffee in hand, waiting to hear Rosie's gossip. They'd spent hours sat on those kitchen stools talking about life, watching their husbands preparing the barbecue in the garden, and dreaming of when their children would be running around playing together.

"It was a mistake."

"Why?"

"I can't allow myself to get close to another man. What if he breaks my heart?" Rosie climbed out of bed, wrapped her dressing gown around herself, and went to make a cup of coffee. If she sat at her own kitchen table, she might feel that bit closer to her friend.

"Rosie, I know you think what Oliver did to you was awful. But, I knew you during the good times and you were so happy in a relationship. You wanted to spend your life with him. We were hoping for our children to grow up together. I know Oliver has ruined that, but can you really not imagine still having that life? You could have all of that still."

"I don't think I could risk putting myself through that again. Sofia, it broke me." Rosie's voice cracked.

"Oh, Rosie. I'm sorry, and I'm so sorry I wasn't there for you."

"It's fine, honestly. It's just nice being able to talk to you now. I've made friends here, but it's lovely to have someone that knew me before and during Oliver."

"Rosie, I need to go. Ava's waking up. Don't give up on the future we dreamt of."

"We'll see."

"Anyway, I meant to call you to ask you whether there's anything you want me to bring you from London?"

"Sofia, I'm in Cornwall! There are still plenty of shops and online shopping available."

"Oh, I forgot about that."

Rosie chuckled, "you'll get to see it soon."

"Yes, I'm already all packed!"

Rosie said goodbye to her friend and finished her coffee. She wished she had Matt's number so she could at least text him and apologise for running away. Instead, she would have to speak to him face-to-face. Dread filled her at the thought.

Getting ready for the day came as a relief to Rosie. She focused on her makeup, put her hair up into a messy bun and took her time choosing her outfit. Finally she settled on a plaid pinafore, over a black long-sleeved top and tights. It was a relief to keep her mind busy while she was getting ready. The last thing she wanted was to allow her thoughts to wander to Matt's beautiful eyes.

It was an uneventful day in the shop. Despite Rosie's best attempts to forget about Matt, every time the door opened, her head shot up, wondering whether it was him. It wasn't. Her emotions were all over the place and Rosie was eternally grateful for her mum suggesting she find a therapist. That evening's session couldn't come soon enough.

The therapist Rosie had chosen offered telephone appointments. After locking up the shop, she made herself a quick sandwich for dinner and waited for the call. Rosie felt sick as her phone lit up with an unknown number. She knew that whatever happened, they would drag a lot of unpleasant memories and emotions up over the next hour.

The hour passed in a blur, and Rosie felt surprisingly positive when she put the phone down. It had been almost cathartic telling a stranger about what had happened to her over the past year. The therapist had pinpointed her lack of confidence that stemmed from Oliver's betrayal.

They agreed it was something Rosie needed to work on. She had to know her own worth to know that she was worthy of another relationship. Rosie was also disheartened to hear she needed to work on trusting people. It was something she already knew, but not necessarily something she wanted to confront.

Rosie rolled her eyes as she saw her phone ringing. It was her mum.

"How did it go?" her mother asked as soon as Rosie answered the phone.

"Mum, I've only just put the phone down!"

"Sorry, I just wanted to know how it went." Rosie could hear from the echo on her mother's end of the line that she had her on loud speaker.

"It went well. We're going to focus on growing my confidence and trust."

"Oh, Rosie. That's such good news."

"This will be the turning point for you, love." Rosie's father called out.

"Thank you, dad. I'm quite positive."

"How did your date go?" Trust her mother to call with a barrage of questions.

"It wasn't a date. I need to go now as my dinner's burning." The lie slid effortlessly off of Rosie's tongue. Usually, she loved speaking to her parents. However, the last two days had been emotionally draining and Rosie just needed a break. She said her goodbyes and sat down on the sofa, breathing out a sigh of relief.

With her mind spinning from everything, Rosie opened up her laptop and started work on designing some leaflet for the Sunday market she attended. She needed to refocus her attention, and her business was the perfect distraction.

CHAPTER NINE

Rosie woke Wednesday morning to the sound of seagulls squawking outside her bedroom window. They were perched on her window ledge making the atrocious noise. She glanced at her phone to see the time. It was just gone eight. The shop was closed Wednesday mornings, allowing Rosie to run errands. Today she was planning to get the bus to the next village to print the leaflets she'd designed last night. The first time she had got on a bus in Cornwall had been a shock to the system. She'd become spoilt by the consistency of public transport in London. At any time of the day, Rosie could jump up and be on a train in a few minutes. However, here in Cornwall, buses adhered to a strict timetable and so she would need to be quick to catch the eight-thirty bus.

Throwing on a pair of vintage jeans and an

old jumper, Rosie tied her hair up into another messy bun and grabbed a coffee in a travel mug. With a USB stick in hand with the designs on it, she ran out the door. Quickly, she made her way down to the harbour where the bus would stop.

"Rosie!" called a voice from behind. Rosie felt her heart hammer in her chest at the sound of the voice. She slowly turned around to face Matt. "I was wondering if I could have a word?"

"I'm in a bit of a rush."

"Oh, sorry." He sounded disappointed, and Rosie saw a flash of something in Matt's eyes.

"I'm catching the bus in to the next town. Sorry, they only run one every two hours, so if I miss this one, I won't get back in time to open the shop." Rosie explained. Her words were coming out at a hundred miles per hour.

"Sorry, I don't want to make you miss your bus. Could I pop into the shop this afternoon?"

"Of course. I'll see you later." Rosie waved as she ran towards the bus stop. She could see the bus at the end of the road.

Out of breath, Rosie took the first seat available. It was busy today. She really needed to look into getting a car, but she was so busy in the shop that she rarely went out of Ives-On-Sea. She sucked in a few deep breaths as the bus climbed the hill out of the costal village that she'd grown to call home. Relief washed over her as the wheels kept turning, putting distance between her and Matt. Her relief was short-lived when she realised she would have to speak to him that afternoon. She couldn't put it off any longer.

The bus continued along the costal road, stopping occasionally to let a few more people on. Rosie rested her head against the window and stared out across the sea. It was a beautifully bright day, and the sea was an inviting, sparkling blue. If Rosie hadn't known how cold it was, she might have been tempted to dip her toes in.

Finally, they arrived in town and Rosie went straight to the printing shop to have her leaflets printed. Once they were safely stowed away in her tote bag, she had a rummage around the charity shops. She had a couple of hours until the bus returned. She picked up a few dress rings for the shop, knowing they matched a couple of outfits she already had in. Once she was finished shopping, she popped into the village cafe and ordered a hot chocolate. With half an hour until the next bus, she wandered down to the beach and sat on a bench. There was a young family walking across the sand, a child strapped to the woman's chest and their spaniel bounding across the sand in front of them. Rosie felt her heart constrict at the sight of them. Despite wanting to avoid another relationship, it was still a future she yearned for.

Rosie's phone vibrated in her pocket. She pulled it out to find a picture from Sofia. It was of Ava, holding a box of Rosie's favourite chocolates. Sofia had captioned the picture 'bet aunty Rosie can't get these in Cornwall!'. Rosie chuckled to herself. If life had gone to plan, she might be standing next to Sofia, pushing her own pram. Rosie typed out a reply, finished the dregs of her drink, and made her way to the bus stop.

The journey back to Ives-On-Sea was much the same as the journey there. Rosie found herself staring out of the window, but she was no longer seeing the view. Her mind kept wandering back to the family on the beach. But her mind kept replacing the woman with her own image. Rosie was finding it harder and harder to ignore the fact that her heart yearned for a family of her own.

Once Rosie had dropped the leaflets at the shop, she popped up to Chloe's cafe for some lunch. She'd been ignoring her friend's phone calls since her not-quite-date with Matt.

"There you are! Why don't you answer your phone?" Chloe honed in on her as soon as she stepped through the door. Rosie laughed at her friend's dramatic greeting. She walked over to the counter and inhaled the smell of fresh bread. Chloe was always baking something in the little cafe. Whatever you chose from the menu, it would be delicious.

"Hello, Chloe!" Rosie smiled sweetly at her as she pulled out her purse.

"Don't you 'hello, Chloe' me!" Chloe put her hands on her hips and narrowed her eyes. Rosie had to suppress a giggle at her friend's reaction.

"Look, I'm sorry. Why don't we have a proper catch-up at the weekend? Let's have fish and chips with Aisha?" Rosie hoped her friend would accept the olive branch. It would also be nice to catch up with the women in Cornwall, who had quickly become her closest friends.

"Fine, but I want all the gossip!" Chloe rolled her eyes and went about making Rosie her usual order.

"Thank you."

With her sandwich in hand, Rosie opened the shop. The bright weather had brought out a few tourists today, meaning Rosie was only halfway through her lunch before her first customers came in. After that, there was a steady stream of people popping in. Rosie did her best to find the items they were looking for. Each person left with a smile on their face and a leaflet for Rosie's Sunday market in their bag. It was proving to be a very successful afternoon. At least, it was until Matt turned up.

"Hi." He stood awkwardly in the doorway. "Should I come back later?" His eyes swept over the customers in the shop.

"No, come in. It's been busy all afternoon."

"Did you catch your bus?" he asked. Rosie had to stifle a giggle at the small talk.

"I did, thank you." She kept her answer short.

"I'm sorry about the other night." Matt's voice was a whisper. Thankfully, there were no locals in the shop. Rosie could only imagine how quickly news of her failed date with Matt would whip around the village.

"Matt, it really wasn't you. I'm getting over a

bad relationship." Rosie didn't want to say too much. She didn't want him to know that she was damaged goods. To know that even her own husband had decided she wasn't worth having around.

"I'm sorry." His eyes moved from hers, and he looked at the counter below. Rosie felt herself grow cold at his reaction.

"You weren't to know." Rosie wanted him to just make his excuses and leave.

"I wouldn't have kissed you if I'd have known." His words cut through her. Rosie felt the tips of her ears burning. She had never felt so embarrassed in her life. He was openly admitting to regretting kissing her.

"Well, thanks for that. Now, if you wouldn't mind, I've got customers to tend to." Rosie was incredibly grateful to see a woman walk towards her, holding a bundle of clothes. Matt looked suitably embarrassed.

"Of course, sorry. I'll see you around." He gave her an awkward wave and left the shop. Rosie wanted to curl up in a ball and shut out the world, but she had customers waiting to be served. She took a deep breath and held her head up high. Just because Matt regretted kissing her didn't mean she couldn't be confident about herself as a shop owner.

CHAPTER TEN

Rosie was still seething from Matt's visit when she shut the shop and made her way up to the flat. She could barely contain how annoyed she felt. Grabbing a bottle of red wine from the cupboard, she poured herself a large glass and turned some music on. Rosie had neighbours on either side, so she couldn't turn it up loud enough to drown out her thoughts, but at least it was something to disguise the lonely silence. She felt the tears pooling in her eyes, but she refused to give in to them.

In an attempt to distract herself, Rosie grabbed her sketchpad and started fleshing out the designs for Grace's dress. She wanted to see the girl look confident in the outfit. Her own confidence was at rock bottom, but that didn't mean she couldn't help others with theirs. Rosie must have missed the sound of her phone pinging as *Wham!* echoed throughout her flat. Matt had texted her half an hour ago. Rosie took a gulp from her wineglass before opening the message.

Hope you don't mind, but Chloe gave me your number. I wanted to apologise for earlier. I don't think I came across how I wanted to and I'm worried I might have upset you. Matt xx

Rosie scoffed at the message. He had come across exactly how he wanted to. Rejecting the woman with emotional baggage. With the wine sloshing around in her empty stomach, Rosie typed out a reply.

No need to apologise. I know exactly what you meant. Don't worry, I'll keep the kiss a secret. You don't have to suffer through the embarrassment of being connected to the divorced woman.

As Rosie hit send, she couldn't hold off the tears for any longer. The future she yearned for would never happen. She wasn't worthy of it. Oliver had made that very clear. Matt didn't reply, but that didn't stop Rosie keep checking her phone. For the next half an hour, she checked her phone every two minutes, in between finishing the bottle of wine.

Dread weighed down in the pit of Rosie's stomach as she heard a knock from downstairs. She crept over to the window, trying to duck down out of sight. Standing outside her front door was Matt. A gasp escaped her lips as he looked up. Rosie tried to move out of the way, but she was too slow. He saw her. He knew she was up there. She had to open the door. Her legs wobbled a little as Rosie walked down the stairs to the door. She wasn't sure whether it was from nerves or the effects of the bottle of wine.

"Hi." She swung open the door, almost hitting Matt in the face.

"I got your text." He shrugged and pushed his hands into the pockets of his suit trousers.

"Thank you for popping by to tell me my phone's working." Rosie went to shut the door, but he reached out in time to stop her.

"Rosie, I didn't mean to offend you. I just got a bit awkward in the shop earlier and didn't know what to say. You've probably noticed, but I'm not very good at emotions. My parents weren't the best role models." He was looking down at his feet, refusing to meet her eyes.

"You don't regret kissing me?" Rosie's voice came out as a squeak.

"I loved kissing you, but I hate how it made you feel." He sighed.

"Would you like to come in?" As the words tumbled out, Rosie knew it was a bad idea. She'd already had too much to drink. The last thing she needed was to invite Matt in, pour another drink, and tell him all about her messy break up.

"No, I don't want to disturb your evening. I just wanted to apologise for how I came across earlier."

"I'm also sorry for my text. I've had a bit too much liquid courage." Rosie was sure Matt had already guessed that from the way she was swaying in the doorway.

"Can we start again?"

"You want to forget the kiss?" Rosie could hear the despair in her own voice.

"No, I don't want to forget the kiss. I was just thinking perhaps I could take you out for dinner again? Even if it's just as friends. I'd like to get to know you better."

"That would be nice." A huge smile spread across Rosie's face, mirroring Matt's own reaction to her answer.

"Good. I'll pick you up tomorrow evening and we'll go for dinner. Perhaps down at the harbour restaurant?"

"That would be lovely. Thank you, Matt."

"I'll see you at about seven-ish?"

Rosie nodded, and Matt raised his hand to wave goodbye. Both of them walked away with a soppy smile on their face. Rosie was sure her therapist would have been proud of her for saying yes. Although, she might not have agreed with Rosie's consumption of a bottle of wine and her reply to Matt's text.

CHAPTER ELEVEN

"Excuse me, dear?" Rosie jumped at the sound of the voice, pulling her from her daydreams. Stood opposite her was an older lady, holding a 1950s swing coat.

"Sorry. How can I help you?" Rosie quickly tried to appear professional.

"I asked if you had anywhere I could try this on?" The woman had a kind smile, but her tone suggested she was becoming frustrated.

"Of course. Let me show you." After leading the woman to the changing rooms and making sure she had everything she needed, Rosie returned to the till and finished the dregs of her cold coffee. She'd been useless all morning. All Rosie could think about was her date with Matt that evening. Nerves were bubbling away in the pit of her stomach, sloshing around with last night's alcohol.

"It fits perfectly. I'll take it." The woman placed the coat on the counter.

"Wonderful. I'll just see whether there's any picture of documents to go with the item." Rosie looked down at the tag. She was disappointed to see that the item had nothing to accompany it. "Sorry, it looks like its history is unknown."

"That's okay. I've got plenty of history to share with it." The woman beamed back at Rosie.

She rang the item up on the till and then wrapped it in tissue paper, before putting it in a bag and waving the woman off. It was heart-warming seeing a piece of history leave with someone who would cherish it. Rosie glanced at the clock. Only another hour until closing time. She could use that time to decide what to wear.

Finally, it was time to close the shop. There had been a steady stream of customers all afternoon, keeping Rosie busy. But most importantly, keeping her from deciding what to wear. Chloe had been so good at choosing the last time she saw Matt that she was almost tempted to text her and ask for some help. However, Rosie couldn't face the barrage of questions that Chloe would no doubt have. Instead, she closed the shop and went up to her flat. She was sure there would be something in her wardrobe.

The harbour restaurant was fancy. Rosie didn't know whether they had an evening dress code, but she knew she would have to dress up to fit in. She glanced inside her wardrobe while the shower was heating up. Tucked away at the back was a gorgeous suit that she had planned to wear for her wedding anniversary. The outfit was so beautiful that Rosie couldn't bring herself to throw it away, despite the associations. With a deep breath, she pulled the outfit out and hung it on the front of the wardrobe. It was all white. Waist high, flared, tailored trousers, with a bralette top and an oversized blazer to match. It would be perfect for tonight's dinner, and Rosie was sure her therapist would be happy with her confronting the association.

Once she had showered, dressed, and had applied a little makeup, Rosie grabbed her handbag, and slipped on a pair of black heeled sandals. She made her way down to the harbour. Her toes were freezing, but the shoes suited the outfit. She would have to tread carefully so she didn't slip over on the icy cobbles. It was dark by now, but the stars twinkled above and there were still people milling around. Some heading up towards the pub, others walking down to the harbour restaurant or the chip shop. There was a relaxed atmosphere. The end of another week, and everyone was ready to enjoy their well-earned weekend.

"You're early this time!" Matt's voice interrupted Rosie's musings. She rolled her eyes at him, but couldn't stop the smile that spread across her face, giving away her joy at seeing him.

"Good evening." She smiled coyly up at him. Despite her heels, he still towered above her. He was wearing a navy tailored suit tonight.

"Look who's wearing a suit!" he teased.

"I should have texted you to make sure we didn't match!"

"Yes, I almost wore that exact outfit." He raised his eyes brows as he opened the door to the restaurant, standing aside to allow Rosie to walk ahead of him.

"Hello, do you have a reservation?" A waitress approached them as they walked in. Rosie was glad she had dressed up as she glanced around the restaurant. There were only a handful of free tables, and everyone was dressed up for the occasion.

"Yes, there should be a table for two booked under the name of Carter." The woman checked her iPad before leading them to a table in the corner. It was disappointing not to have a view of the harbour, but she could make do with looking at Matt instead. The waitress handed them each a menu and left.

"Have you been here before?" Rosie asked, glancing down at the menu. As soon as the question left her lips, she regretted it. Hearing about how many other women Matt had wined and dined here would not help her in her attempts to learn to trust others.

"I've never been. It's quite new, isn't it?" He looked up from the menu, meeting her eyes for the first time since they had sat down. Rosie found herself getting lost in them. She had to force herself to look away. Hadn't he just asked a question? Thankfully, the waitress came back to take their drinks order, saving Rosie from her embarrassment.

"Shall we share a bottle of Rosé?" Matt suggested.

"That sounds perfect." She beamed back at him. Oliver never shared wine with her. He would only ever drink beer. She shook her head, forcing any thoughts of Oliver to scatter. There was no place for him here on her date with Matt.

"Have you been here before?" Matt asked once the waitress had left.

"Once. I came for dinner with my parents when I picked up the keys for the shop. It was a bit of a celebratory meal." Rosie smiled fondly at the memories or her dad standing up to make a toast. The entire restaurant had turned to watch and Rosie's cheeks had burned with embarrassment, but her father hadn't cared. He had been too proud of his daughter to think about whether others might have been watching or listening.

The waitress brought over the bottle of wine and took their food order. As they waited for their food, Matt asked Rosie a few questions about her parents. She didn't return the questions, worried that he wouldn't want to speak about his mother so soon after her passing. Dinner came, but that didn't halt their conversation. They both spoke about their time at university and their jobs. Rosie told Matt about her time as an interior designer.

"Do you miss it?" he asked. He placed his cutlery down on his empty plate, giving her his full attention. Rosie chewed her mouthful as she thought about the question.

"No, I don't. Everything I loved about the job, I still get from the shop. The joy of seeing someone choose the right style for them is the same when they try on a new dress as it was when they found the perfect carpet."

"That sounds lovely." Matt's eyes had glazed over as Rosie had spoken.

"Do you enjoy your job?" she asked.

"Sometimes, but I'm wondering whether my job has taken over my life."

Rosie didn't know what to say to that. Matt took a sip of his wine and Rosie did the same as she considered his answer. Right now, her job was her life. It was what she wanted. But was it stopping her from living her life?

"Anyway, I have the most important question of the night…" he paused for effect as he swirled his wine around in the glass. "Pudding or no pudding?" Rosie giggled to disguise her relief.

"Of course we have to have pudding! It's not dinner out without pudding."

Once their sticky toffee puddings with custard had been devoured, Matt suggested he walk Rosie back to her flat. It was much later now, and there were far fewer people milling around.

"Thank you." Rosie smiled at him. It had been a while since a man was worried about her getting home safely. Well, someone other than her dad.

Rosie tried to hide the smile on her face as they stepped outside the restaurant, and Matt took her hand in his. Their hands swung together in between them as they walked up the cobbled hill. Rosie could feel the tension between the two of them growing. Sparks were firing from their connected hands. His fingers intertwined with hers. Rosie tried to control her breathing as her heart hammered in her chest. The world felt like it might shatter around her if she took the wrong step.

"Here we are." Matt looked down at his feet as they stopped outside her front door.

"We're here." Rosie confirmed. She didn't know what to do next. All she knew was that she didn't want to let go of Matt's hand.

"I should go." He made no move to let go of her hand and walk away.

"Would you like to come in?" Rosie's mind was shouting at her. Screaming at her to stop and thinking about what she was doing. However, she couldn't stop herself. It was too late. It had been too late the moment she had lost herself in Matt's eyes.

"I'd love to."

Rosie fumbled for her keys, still refusing to let go of Matt's hand. This might be the biggest mistake she would ever make.

CHAPTER TWELVE

Rosie woke with a fright. She had been on a date with Matt. Not only had she been on a date with him, but they had stumbled home together, unable to take their eyes off of each other. Rosie's heart rate quickened as she remembered kissing Matt as she fumbled for her keys outside the door. Eventually, she'd found them and they stumbled through the door together. Rosie stilled her breathing, taking a second to quieten the deluge of memories. She focused on her surroundings. She was sitting up in bed. The curtains were wide open, and she could feel heat emanating from beside her. Rosie turned her head to see Matt lying on the pillow beside hers. His dark hair was tousled and his muscular chest was on display. He was very handsome. Rosie groaned internally. What had she been thinking? They would regret this burst of passion. Well, she might regret it if she could remember it. Rosie's memories became rather blurry once they had entered her flat. If only they had gone back to his place, she could have snuck out this morning. Unfortunately, that wasn't an option. Instead, she slowly climbed out of bed, careful not to wake him. Once untangled from the duvet, she tiptoed over to the bathroom and firmly locked the door behind her. A shower. That was what she needed. Rosie took a deep breath and fanned her face in an attempt to calm herself down.

A long shower later, Rosie towel dried herself and reached for her clothes, where she usually left them on top of the washing basket. They weren't there. All she had was a tiny towel to protect her modesty. With her fingers crossed, she wrapped the towel around herself and hoped Matt was still asleep. He wasn't. Not only was he awake, he was sitting on the bed dressed in his boxers with two freshly made coffees on the bedside table. It was refreshing to see him in something other than a suit.

"I thought you might like a little caffeine boost after you jumped out of bed this morning." He was teasing her already.

"I thought I was being quiet. Do you mind?" She motioned for him to turn around while she slipped on her dressing gown.

"No, that's fine. You had no inhibitions at taking your clothes off in front of me last night." He chuckled at her apparent shyness this morning. Rosie groaned, and he turned around. Steam had covered the bathroom mirror, so she hadn't seen her reflection, but Rosie knew her face was bright red. It always was after a hot shower. The bright white of her dressing gown would only frame her fiery face and hair. It was one of the few items of clothing that Rosie owned which wasn't from the shop. Instead, it was a present from her mother from The White Company. An indulgence, but her mother had insisted on treating her during one of their first shopping trips after Rosie left Oliver. She was just so happy to see her daughter out and about again, she wanted to celebrate the moment.

"You don't have to stay and make small talk. You can leave." Embarrassment was filling Rosie. As much as she loved his company, she would have liked to have been on her own to wallow in her humiliation.

"I don't want to leave. Rosie, you know nothing happened last night?" A lazy smile spread across Matt's face as he reclined on her bed and took a sip from his cup of coffee. Unsure how to proceed, Rosie walked round to her side of the bed and joined him, taking the other cup from him.

"What do you mean?" she asked.

"I mean, you sat down at your kitchen table and fell asleep. I brought you into your bedroom, where you pulled off all your clothes and begged me to stay."

"Oh, no!" Rosie wanted to scuttle under the duvet and never emerge again.

"It was rather entertaining. You were asleep as soon as your head hit the pillow. I'd already promised to stay, and I didn't want to break my promise to you." Matt glanced down at his coffee as a light blush spread across his cheeks.

"Thank you, Matt." There was an awkward silence as she digested Matt's words. Rosie was relieved that nothing had happened between them. Especially since she couldn't remember it.

"What time is it?" she asked. It could be midday for all she knew.

"It's only eight. Are you opening the shop today?"

Rosie thought about it and wandered over to the window. It was raining and blustery outside, so it was unlikely any tourists would stop by. Everybody would stay wrapped up indoors, with a hot chocolate, refusing to venture out into the near arctic temperatures.

"I could leave it shut?" It came out as a question. Was Matt suggesting they took the day off together? A day in bed with Mr-handsome-suit-man could be just what Rosie needed.

"I have a meeting in an hour," he said. Rosie's cheeks immediately flamed red. He hadn't been asking her to spend the day in bed with him. All thoughts of their day in bed together fled her mind as she hid her face in her hands.

"Sure. I need to get working on some tailored items even if I shut the shop." She brushed off the feelings of rejection and reminded herself of just how busy she was. She certainly did not have the time to laze around in bed all day. However nice it sounded.

"Why don't I meet you for lunch?" Matt's tone was tentative as Rosie refused to meet his gaze. It still mortified her how she had allowed her mind to run away with itself. It seemed she just couldn't stop embarrassing herself in front of him.

"That would be lovely." The words escaped Rosie before she could even consider her response. She wanted to see him again, and he hadn't even left yet. She finally looked up to meet his eye and saw his smile reflected in them. He genuinely wanted to see her again.

"I'll swing by around lunchtime." Matt finished his coffee, pulled on his clothes, and leant down to kiss her before leaving.

Rosie stared longingly after him as he let himself out of her flat. "What am I doing?" she whispered to herself. She closed the door and leaned against it. "This isn't me."

Aware she would see Matt again later, Rosie took her time choosing her outfit. She picked out a grey roll neck, long-sleeved top, and a pair of chequered cigarette trousers that hugged her curves. With her curly hair tumbling down her back, Rosie grabbed her sketchbook and went to open up the shop. She had a certain glow about her today. Her time spent with Matt had left a smile on her face.

With a fresh coffee in hand and the sign on the door turned to open, Rosie took advantage of the morning lull. She unlocked her phone to see a few missed calls from Chloe. As she was pondering calling her friend back, her phone started vibrating in her hands. It was Chloe.

"Hello?" answered Rosie.

"Finally! You better have a good excuse for not telling me you were having dinner with Matt last night! I had to hear it from my sister who saw you there." Chloe's shrill tone came down the phone. Rosie could just imagine her buzzing around the kitchen, getting everything ready for the lunch orders, while shouting down the phone. "You should have at least told me you got home safely."

"I got home *very* safely." Rosie blushed as memories of the previous evening came back to her.

"What does that mean?" Chloe squealed down the phone.

"I mean, I had company."

"Oh, my god. Really? Is he as good looking naked as he is in his suit?"

"Nothing happened! I'm going now, Chloe. I'll see you tonight!" Rosie was rolling her eyes as she cut her friend off. She was not ready for a full debrief just yet.

The morning sped past as Rosie busied herself by making Grace's 1950s style bridesmaid dress. The fabric had finally arrived and Rosie was eager to bring the dress to life. She had opened the shop, but only a few locals had popped in for a chat and a browse. Rosie was sitting at the reconditioned singer sewing machine in the corner, making a rough template for the dress. Even the template looked beautiful. Rosie couldn't wait for the moment she could reveal the dress to Grace and Audrey.

"You look beautiful." Rosie jumped at the voice and spun around to see Matt stood in the doorway, laden down with sandwiches and coffees from the Chloe's cafe.

"Thank you. You look rather nice yourself." He was wearing yet another suit. Although, he'd gone casual today and not put on a tie. Rosie finished the line she was working on before making her way over to Matt. She reached up on her tiptoes to give him a kiss. Thankfully, his hands were full, so he couldn't wrap his arms around her waist and pull her closer. They didn't have time for that and lunch. He looked strangely out of place in the middle of all the vintage items. His modern suit and shiny shoes. And yet, Rosie couldn't take her eyes off of him.

"Come on, let's go upstairs and eat." Rosie didn't want any of the locals wandering past and peering in.

Rosie led Matt up to her flat and into the kitchen, where there was a table and chairs. It was small, but until that morning, it hadn't been something Rosie had to worry about. On one wall was a single line of white kitchen cabinets with a wooden worktop. The other wall was a window with the table and two seats beneath it.

"I didn't know what you liked, so I asked the woman in the tearoom and she said this was your usual." Matt gestured towards the sandwich he had just put down.

"Thank you." Rosie replied, sitting down opposite him. "How has your morning-" The sound of Matt's phone ringing interrupted Rosie. He pulled it out of his pocket and frowned at the screen.

"If you need to get it, then please do." Rosie busied herself by taking a sip of her coffee. She was trying to ignore the interruption.

"It's fine. I'll just send them a text telling them I'm busy." Matt cancelled the call and quickly tapped out a message. "Sorry about that. Anyway, I brought the pictures we forgot to go through yesterday. They're all copies. I thought you might like to keep them." Matt produced a backpack and pulled out a wedge of photographs.

They spread them out across the table as they ate, careful not to leave any grubby fingerprints on them. Matt told Rosie the story behind each one, and had even written the story on the back. Such as the 90s dress he remembered his mother wearing on one of their holidays abroad. He had really taken the time to ensure their history lived on with them.

"Thank you for this." Rosie smiled as she thought about how much time it must have taken him.

"They're just copies. I wrote it on the original so I could always look back and remember. You gave me a reason to remember my mother, and as much as it hurt, I was glad I did it." Rosie reached out to take his hand in hers. With his attitude of indifference, it was easy to forget Matt was still grieving for his mother.

"She'll always be a part of you and your memories. Please, don't feel you have to hide your grief from me."

Matt sniffed before taking a deep breath and smiling at her. "I'm fine. Thank you. It's just been a tough time. Once I get back to London and throw myself back into work, it will all be okay." Back to London. Rosie had forgotten that little detail. They lived hours apart. He lived somewhere she could never see herself moving back to.

"Why did you leave Ives-On-Sea?" Rosie asked.

"I wanted more than this little seaside village offers." Matt's reply was curt, and Rosie suspected there was more to it.

"Do you see yourself ever moving back?" She had to ask or else she'd keep wondering.

"No. Once I've sold my parents' properties here, then I have no reason to return. There's too many bad memories here." No reason to return. Rosie felt her cheeks flush as she realised what an idiot she had been. She was just a distraction for while Matt was sorting things out. Perhaps she was even his rebound from his recent breakup. Her stomach flipped, and she put down the half of a sandwich she had left, no longer hungry.

Matt's phone rang for the fifth time. "I should probably answer this," Matt commented. Putting down his half-eaten sandwich, he stood up.

"Of course. I need to head back to the shop now, as I have an appointment this afternoon." That was a lie. Rosie didn't have any appointments this week. She was keen for him to leave. Some time on her own was what she needed. She'd broken down her walls and allowed Matt to spend the night, but it was clear there was no chance of a future for them.

"Shall I come over tonight?" Hope lit up his eyes.

"Sorry, but I said I'd meet Chloe and Aisha for dinner."

"I can always pop over when you get home. Just give me a message. If not, then what about tomorrow?" He looked disappointed. Perhaps he was hoping for one last night of passion before he returned home.

"I have to be up early tomorrow to take the bus to the market. Why don't I text you?" Rosie knew he would turn on the charm and change her mind if she said no, and so this felt like the sensible option.

"Sounds good. I'll see you tomorrow." He didn't ask Rosie any questions about what the bus was or where the market was. Instead, he leant across the table and gave her a chaste kiss before picking up his phone and leaving. Rosie looked after him, feeling empty inside. Sundays were Rosie's favourite day of the week. She took her vintage bus over to the neighbouring town for the market. There she displayed some of her more modern vintage clothes and often came home with an empty bus. Matt could come along with her and experience it. There was something about the bus that relaxed Rosie. She had bought the bus before the shop.

Whilst still living with her parents, her father had spotted the bus for sale and had bought it for her. Together, they worked on it and brought the vehicle back to life. As they fixed the bodywork, her mother was busy stitching new seat covers. It pulled Rosie from the depths of her wallowing and was the start of her finding a new direction in life.

CHAPTER THIRTEEN

After work, Rosie ignored Matt's phone call as she got changed to go over to Chloe's for dinner. She changed out of her figure hugging outfit and into something more suitable for an evening of gorging on food and wine. Rosie grabbed a bottle of rosé from her fridge and made the short walk over to Chloe's cottage. The whole time, Rosie was dreading bumping into Matt.

    Chloe's cottage was down by the harbour. It was a beautiful home with the sea almost on the doorstep. The cottage had once been home to one of the many fishermen, and their families, that inhabited Ives-On-Sea. Rosie walked straight in, not bothering to knock. Chloe had messaged her to say she would be in the shower after work and to let herself in. The smell of freshly baked scones hit her as she stepped through the door. Despite spending all day, every day cooking, Chloe still enjoyed baking treats at home for when her friends popped over.

"It's just me!" Rosie called out. Although Chloe was expecting her, she didn't want her to worry that just anybody had walked in. A muffled reply came from the bathroom and Rosie wandered over to the kitchen to put the bottle of rosé in the fridge for later.

The shower shut off and Chloe called down, "I'll just be a moment! Help yourself to anything."

"Take your time. I'm fine waiting." Rosie wandered into the living room and took a seat on the blue and white striped sofa. Chloe had embraced the nautical theme. She pulled out her phone and checked her messages.

There were two, one from Matt and the other from Oliver. Rosie sighed. Her life was confusing enough when she only had Oliver to think about. Why had she complicated matters further? She didn't know whose message she dreaded the most and so she chose to just open the one that was sent first. It was from Matt.

Really would love to see you tomorrow. Have a lovely evening xxx

Rosie almost wanted to throw her phone across the room and ignore the message. He was very full on for someone who was just indulging in a holiday romance. With a deep breath, Rosie opened the other message. She had never replied to Oliver's previous text and so she dreaded what this one would say.

My solicitor said you've signed the papers. Please speak to me, Rosie. I'm not signing until we speak. I love you xxx

It took a lot of restraint to stop Rosie from actually throwing her phone this time. Why did he want to speak to her? Hadn't he put her through enough? Rosie texted Matt back, saying she was looking forward to seeing him tomorrow, and gave him the details of where to meet her the following morning. She then turned her phone off and turned her attention back to the evening.

"Sorry, I just really needed to wash the flour out of my hair." Chloe apologised as she walked into the room dressed in her pyjamas and her hair up in a towel.

"No, Chloe, it's me who should be apologising. I should have offered to have you both over to me. I'm sure you'd much rather have a quiet night than hosting. After everything that's happened, I just need to talk to someone."

"Rosie, it's fine. Aisha should be here any minute and she's going to bring some fish and chips with her for dinner. Hope you don't mind, but I filled her in on your date with Matt."

"Thanks. At least I don't have to go over it all again when she gets here." Rosie sighed. "Why don't you dry your hair and I'll pour us some wine?"

"Are you okay?"

"Not really, but I'd rather tell you both at the same time."

Half an hour later, Chloe's hair was dry, Rosie was on her second glass of wine, and Aisha had just arrived with dinner. The girls sat on the floor of Chloe's living room with their dinner on their laps.

"So, what's wrong?" Chloe asked.

"I'm so confused. I went on a date with Matt last night."

"Why didn't you tell me about Matt? I had to hear second hand gossip from Chloe!" Aisha interrupted.

"I'm sorry, Aisha. It's all just been a bit of a whirlwind."

"It's okay. Come on, tell us what's wrong."

"We went on a date last night. It was perfect, and he came back to mine. Nothing happened."

"Why didn't you immediately message me?" demanded Aisha.

"I was a bit too busy embarrassing myself to get my phone out." Rosie threw a chip at her friend, who caught it.

"How was your date?" Aisha asked, her eyes wide.

"Amazing, and then at lunch today he was talking about why he moved away from Ives-On-Sea. I don't think he'd ever return. There's no hope of a future for us."

"Did he say that?" Chloe asked.

"He said he doesn't see himself ever moving

back to Ives-On-Sea. I don't think I could ever move back to London, so we've hit a bit of a dead end."

"Are you ready for a relationship?" asked Chloe.

"I'm not sure." Rosie sighed and took a sip of her wine. She'd been asking herself the same question.

"Then that's your answer. Just have some fun with him, but know it's not going anywhere. Just make sure you're both on the same page." Aisha made it sound easy.

"I don't know. Can I really do this? He's very full on for a holiday romance. I'm already getting caught up in the possibilities of what we could be."

"I think it would be good for you. It might help you properly put Oliver in the past." Chloe took Rosie's empty glass from her hand and refilled it.

"Oliver is in my past. He just won't accept it."

"Are you happy when you're with Matt? How does he make you feel?" Aisha asked.

Rosie thought about the question. She didn't need to think for too long because as soon as she thought about Matt, a huge smile spread across her face. "I had butterflies the moment I saw him. It felt so different from when I first met Oliver, but perhaps that was because we were younger. There was no anticipation of what was to come. I don't know. There's a spark between us, but I hardly know him. Whenever I think of him, this huge soppy smile spreads across my face."

"You're happy when he's by your side, so just

enjoy that. You hardly know him, and you might never get to know him, but that doesn't mean you can't enjoy his company now." Aisha was adamant that this was the best thing for Rosie.

"Look at it as an exercise to learn to trust a man again." Chloe pulled Rosie in for a hug.

"I don't know if I can ever trust anyone again."

"Then isn't this the perfect option? Just have some fun and see how you feel about having a man by your side again. Rosie, you deserve some fun in your life. Don't ruin it for yourself because you're scared." Aisha moved to sit on the other side of Rosie and took her hand in hers.

"Okay, but you girls better be there with the wine when he leaves for London." Rosie sighed. She had decided. Her heart was already broken. She could cope with this. A few fun dates and evenings with Matt would boost her confidence. That was all. There was no future between them. It would be fun to spend tomorrow with him.

CHAPTER FOURTEEN

"I didn't realise you could drive," Matt commented as he took in the mint green vintage school bus. His eyes were wide as he looked between her and the bus.

"I can. I just don't do it very often. Living in London, I didn't need a car and I'm so busy here with the shop that I hardly have time to go anywhere. Welcome to The Cornish Vintage Dress Shop on Wheels." Rosie dramatically flung her arms out to introduce him to her bus. He chuckled nervously at her reply and reluctantly followed her aboard.

"This is amazing." Matt wandered down the aisle of the bus. His eyes were flickering to one side and then the other, unable to settle. Rosie and her dad had turned the seats into rows of racks, bursting with vintage clothes from the 60s onwards.

"Thank you. My dad bought the bus as a project for us when I was at my lowest. As it came to life, I created The Vintage Dress Shop on Wheels. Once I had the proceeds from the sale of the home I shared with my ex, I realised I could buy an actual shop. So I'm now technically the proud owner of two vintage clothes shops. I keep the newer clothes on here to entice people to the shop to see the real gems." Rosie's eyes lit up as she explained the set-up to Matt.

"You should be incredibly proud of yourself for this, Rosie. Look at what you've made from an awful situation. You've channelled heartbreak into something amazing." He walked over to her and hugged her from behind, dropping a kiss on the top of her head. It was almost too good to be true. Then Rosie had reminded herself it was too good to be true. He would return to London soon.

"Rosie?" Matt interrupted her thoughts.

"Sorry, what was that?"

"I asked if you're ready to leave? I don't want to make you late," he said.

"Belt up! My driving can get a little dicey around those country lanes, especially those with a sheer drop to the sea." Matt's face took on a greenish tint.

"Did you have to take an additional driving test to drive this?"

"I did. Despite all the joking, you're safe with me." Rosie manoeuvred the bus out of the yard and embarked on the short drive to the market.

They arrived just before eight and Matt had only gasped at a couple of hairpin bends. Having learnt to drive in her father's 1970s Ford Capri, Rosie was no stranger to driving an older car, or bus in this case. The market was small and was in the village's town hall carpark. Rosie was the only clothes stall. Artisan cheese makers, candle sellers, a couple of confectionary stalls, and a few stalls with children's toys and souvenirs surrounded her. It would be much busier in the summer. Truthfully, at this time of year the market wasn't financially bountiful for Rosie, however the locals enjoyed seeing her clothes and she was eager to promote friendly relations to encourage all-year-round shopping. There was a community spirit amongst the market traders. With years of knowledge to draw on, Rosie knew the early mornings and steep pitch fees were worth it.

"This is really sweet." Matt commented as he helped Rosie lift a clothes rack outside. On days when the rain wasn't pelting down, Rosie displayed her favourite pieces outside the bus. Often to encourage customers inside. Nobody ever left The Vintage Dress Shop on Wheels with just a single item. As soon as the clothes were out on display, the first few locals made their way over. Matt was wonderful with them, charming them and convincing them they had to leave the market today with a new dress. Rosie marvelled at his people skills. For the first time since she had met him, Matt wasn't wearing a suit. Today he was dressed in navy chinos, a black jumper and a black overcoat. His style was very bland, especially for someone trying to sell a pair of 1980s psychedelic, flared trousers.

The morning was a success. Despite the dreary October weather, lots of locals were milling around. It was also the start of half-term and so a handful of tourists had descended on the small village. Rosie had been slipping leaflets into the bags of everyone that had visited the shop in the last couple of days. It seemed to have worked to get people to the market. They'd sold a variety of styles that morning. From a 60s mini dress - which her mother had donated - to a pair of 90s jeans that she had repurposed as a pair of shorts. Each item had a little card with its history which Rosie slipped into the bag. Her mother had even provided a picture of herself wearing the dress. Matt had watched Rosie's eyes light up every time she showed an item of clothing to a potential buyer. The idea of all the history continuing on to a new owner. New memories to be made.

"How much longer are we here for?" Matt asked, rubbing his hands together. It was almost midday and cold was seeping through to their bones. Rosie could still see his breath lingering in the air.

"I'll be packing up in about ten minutes." Rosie glanced at her watch. Despite her teeth chattering, she was sad to pack up today. It had been successful and fun with Matt by her side.

"I'm going to run over and grab us bacon

sandwiches and coffees from the van over there." Rosie could have lunged at him and kissed him. There was nothing she fancied more, well, apart from him.

Rosie brought the clothes inside the bus, ready for when Matt returned with their greasy feast. It was a few minutes early, but she didn't want to risk staining any of the gorgeous clothes.

"Here you go." He returned and handed her a sandwich and coffee. They sat side by side on the steps to the bus and watched as the other stalls packed up.

"Do you have to go back to the shop?" Matt asked as he finished the last bite of his sandwich.

"Normally I do, but I don't have to today. Lilly is working today. She's a student and is saving up to buy her family Christmas presents, so she's looking for some extra hours. Why did you have any plans for this afternoon?"

"I thought we could head back to yours and I'll cook us some dinner?" Matt's suggestion sounded wonderful.

*****

Rosie poured herself and Matt a glass of wine while he stirred their dinner that was bubbling away on the hob. He was making risotto.

"Here you go." She handed him the glass and went to sit on one of the chairs.

"Rosie, I probably should have said

something earlier. I'm going back to London first thing in the morning." The words hung in the air as Rosie let them sink in. She wanted to shout at him for not warning her sooner. However, she reminded herself of the promise she had made. She knew their relationship wasn't going anywhere. He didn't owe her anything. She always knew he would have to go home.

"I'll miss you." Rosie's voice broke as the words escaped her.

"I'll miss you, too. I don't want things to end here. Rosie, I'll be back and forth for a while sorting out my parents' affairs. After that, we'll think of something." His voice was sincere, but Rosie couldn't see how they could ever make anything work. He lived somewhere she vowed never to live again, and she lived somewhere he vowed never to live again. It was an impossible situation.

"Let's not think about it. Let's just enjoy tonight." She placed her wineglass down and wrapped her arms around him.

CHAPTER FIFTEEN

Rosie woke to the sound of her phone buzzing on the bedside table. It was a text from Sofia saying they were just leaving London. They weren't arriving until lunchtime and they would get settled in to their home for the week before coming over to say hello. Rosie had almost forgotten her friend was coming to stay. As much as she was looking forward to seeing her oldest friend, she couldn't shake the empty feeling within. With a final kiss goodbye, Rosie had waved goodbye to Matt from her doorstep last night and watched him walk away. He'd texted her as soon as he got back to his parents' house to wish her a good night's sleep and promised he'd be back soon.

Trying to ignore the ache in her chest, Rosie got up and got ready for the day. She wanted to throw on something comfortable and hide from the world, but she couldn't do that. Today was a happy day. Sofia was coming and Rosie could show her everything she had achieved. Despite saying goodbye to Matt, Rosie had a lot to be happy about. With that in mind, she grabbed her new patchwork denim dress out of the wardrobe and pulled it on over a black long-sleeved top and tights. For a vintage dress shop on the Cornish coast, Rosie received lots of pairs of jeans in her donations. With piles of them from floor to ceiling in her storeroom, she decided she needed to do something about it. The dress she was wearing was her prototype. It had gone well and so Rosie was planning to create lots more in all shapes, sizes, and styles. They would adorn the recycled corner of the shop - helping old pieces find a new lease of life. The truly wonderful thing about these dresses was just how many memories they held. As Rosie ran her hands over the dress, the history of each square of denim flooded her mind. The light denim square just above the waist was from a pair of her mother's jeans. Rosie had pictures of her mother wearing them on one of their holidays to Ives-On-Sea. The edges of the patch were fraying and the colour dull from years of washing, but the memories glistened beneath the signs of wear.

With her hair wild and free, much like her emotions, Rosie opened the shop for the day. It would be a long and boring day filled with a stock take. A necessary evil of running your own business. However, Rosie couldn't be too annoyed. It would give her the chance to look at all the items in the shop and remember the story behind each one. It was nowhere near as laborious as her first ever stock take had been working in a boutique clothes shop as a teenager. Every dress was the same, and each brand new, with not a single shred of history to its name. There was the simmering excitement of each piece going out into the world to begin their lifecycle. However, they never quite caught Rosie's attention in the same way as pre-loved pieces.

"Surprise!" Rosie was in the middle of typing up the results of her stock take when Sofia burst into the shop.

"Oh my god!" Rosie dropped the papers from her hands and ran around the counter to hug her friend.

"Ava's having a nap, so I couldn't resist popping in to see you." Her friend was beaming. Rosie took a step back and took in her appearance. She was glowing. Her friend's hair fell in soft waves, her green eyes shone with excitement, and her smile was almost taking over her face. Dressed in white linen trousers and a black vest, with a designer cross body bag, and a designed jacket across her shoulders, she looked stunning. She also looked every inch the visiting London tourist.

"It's so good to see you!" Rosie let go of Sofia and stepped back.

"Look at this place." Sofia was spinning in circles, taking in the shop. Rosie felt her heart swell with pride at her friend's reaction. With the winter sun shining through the windows, the shop looked particularly lovely today. The antique beads on the dresses glistened in the sunlight.

Rosie showed Sofia around, basking in her delight as she took it all in. Seeing her friend stood in the middle of her shop was strange. It was like her two lives had merged into one. That would be something to talk to her therapist about during tonight's appointment.

"This place is so cute!" Sofia exclaimed, sitting down behind the counter with the coffee Rosie had just made her.

"Thank you." Rosie's smile was tight. She had never heard Sofia refer to anything as 'cute' before, and she wondered what her friend was really thinking.

"Are you here all the time, or do you have people to run it for you?" Sofia's nose scrunched up as she took a sip of the coffee.

"I have help at the weekend from a local girl. I spend Sundays at a local market with my vintage bus."

"Oh, that's cool." Sofia's voice sounded distracted as she looked out of the window. "Do you not miss London? Having everything to hand? Decent coffee?"

"No. I love it here." Rosie shrugged. She felt a little deflated. It hurt to have her oldest friend questioning her choices.

"Are you just saying that?" Oh, Rosie, you know you could come back with me. Our summer house is empty. You could stay there while you get yourself back on your feet."

Rosie took a deep breath. "Sofia, I'm happy here. Yes, I left London because of Oliver, but I couldn't ever see myself coming back. This is my life now."

Sofia's phone pinged. "Ava's awake. I best head back. Why don't we meet at that lovely looking restaurant by the harbour?"

"Sure, sounds great. I'll book us a table for 7." Rosie had been about to suggest they meet for dinner at the pub. However, as she took in Sofia's appearance, she realised the pub really wasn't her scene. In London, they would have gone to a fancy wine bar in Chelsea. Rosie would have loved to take Sofia to the pub and introduce her to all of her new friends, but in that second she knew they never would have got along. They were too different. The Rosie who lived in London and visited wine bars in fancy strappy heels was worlds apart from Cornish Rosie. She had changed for the better. Her friend seemed exactly the same, just with a baby in tow. With a kiss to each cheek, Sofia left in a cloud of expensive perfume and Rosie felt herself breathing a sigh of relief. She could relax again. As nice as it was having her old friend back, she felt as though she couldn't truly relax around her. Was that how she had felt the entire time she was living in London with Oliver?

Rosie closed early that afternoon. She needed time to process the hurt from her friend's reaction.

Rosie hoped Sofia would see everything she had achieved and be happy for her, instead she had been left feeling as though her choices weren't good enough for her oldest friend.

It was with a feeling of relief that Rosie answered the phone to her therapist that evening. She spoke about how her friend's visit was making her feel. All thoughts of Matt had temporarily left her. She had wanted to tell Sofia all about him and ask for her opinion, and yet after this afternoon's meeting, she felt as though she couldn't confide in her. Rosie hated to admit it, but she was looking forward to Sofia leaving so she could go to the pub with Aisha and Chloe.

Her therapist was happy to hear her confronting her fears and exploring her relationship with Matt.

"It may be tough, and there may be times when you do hurt," she had said. Reminding Rosie that it's okay to feel.

Once she had finished with her session, Rosie got herself ready for dinner with Sofia. She felt pressure to make an effort - even more so than when she had gone for dinner with Matt. In London, she would have gone to her cupboards filled with designer clothes and picked something from it. Oliver was always keen for her to make an effort. He liked her shining on the end of his arm while he was networking. Rosie didn't mind. It was what was expected of her, and it was helpful in finding clients. Bored housewives who redecorated the house as a distraction.

There was a dress on the shop floor, locked away behind a glass cabinet. Rosie didn't own the dress. It was on hire to her shop with the agreement that Rosie would take a percentage from any sale. There was no way she could wear it out for dinner. She drummed her nails on her vanity table. Nobody would know it was gone. Only Rosie had a key for the cabinet and the true owner was unlikely to come looking for it on a Monday evening when there was another three months left on their contract. Sofia would know the dress immediately. Especially since she worked for the designer. Rosie was sure Sofia would have seen pictures of the 50s vintage Dior dress. With a mixture of fear and excitement, Rosie went to get the dress from the cabinet. If she damaged it she would have to sell the shop to pay for it.

Dressed in the waist clinching black dress with its full skirt, Rosie pulled on a pair of black heels and left her curls cascading down her back. If anyone but Sofia asked, she would tell them it was a replica of a vintage Dior. She was risking a lot, but she had a lot to prove. Rosie didn't want to risk Sofia inviting her to stay in their summer house again.

Rosie's teeth chattered on the walk down to the restaurant. She had thrown a faux fur stole around her shoulders, but it wasn't doing much to keep the bitter chill from seeping through to her bones. The restaurant was quiet, with only one other table occupied. As Rosie stepped inside, she spotted Sofia sat by the window. She was dressed in a fitted black lace jumpsuit with fur on the wrists. Her hair had been perfectly blown-dry into bouncy curls. Rosie had to admit she looked flawless.

"Darling!" Sofia bounced up from her chair and kissed Rosie on both cheeks. "I ordered champagne."

Rosie smiled and took her seat, internally cringing at how much this would cost her when they inevitably split the bill. The bubbles filled her nose as she took a sip. It might be expensive, but Rosie had to admit it was nice. Nights out like this in London were common. Between her and Oliver's joint income, they could enjoy a certain lifestyle. Looking back, it was empty. What good were expensive bottles of champagne when the company didn't want to be there with you?

"Your dress is stunning. Is it a replica?" Sofia looked up from the menu. *Replica?!* How dare she. Rosie felt her teeth grinding. She took another sip of her drink to calm herself down.

"No, it's an original. One of the perks of running a vintage dress shop." Rosie smiled sweetly back at Sofia.

"Oh, I didn't realise you had anything designer! You'll have to show me tomorrow." Sofia turned her attention back to the menu, leaving Rosie seething. Now her cute little shop was interesting to her. Rosie wondered whether a few years ago she would have visited Ives-On-Sea, stepped into her shop, and treated it the same way Sofia was. Deep down, she knew the answer. This was her. She no longer had to play a part in London.

The night went as expected. Lots of Sofia bragging about her life in London and all of her new 'mum friends'. Quite frankly, Rosie couldn't think of anything worse than sitting in a cafe on Kings Road discussing the latest baby fad. Once upon a time, it was everything she ever wanted. She'd almost got it, too.

They split the bill and Rosie crossed her fingers under the table as the card machine processed her payment. Thankfully, it went through and she was spared the embarrassment of her card being rejected. They had air kissed at the door, and Sofia had stepped into her taxi and drove off into the night. She hadn't bothered to ask Rosie if she wanted a lift back to her flat.

CHAPTER SIXTEEN

With the champagne lying heavily in Rosie's stomach, she barely slept that night. To make matters worse, she hadn't heard from Matt since he'd arrived home. By the time 5am rolled around, Rosie had showered and was sitting in her dressing gown looking out to the sea. It was tranquil, with only a few seagulls strutting around on the sand. She pulled out her phone and scrolled down to her mother's number. She really needed to hear a familiar voice.

"Rosie dear, what's wrong?" Her mother's answer was instant.

"I'm okay. Just fancied a chat." Rosie cursed her voice for wobbling.

"Rosie, you're forgetting I've known you your

entire life. What's wrong?"

"Sofia's here." There was silence as her mother processed the information.

"You're not happy about her being there?" Came her mother's strategic reply.

"It's reminding me how much I've changed. Well, not changed. It's making me realise how unhappy I was in London. I was playing a part, whereas here I'm happy."

"That's a good thing, Rosie. Don't upset yourself. I'm sure Sofia is a lovely girl, but she's always been competitive. Even as a child, when she'd come round for tea, she would act as though she was the queen. Rosie, it's okay to leave friendships in your past."

"I seem to be leaving a lot in the past."

"We can't carry our baggage around forever," her mother said. Rosie sighed. How could her mother be this wise at this time of the morning?

"I know."

"Your father and I will be down soon."

"I'm looking forward to it, mum. It'll be nice to have some company I can relax in."

"Asides from your blast from the past. How is everything?"

Rosie chewed her lip, wondering whether to tell her mother about her date with Matt. She kept very little from her parents, and she wasn't about to start keeping things from them.

"I've been on a couple of dates." It felt like a weight lifted off of her shoulders to say it out loud.

"Oh, tell me."

Rosie told her mum about dinner with Matt. She told her about how his life was based in London and how she was scared to get too involved. But at the same time, she was enjoying his company and feeling wanted by a man again.

"He sounds lovely, but I think you're right to be cautious. Seeing Sofia has reminded you how unhappy you were in London. No man is worth that. Enjoy his company, but be sensible."

"Thank you, mum."

They said their goodbyes. As Rosie went to put her phone back down on the bedside table, she spotted a new message. It was from Matt.

Sorry for not getting in touch yesterday. Work was chaotic! I think I might be holding this entire place together. Is it forward of me to say I miss you? It was nice being in Ives-On-Sea with the possibility of bumping into you at any turn. Hoping to come back down at the weekend, will you be around? Matt xxx

Rosie let out a little giggle in relief. He hadn't been trying to let her down; he had just been busy at work. She smiled to herself. Having plans with Matt at the weekend would make a week of Sofia a lot more bearable. Rosie quickly typed out a reply saying she would be around and would love to see him. Then she deleted it and reworded it to say she would *like* to see him.

It was yet another busy day in the shop. Rosie had lots of clients coming in to be measured for tailor-made items. She messaged Sofia telling her she would be busy most of the morning. Rosie was grateful to be back in the shop. She'd carefully steamed the vintage Dior and put it back in the cabinet. Every time she glanced over, she felt her chest tighten and the guilt settle in the pit of her stomach. Why had she done such a stupid thing? She had risked everything she had built just to impress a friend from London.

At lunchtime, Chloe popped in with a sandwich for her. Rosie felt the guilt lift as her eyes settled on her friend, still in her apron from baking all morning.

"Lunch delivery! I thought you might be too busy to pop out and get something." Chloe placed the paper bag down on the counter. There was a sandwich, a packet of crisps, and a scone.

"Thank you! I'm starving." Rosie had forgotten to eat breakfast, as she had been in such a rush to get down to the shop to put the dress back in its display cabinet.

"You're welcome. We're meeting at the pub tonight, if you fancy it?" Chloe stole a crisp from the packet Rosie had just opened.

"I can't. I've got a friend from London visiting." Rosie busied herself by unwrapping the sandwich. She would have loved to meet her Cornish friends in the pub for a drink this evening, instead she was off out for dinner with Sofia, Harry, and baby Ava. Rosie was looking forward to meeting Ava. However, she was dreading spending the evening in Sofia and Harry's company. Watching the happy couple would no doubt dredge up a lot of memories and heartbreak.

"They're welcome to come along." Chloe's smile was genuine, and Rosie knew that none of her Cornish friends would mind her bringing Sofia along. However, she knew exactly what Sofia would think of the pub. Whilst Rosie's therapist told her merging her past life and her present life was a good thing, Rosie knew that this particular merging would not go well. Chloe would never look at her in the same way if she saw the company Rosie had kept in London.

"I think they've already booked a table somewhere." Rosie took a bite of her sandwich. It was delicious. Sofia would have turned her nose up at the amount of calories in the cheese. Rosie tried to remember back to her days in London. Would she have done the same? She probably would have taken half the cheese out, in fear of not fitting into her designer wardrobe.

"Perhaps another time. I better run back. We'll have a catch up soon." With a wave, Chloe left, leaving Rosie to her lunch.

The afternoon was just as busy as the morning had been. Sofia didn't pop in. She texted Rosie to say they had taken a drive out to one of the big towns to do some holiday shopping. They were going to pick Rosie up at seven to drive to the restaurant. Rosie wasn't sure where they had booked, but Sofia had promised her that one of her travel blogger friends had recommended it, and so it was sure to impress.

As promised, they picked Rosie up at seven and she climbed into the back of their Range Rover to sit next to Ava.

"How was your day?" Rosie asked as she cooed over the baby, who was the spitting image of her mother.

"Oh, it was wonderful. I didn't realise Cornwall had such lovely shops. There was an adorable little boutique selling Balenciaga shoes, so we purchased Ava's first pair."

Rosie tuned out as Sofia listed everything else she had bought.

It was over an hour to the restaurant, and Sofia had barely stopped to take a breath. She had been telling Rosie all about the new shops and cafes in London. Rosie had made a few comments and smiled, happy to let her carry on. There was very little Rosie could say that would interest Sofia and so it was easier to let her lead the conversation. Finally, they arrived at a restaurant built at the top of a cliff overlooking the sea. Fairy lights covered the doorway. Rosie followed Sofia into the restaurant as Harry stayed behind to get Ava out of the car. There was once a time when Rosie envied Sofia and Harry's relationship. He was always so attentive towards her and eager to please. She had once argued with Oliver when she suggested he should be more like Harry. However, seeing them together tonight made her realise how lucky she was not to have a Harry in her life.

Sofia ordered more champagne and Rosie cringed, hoping she had her back-up credit card stowed somewhere in her purse.

"I played golf with Oliver before we came down." It was the first thing Harry had said all evening and Rosie couldn't help but wish he had kept his mouth shut.

"He never was a very good player," Rosie murmured, keeping her eyes focused on the menu below her.

"Awful player. He told me you've signed the divorce papers."

"There's no point letting it drag on. This way, we're both free to move on." It was an answer that Rosie had rehearsed in her head, but not one she'd ever needed to say out loud. Everyone else had understood when she announced she was starting the process of getting divorced.

"He misses you." Harry wasn't letting the matter drop.

"Harry, he should have thought about that before he had an affair. Just because he's realised life with someone else isn't all rainbows and butterflies doesn't mean I should take him back."

"Rosie, he has a stressful job. He just needed to let off some steam."

Rosie's jaw dropped as Harry tried to defend Oliver's behaviour.

"That's absolutely no excuse. Is that really what you think? Would you really sleep with someone else and break Sofia's heart just because you're stressed at work?" Rosie could feel the people on the table next to them staring as she raised her voice. Usually, she hated drawing any attention to herself, but she refused to let Harry speak to her like this. How dare he try to justify Oliver's behaviour?

"No… that's not what I'm saying." He tried to backtrack.

"That's exactly what you're saying."

Thankfully, the waitress came over to take their order. Rosie ordered the lasagna and a glass of red wine. As the others ordered, she tuned out and thought about what Harry had said. He'd always appeared to be the model husband, and yet here he was trying to justify Oliver's affair. Rosie was starting to wonder just how much of Sofia and Harry's relationship was for show. Actually, she was wondering just how much of their life was for show.

The night dragged as Harry kept quiet, and Sofia kept the conversation flowing. However, all she talked about was London and how wonderful it was. Rosie found herself wishing she had never invited Sofia to stay. Perhaps some old friends were better left in the past.

CHAPTER SEVENTEEN

The week dragged by terribly slowly. Sofia didn't appear to pick up on any of Rosie's hints and instead kept suggesting they go for coffees, lunches, and dinners. Rosie tried to point out she would be in the shop working all week, but Sofia didn't understand the concept of work. She thought Rosie could just close the shop whenever she felt like a long lunch. On Friday morning, when Sofia, Harry, and Ava pulled up outside the shop, Rosie was grateful to be saying goodbye to them. Sofia had invited her down to London, but Rosie had tactfully pointed out that she wouldn't be able to close the shop for that long. As she watched them drive away, Rosie let out a sigh. It felt as though a weight had lifted from her shoulders. She walked back into the shop and pulled out her phone before she texted Chloe and Aisha to see whether they wanted to meet at the pub for dinner that evening. They immediately replied, saying they couldn't wait.

"Hello?" someone called from outside the shop's door. Rosie wasn't open yet, but the woman must have peered through and seen her.

"Hello, can I help you?" Rosie opened the door and greeted the woman.

"I'm here for my son's wedding, but my perfume has leaked in my suitcase and ruined the dress." The woman was close to tears.

"When's the wedding?" Rosie stood aside to allow the woman to step into the shop. She might not be open, but there was no way she could turn this woman away.

"Midday." The woman let out a sob as Rosie gasped.

"Okay, deep breath. My name's Rosie. What did you dress look like?"

The woman introduced herself as Jada and described her dress to Rosie. As Rosie listened, she took in the woman's appearance. Jada was wearing in a pair of high-waisted black trousers and a bright red cashmere jumper. Her dark skin glowed against the red of the jumper. Rosie's mind was an inventory of all the items of clothing she held in the shop. She flicked through each item, focusing on the ones in a similar shade of red. Towards the back of the shop, there was a beautiful red midi dress with sheer puffy sleeves.

"What do you think of this?" Rosie pulled it off of the rack and held it up.

"It's gorgeous, but I'm not sure I could pull it off." Jada's eyes lit up at the sight of the dress.

"Let's try it on and see. At the very least, we'll know what you don't want." Rosie led her to the dressing room and left her to put the dress on. She couldn't help but glance at the clock. Jada had four hours until the wedding was to start. Rosie crossed her fingers that the dress would fit.

"It's gorgeous." Jada emerged from the changing room with a huge smile on her face. The dress fitted almost perfectly. The only problem was the plunging V neck was a little too revealing for the mother-of-the-groom. "Do you have any safety pins?"

"Let me grab some pins. I'll alter it for you." Rosie busied herself pinning the dress, so she knew how much to alter the neckline. Once Jada had slipped out of the dress and was back in her own clothes, Rosie instructed her to pop next door to Chloe's cafe for a cup of coffee and some breakfast while she made the alterations.

*****

"I can't thank you enough, Rosie." Jada threw her arms around Rosie as she emerged from the dressing room after trying on her altered dress.

"I'm so glad I could help!" Rosie couldn't wipe the smile off her face. She priced up the dress and alteration before waving a very happy Jada off to her son's wedding. After the awful week spent with Sofia, it was a reminder that she was exactly where she needed to be.

As she stepped into the pub that evening, Rosie felt a warmth spread over her. This was home.

"I've got wine!" Chloe was waving her arms frantically at her from their usual table. Rosie chuckled and made her way over.

"You read my mind." Rosie slid down into the chair and took the glass of red Chloe had just poured for her.

"Long week?" she asked, pouring another glass for when Aisha arrived.

"Far too long. Remind me never to invite any of my old friends from London to stay."

"Didn't go well?"

"It was a reminder of a life I'm happy I've left behind me." Rosie didn't mention the worries that had been playing around in her mind. The confirmation that she could never be happy again in London only made her question whether she should be seeing Matt again. She pushed the thoughts from her mind. She would worry about that when she saw him tomorrow. Tonight was about unwinding and catching up with her best friends.

Aisha arrived shortly after Rosie and took a big gulp from her glass before speaking. "Remind me NEVER to invite the local school to the shop ever again."

Rosie's phone beeped. It was a text from Matt

to say he was just leaving London. Rosie texted him back to wish him a safe journey. It would be too late for her to see him tonight, instead they had agreed he would pick her up tomorrow morning and they would go out for the day.

"Is that your lover boy?" Chloe teased Rosie as she watched her typing out her reply.

"Oh. What's it like to have a man interested in you? It's been so long I can't even remember." Aisha was already pouring herself a second glass of wine. Rosie chuckled. Despite the teasing, it was lovely to feel so relaxed in their company. She had always felt like she had to try with Sofia and do everything she could to please her. With Chloe and Aisha, she could just be.

"Tourist season is the best time for male attention. The only problem is we're so busy working that we don't get a spare moment to speak to them." Chloe rolled her eyes. Despite her moans, Rosie knew she loved running her little cafe and wouldn't give it up for any amount of male attention.

They spent the evening talking about nothing in particular, and yet they didn't stop chatting all night. The girls had offered to listen to Rosie moan about her week with Sofia, but she didn't feel ready to talk about it yet. There was a lot for her to process. It wasn't just about Sofia; it was about Rosie confronting the person she once was. Or at least, the person she was once trying to be.

CHAPTER
EIGHTEEN

Matt texted Rosie saying he would pick her up at ten and so she was up bright and early Saturday morning to get ready for the day. She crept down to the shop before it opened to find an outfit. Rosie wandered over to the reclaimed section, which contained clothes she had repurposed. She grabbed a pair of dark green, waist high trousers which had once belonged to a lady called Mary in the 1940s. Rosie had bought them at an auction. She had travelled to the Clemonte auction house in Ivy Hatch after reading about it in a magazine. Without a car, Rosie had travelled on the train. The auction and the auction house had been breathtaking. Filled with items from other people's lives. Rosie had bought several lots, ranging from clothes to accessories. The trousers had been an accidental purchase, hidden inside a vintage suitcase with some of Mary's personal possessions. Thankfully, Rosie had bought enough for the auction house to deliver the items to her, which meant she didn't have to bring it all home on the train with her.

When the delivery arrived, it shocked Rosie to discover clothes and other belongings filling the suitcase. These trousers had started life as a dress which had been at the bottom of the case, the fabric frayed and worn in places. There had also been a pile of photographs and letters. As Rosie had flicked through them, she recognised the dress in a black-and-white picture. A young woman stood in the street, smiling at the camera. She was beautiful. The letters had revealed the tragic life of Mary Booker. After her husband died at war, Mary had written a suicide letter, packed the suitcase and made her way to the bridge in town. She had wanted her life and her pain to be remembered. Rosie could only guess what had happened next. Mary must have left the suitcase to be found near where she jumped. It was sad, but Rosie would not allow Mary to be forgotten. The pictures and letters were part of a collage on the far wall, which comprised copies of all the photographs or letters that had passed through the shop.

Rosie's phone pinged, pulling her from her thoughts. She pulled her phone out of her pyjama pocket and saw Matt had texted to say he would be there shortly. Rosie let out a little squeal, grabbed the trousers, and ran back upstairs to get ready. Ten minutes later, she had dressed in the green trousers, a black jumper and her hair was up in a messy bun. She glanced in the mirror one last time as she heard a car pull up outside. Rosie knew she was obsessing over her outfit, but it helped to keep her mind from wandering. She wrung her hands as she thought about all the possibilities of what could happen today. She didn't know how to stop herself from feeling anything towards Matt. Shaking her head, she grabbed her coat and bag and made her way out to the car. She didn't have time to worry; he was outside.

"Hello!" Matt called out of the window of his car. Rosie waved back and walked around to the passenger side.

"Hello you," she said, climbing in. It was a big four-by-four and Rosie struggled to climb in.

"How's your week been?" asked Matt. Rosie didn't have the chance to reply before he leant across the centre panel and kissed her.

"It's just got a lot better. How was yours?" Rosie pulled back from the kiss and busied herself with putting her seatbelt on. She had to remind herself to keep emotionally detached. Her week with Sofia had reminded her that any future with Matt was impossible.

"I just worked. Anyway, let's get going." Rosie looked over at him as he put the car into drive and started down the road. His eyes had dark circles underneath them and the stubble on his chin was out of character for his usual pristine appearance. He looked like he'd had an awful week.

"What are we doing today?" asked Rosie. She was trying to distract herself from worrying about him. She'd have to care about him to worry about him, and she did not care about him. At least, that was what she was telling herself.

"There's a small village about an hour's drive away. I thought we could have some brunch and then go for a walk."

"That sounds perfect." Rosie's stomach rumbled at the mention of food.

They fell into a comfortable silence as Rosie watched the scenery pass them by. The sea was behind them and they were heading into the countryside. Fields stretched out for miles as the October sun slowly rose above them. By the time they arrived in the village, it was eleven o'clock and Rosie was starving. She had skipped breakfast that morning, as she was feeling so nervous about their date.

Matt led her towards a small cafe in a Tudor cottage. The inside of the building had the original wood and brickwork exposed. A waitress showed them to a table by a window where the autumnal light was streaming through. It was beautiful and very quaint. Almost romantic.

"How do you know about this place?" Rosie asked. She peered at the extensive menu in front of her, trying to decide what she fancied. She was finding it difficult to choose between the eggs

Benedict or the full English.

"My mother used to work here. It was our sanctuary away from my father. In more recent years, I took her here the few times I visited." Matt kept his eyes on the menu as he spoke. Rosie's breath caught as she let his words sink in. Did this date really mean nothing to him if he was taking her to such a special place? Confusion threatened to consume Rosie, but she pushed it away, determined to just enjoy the day for what it was.

"It's lovely." Rosie diverted her eyes from Matt to her surroundings. Towards the back of the room was a counter filled with delicious cakes and pastries. Her mouth watered at the sight.

"My mum was their baker. She cooked them at home and then each morning, until I was about ten, I would come with her on the bus on the way to school to drop them off. This little cafe was our safe haven away from my father's temper." Matt kept his eyes on the table, refusing to meet her gaze.

"Oh wow. You must have had lots of yummy cakes growing up. My mum can just about manage a packet mix." Rosie's mum had always been too busy sewing and tailoring clothes to be baking in the kitchen. However, she wouldn't have changed a thing about it since it was where her love for pre-loved fashion came from. She was trying to keep the conversation light. If she delved into his feelings of loss, then she might start caring, and she couldn't do that. Rosie knew her therapist would encourage her to care for another person, but she knew she wasn't ready for that. And definitely not with someone who would break her heart when he left again.

"She made the most amazing food. Whenever my father was away for work, my mother would cook me lots of treats. I think it was her way of apologising for how he treated us. She couldn't leave him, so she just tried to make the best of life when he was away."

"I'll have to ask you for lots of restaurant recommendations." Rosie pulled her hand from his as the waitress brought over their drinks. She had ordered a hot chocolate with marshmallows and cream, whilst Matt had ordered a black coffee. She chuckled inwardly as she realised their choice of drinks aptly showed their differences. Matt was a serious, straight-talking person. Meanwhile, Rosie was trying not to take life too seriously and embrace the fun wherever she could find it. They were opposites, and yet somehow they worked. Rosie shook her head to rid herself of the thoughts. They didn't work. They couldn't work. He lived in London, she lived in Ives-On-Sea.

"So, tell me about your week. Did you have fun with your friend?" Matt's eyes sought hers as he waited for her answer. It struck Rosie that he truly cared about her answer.

"To be honest, it was awful."

"What happened?" He reached out and took hold of her hand and gave it a squeeze. Rosie felt her heart flutter at the action.

"It only emphasised the difference between

my old life in London and my new life here. I found it difficult to put up with Sofia and her snootiness. Honestly, I was happy when they left."

"I'm sorr-" Matt's phone rung, stopping him mid-sentence. His phone was lying on the table and Rosie couldn't help but glance down at it. The screen was flashing with a call from Mimi. Rosie pulled her hand away from his, recoiling at the sight of the heart next to the name.

"What? Who's Mimi?" Her voice shook. Rosie wrapped her arms around herself. She'd just broken another woman's heart. She was the other woman.

"Wait, Rosie. It's not what you think. She's my ex."

Rosie let out a bitter chuckle. "Of course she is. Do you really think I'm that gullible?"

"Here, look at my recent messages with her." Matt unlocked his phone and handed it over to Rosie. She was torn. Should she be looking through his phone? She had to know the truth and so she clicked on the icon and watched as the messages flashed in front of her eyes.

Mimi: Matt, don't ignore me.

Mimi: I miss you.

Mimi: Why don't I meet you in Cornwall?

Mimi: I love you.

Mimi: I missed you at work today.

Mimi: You can't keep ignoring me.

Mimi: We belong together.

Rosie stopped scrolling. She'd seen enough. Matt was telling the truth, Mimi was his ex. However, that didn't make Rosie feel much better. Just knowing his ex was still around made her heart pound with fear. Their relationship seemed doomed from the beginning. Perhaps they just weren't meant to be.

"Rosie, please believe me when I say there's nothing between myself and Mimi. We dated for a few months and that was that."

"I need time to process this." Rosie's mind was hurtling along at a hundred miles an hour with multiple scenarios playing out in her head.

"Do you want me to take you home?" Matt's face dropped, but she knew he meant it. If she wanted to go home, then he would take her.

"No, I don't think I do. I'm going to go to the bathroom." On shaking legs, Rosie walked to the small bathroom at the back of the cafe. She shut the door behind her and leaned against it, letting out a ragged breath.

Did she believe Matt? The messages suggested he was telling the truth, but Rosie knew all-too-well that messages could be deceiving. He could easily have just deleted his own replies. Rosie walked over to the sink and splashed her face with cold water. What would her therapist say? She'd tell Rosie to trust he was telling her the truth. She couldn't go through life second-guessing everything people told her. There was nothing to suggest Matt was lying, so she had to believe him. Rosie took a deep breath, dried her face, and walked out of the bathroom.

"Sorry about that," she apologised, taking her seat. Their food was on the table, but Matt hadn't started his.

"Are you okay?" he asked her.

"I'm not sure, but I'd like to try to move forward. My ex-husband cheated on me, so I'm finding it difficult to trust people again."

"Rosie, I can assure you I am single." His voice was calm and collected. It was Matt's personality. Nothing seemed to phase him. He gave no hint of being affected by Rosie's revelation about her past. "Mimi saved her name in my phone and I just haven't changed it since. She wants us to get back together and so she keeps calling me. It's not what I want, and she knows it. We're not a good match, but she won't accept it. We were only together for six months. She's very full-on and just won't leave me alone. We work together, so unfortunately I can't just block her number." Rosie watched his facial expressions as he spoke. There was nothing to suggest he was lying. Her heart wanted her to run and to protect itself, and yet her legs wouldn't move. Was he the type to make his ex look crazy just to cover his own tracks? Rosie didn't think so.

"It's okay, I believe you. I'm sorry."

"Please, don't apologise. I should have been open with you from the start." He squeezed her hand.

"Can we pretend that didn't happen?" Rosie felt mortified at having made such a scene.

"We can, but I'd prefer not to. There may have been better ways of bringing it up, but at least we both know we're single. I also now know that your husband cheated on you and so I'll do my best to explain any future phone calls from my ex." He smiled reassuringly.

"Thank you." Rosie's smile mirrored his. She mulled over his words as she took a bite of her food. Were they really just having a bit of fun together, or did he want more? This morning seemed to have complicated their fun and turned their relationship into something more serious. Rosie took a deep breath and reminded herself that she was just going to go with the flow. Planning everything hadn't worked with Oliver and so it was time for a fresh approach. She had to trust herself and Matt and just see where life took them.

Together, they enjoyed their brunch. Matt shared some memories of the various cakes and pastries he'd eaten inside these walls. By the time they climbed back into Matt's car, both were tired from all the eating and talking. They put their seatbelts on, and Matt turned to Rosie.

"What do you want to do now?" he asked. Matt was doing her best to make her feel comfortable.

"I think I need to walk off brunch! I know a beautiful little costal path on our way back. Why don't we have a walk, then we can go back to the warmth of my flat?"

"That sounds wonderful."

Rosie directed Matt to the car park. Despite the blustery weather, there were a few cars parked. In the far corner was a little cafe, selling hot drinks and bacon sandwiches to those who had ventured out. There were numerous coloured arrows, each showing a different walk.

"This one's my favourite. Come on." They followed the purple route. Matt slipped his hand into Rosie's as they walked along the path. The wind was blowing a gale, but it didn't take away from the beauty of the area. As they moved away from the car park and climbed over a stile, Matt gasped.

"It's beautiful!" he exclaimed. The sea stretched out in front of them, glistening in the midday autumnal sun. Waves raged below and the wind continued to howl. Despite being open to all the elements, there was something so hauntingly beautiful about this spot.

"It's my favourite place. I feel as though I'm standing on the edge of the world when I come here. Nothing else seems to matter. The sound of the waves and the wind drown out your thoughts. Yet, somehow, it's peaceful." Rosie was having to shout above the wind. Their faces broke into laughter at the irony of her words.

"I love it. Thank you for bringing me here."

Silently, they continued their walk. Hand-in-hand, they admired the stunning landscape of

Cornwall.

CHAPTER NINETEEN

They made it back to Rosie's flat, both frozen from the icy Cornish wind.

"Shall I put the kettle on?" Rosie asked as they climbed the stairs.

"That would be lovely."

After taking her coat off, Rosie busied herself in the kitchen preparing hot chocolates. She was acutely aware of Matt by her side.

"I'm going to have to head home in the morning. I've got lots of work to do for Monday." Matt took his drink from Rosie's outstretched hand.

"Oh." Rosie didn't know what more to say. She hadn't been expecting him to leave so quickly. Had he driven all the way down here just to spend today with her?

"I'm sorry. I should have mentioned it sooner."

"No, it's fine." There wouldn't have been time to mention it in between Rosie's fears that he was still in a relationship. A part of her was relieved that he was going home. It would give her time to process everything. She always knew long distance dating would be difficult, but what she hadn't expected was for it to be so intense when he was visiting.

"I'm going to miss you. It's so strange, we hardly know each other, and yet I'm at my happiest when I'm with you." He shrugged his shoulders and stared down at his mug.

"I feel the same. Anything good that happens, I just want to run to you and tell you about it. Is that normal?"

"I'm not sure there's such a thing as normal, Rosie." He stepped towards her, placed his mug down on the worktop, and pulled her into his arms.

"Shall we watch a film?" Rosie was aware of how serious their conversation was becoming. She wasn't ready to tell him just how strongly she already felt for him. What would she do when he returned to London, leaving her in Cornwall?

They flicked on a rom-com and snuggled up on the sofa with their hot chocolates and a blanket. Neither of them uttered a word as they watched the film play out in front of their eyes. As the credits played, Rosie blinked a few times as she realised the room was dark. The day had flashed by in Matt's company.

"Shall we go out for dinner?" Matt suggested, rubbing his eyes and stretching.

Rosie thought about suggesting she cook for them, but she knew it would be dangerous to spend the evening in such close proximity to him. The last thing they needed was to complicate things by sleeping together the night before he left.

They decided to have dinner at the pub. Rosie had to suppress her giggles as they stepped in, and she caught Chloe's eye. Chloe immediately spotted Matt and started wiggling her eyebrows. Rosie rolled her eyes.

"Come on. Let's sit as far away from her as possible." Rosie steered Matt towards the opposite side of the pub. She loved her friends, but she didn't want to share Matt.

Dinner came and Rosie politely asked Matt about his work back home. There was a small part of her mind that was worried it was a lie. Was he going home early to Mimi? Rosie forced herself to focus on the bite of food she had in her mouth. With each chew, she pushed away the thought of Matt going home to someone else. She had to trust him. She had no reason not to.

"How's sorting your mum's estate going?" Rosie asked. She was trying to silence the little voice in her head that was reminding her she thought she had no reason to doubt Oliver.

"Progress is slow. I need to decide what I want to do with the properties." Matt put his fork down on the table.

"Do you feel ready to sell them?" Rosie reached out and took hold of his hand. She felt awful for asking the question. It had been with a selfish intent that she moved their conversation away from his work.

"I'm not sure. When I first came down, I was determined to sell them and leave Ives-On-Sea behind. Now, I'm not so sure."

Rosie felt her heart thumping in her chest. "Why?" The question tumbled from her lips. Was she ready to hear his answer?

"You, Rosie. I thought I had my future planned, then I met you. Now I don't know what I want anymore. All I know is I've never felt more alive than when I'm in your company."

Rosie stared silently back at him. She hadn't been expecting him to be so honest with his answer.

"I'm sorry. I have a lot of regrets over my mum dying. There were so many things I didn't say to her that I should have. I don't want to regret not being honest with you." He squeezed her hand. Rosie felt her breathing speed up. She gasped for breath to calm herself down. Her eyes were wide, and she sought Chloe's face. Their eyes locked and her friend immediately knew something was wrong.

"Rosie, I need your help. Come to the bathroom with me." Chloe was walking towards their table. Rosie couldn't speak. She just nodded and stood up. In a daze, she followed Chloe to the bathroom.

"What's wrong?" Chloe asked as soon as the

door was shut behind them.

"He's very full on." Rosie gasped for breath. There was a mark on the tile she was standing on. She focused her attention on it. With a few deep breaths, she felt her breathing return to normal.

"In what way?" Chloe had brought her glass of wine into the bathroom with her and handed it to Rosie so she could take a sip.

"He says he's not sure what to do about selling his parents' properties because of me."

"Isn't that a good thing? He's thinking about being closer to you, Rosie."

"It should be a good thing, but there's more to it." Rosie told Chloe about what had happened at the cafe with Mimi and Matt's explanation.

"Surely the fact that he's considering changing his plans for you tells you he's serious?" Chloe had listened carefully to Rosie's explanation.

"I'm scared, Chloe. I trusted Oliver and look what happened."

"Look, he's not saying he's moving down tomorrow. Just take things slowly and see what happens."

Rosie knew Chloe was right. She didn't want to risk losing something special with Matt just because his feelings overwhelmed her. She gave Chloe a quick hug, handed her back her now empty glass, and made her way back out to the pub.

"I'm sorry about that." She sat back down in her seat. Concern was etched across Matt's face as his eyes sought hers, looking for an explanation.

"What happened, Rosie? Please talk to me."
He went to take hold of her hand, but pulled back at
the last second. Rosie felt a pang in her heart. She
wanted him to hold her hand, but she knew now
wasn't the right moment.

"I'm just feeling overwhelmed. There's been
so many emotions today, Matt. I like you, but I'm
scared, and I just don't know what to do or say."

"I can understand that. I'm sorry, Rosie."

"No, don't be sorry. The best thing we can
do is communicate. We need to speak about how
we're feeling. It's just something that I'm finding
particularly difficult right now."

"I understand. Why don't I walk you home? I
should be able to come down again next weekend.
It'll give you the week to process everything."

"Thank you."

Matt held the door open for Rosie to walk
through. As they stepped out into the cold evening,
Rosie reached out and slipped her hand into Matt's.
In silence, they walked back to her flat, stopping
outside her front door.

"I'll be back next week." He promised her as
he moved a stray piece of her hair and tucked it
behind her ear.

"I'm sorry. It's been a lovely day. Thank you
for being honest with me about how you're feeling. I
just need some time." Rosie hoped that was true. She
hoped time would allow her to drop her guard and
trust him.

"I understand." He leaned forward and kissed

her. It was brief, but his lips lingered for a moment before he stepped back. "I'll see you next week." He watched as she undid the door. She let herself in and closed the door behind her, and he walked away.

CHAPTER TWENTY

Rosie had forced herself to go straight to bed when she got home last night. She had an early morning to get the bus to the market. It wouldn't do to be tired on that drive. Just before sunrise, Rosie got out of bed and scrubbed last night's makeup off. She got herself ready and left to walk down to the bus. It was just another workday for her.

On autopilot, she walked the deserted streets of Ives-On-Sea. It was bitterly cold as the wind whipped around her. In the distance, she heard a car door slam shut and she couldn't help but wonder if it was Matt leaving for London. Rosie clenched her fists, focusing on the physical feeling to stop herself from shedding any tears. She pushed herself to put one foot in front of the other. The sound of the sea crashing below filled her ears and gave her something to concentrate on.

It hurt to let Matt go back to London with things so uncertain between them. She hardly knew him, and yet, there was so much unexplored potential between them, so many hopes and dreams. Their relationship had endless opportunities, and yet they hadn't had the chance to explore it. She didn't know whether they ever would get the chance.

Once Rosie reached the market, she set up and grabbed a coffee from the refreshments van. She still had a little while until the first customers would climb out of bed and meander down to the market. Instead of checking her stock, she pulled out her phone and dialled her mother's number.

"Morning!" Her mother's chirpy reply rang down the phone.

"Hi mum." Her voice cracked as she was overcome by a longing to have her mother's arms wrapped around her.

"Rosie, what's wrong?"

"I saw Matt again." She told her mother about what had happened.

"Oh, Rosie. You're both grieving in your own different ways, neither of you can make any sensible decisions about life. Matt sounds lovely and if it's meant to, it will happen. He's probably feeling very lost after losing his mother. He's met you and is enjoying feeling cared for. You both need to take it slow and work through your own problems before you can make any big decisions. Why don't I come down a little earlier than planned? Your father can't take anymore time off work. One perk of being retired is that I can take off whenever I fancy! Dad can just join us next weekend."

"That would be lovely." Her mother's company was just the distraction Rosie needed. She had been there for her throughout her breakup with Oliver. Her mother had even offered to cut the arms off of all of his shirts. She was her rock and right now, Rosie needed her.

"I've got a few things I need to sort out, but I'll be with you by this evening. I'll pick up some chips by the harbour and then drive up to you."

"Thanks, mum. I love you."

"I love you."

Rosie put the phone down and finished her coffee as she watched a couple walk into the market. She felt a pang in her chest as she saw they were holding hands. Her mother was right, her and Matt were two broken people, stumbling across each other at the wrong time. Were they destined to hurt each other?

The market was busy and kept Rosie from overthinking. It wasn't until she packed up the bus when she checked her phone before driving home that she saw she had a message from Matt.

I'm sorry last night ended that way. Something's come up at work and I'm not going to make it down next weekend. I promise I'll be down the following xxx

Rosie felt her heart constrict as she read Matt's message. Two weeks without seeing him. At least it would give her time to figure out how she was feeling. The sad thing was, both of them wanted the same thing. They wanted to be together. To explore their newfound relationship. Yet, neither of them could give up their life for the other. Nor did Rosie want him to leave London and resent her for it. Rosie stared down at the message. What should she say back to him?

A few minutes of thinking later and she had typed out a response and hit send before she could overthink it.

I'm sorry, too. We need to talk about how we're feeling and the future, but I'm just not ready. See you in a couple of weeks. xxx

As Rosie parked the bus back at the yard, she spotted Chloe loitering at the entrance.

"I bought you a coffee and a cinnamon swirl." Chloe pushed them into her hands as Rosie stepped out of the bus. "I thought you might need feeding."

"I'm fine, Chloe." Rosie tried to brush off her friend's concerns.

"Nonsense. You need looking after Rosie. When you first arrived in Ives-On-Sea, you were a shell of the person you are. You jumped at your own shadow. It's been wonderful getting to know you and watching you blossom. Rosie, you've turned into a confident and successful woman in front of my eyes in such a short amount of time and I'm so incredibly proud to call you my friend. Please, don't allow a silly fling to ruin all your hard work." Chloe's speech was charged with emotion as she grabbed her friend's hand.

"Thank you, Chloe. I needed to hear that." Chloe was right. Rosie had put her heart and soul into making a success here in Ives-On-Sea. She would not let some silly brief fling ruin everything. She was the kind of person who craved being in a relationship, but she had to remind herself she had tried that, and it hadn't ended well. It was time to focus on herself. To keep rebuilding her life. This time round, it was all about her.

"I better run back. Never forget how amazing you are!" Chloe blew her a kiss as she ran up the hill. Rosie smiled to herself for the first time that day. Chloe had reminded her just how important her self worth was. Although she saw a future with Matt, she would put her life on the line to explore it. If she still felt unsure by the end of the week, she had to let him go. With no other plans, Rosie made her way back to the dress shop to help Lily for the afternoon.

By the time Rosie's mother texted to say she was at the harbour chip shop, the dress shop had been closed for a while and Rosie had lost track of time working on a dress. She left her sewing machine and went upstairs to put the kettle on. After the long drive, her mother would want a cup of tea.

Ten minutes later, Lisa Witham fell through

Rosie's front door laden down with bags filled with fish and chips, clothes, offcuts of fabric, and her ancient sewing machine.

"Mum! Are you moving in?" Rosie joked at the number of bags her mother had with her.

"I'm working on a few pieces, so I had to bring them with me. And you know I hate your fancy new sewing machine. I much prefer my own."

"I have a refurbished singer machine now." Rosie watched as her mother's green eyes lit up.

"I'd love to see it."

"Let's eat first." Rosie ushered her mum inside, grabbing the last few bags on the doorstep. Her mother wore a long patchwork skirt and a black jumper, with her red hair cascading down her back. Lisa was the spitting image of her daughter, just older.

Once Lisa had hung up a few dresses she was working on, Rosie encouraged her into the kitchen, where they pulled out the steaming bags of fish and chips.

"How are you?" her mother asked, placing a cup of tea down in front of her. Rosie had offered to make the drinks, but her mother had insisted on her sitting down to eat instead.

Rosie finished chewing her mouthful before speaking, "honestly, mum, I'm awful. I didn't expect to meet someone so soon after Oliver. I'm not even sure I'm over Oliver. It's all such a mess. I really like Matt, but I'm not sure I'm ready to trust someone again."

"Oh darling. Oliver couldn't see how amazing you are. From what you've told me, he's realised what a mistake he made. Just because one man couldn't see you for who you are, doesn't mean another won't. You can't go through life not trusting anyone because Oliver was a fool." Lisa took her daughter's hand in hers and squeezed it. "Tell me more about Matt."

"I barely know him, mum. How silly am I getting this upset about it? He's wonderful though. Incredibly good looking, thoughtful, and he genuinely seems interested in me." Rosie let out a sigh. It hurt just talking about him. She had felt a connection with Matt, something that she hadn't experienced in all of her years with Oliver.

"What makes him so special?" asked her mother. Rosie knew her mother was genuinely interested. She wasn't just trying to make small talk over dinner.

"I don't know how to put it into words. He just... he gets me. I'm not saying he doesn't have any flaws. He's completely obsessed with his work. He's grieving for his mother, and has lots of regrets about not seeing her much before she died, and don't get me started on his dress sense.   "You've grown up, Rosie. You refused to admit any of Oliver's flaws." Lisa was always honest with her only daughter.

"I was stupid, young, and naïve with Oliver. I thought he loved me and that was all that mattered. Now, I understand. There's more to a relationship than just love. Matt respects me." She sighed, thinking back to how he had accompanied her to the market. He had completely thrown himself into it and helped her sell her beloved vintage clothes. Their styles were worlds apart, but that hadn't stopped him from supporting her.

"Rosie, I'm worried that you're romanticising Matt. You hardly know him. Just because he's the first man to pay you any attention since Oliver doesn't mean he's your soulmate." The comment hurt, but Rosie knew her mother was right. Had she just grasped on to Matt because he was the first man since Oliver? She didn't think so, but she couldn't be sure. He was emotionally vulnerable after his mother's death and here she was playing with his emotions, not knowing whether she could ever commit to him.

"I know you're right, mum. I just can't shake the feeling that he is the one." The words spilled out of Rosie's mouth before she had time to consider them. As she heard herself say it, she realised how true it was. She really believed he was the one. If only she could trust him and they didn't live so far apart.

"Romanticising." Lisa muttered as she speared a chip with her fork. She refused to look up to meet her daughter's eye, knowing she would plead with her to accept what she had just said. "Rosie, you've just made a life for yourself here. Focus on you. Don't throw it away for a man."

Following those words of wisdom, mother and daughter agreed to put the subject to rest for the evening and enjoy their time together. Rosie took her mother down to the shop to show her the bridesmaid dress she was working on. She had almost finished it. Her mother marvelled at its beauty. With their shared love of vintage clothes and repurposing clothes, they lost themselves within The Cornish Vintage Dress Shop, and for a few blissful minutes, they forgot about Rosie's unfortunate love life.

CHAPTER TWENTY ONE

Having her mum there was just the distraction Rosie needed. Lisa ensured every second of the day kept Rosie busy enough to stop her mind from wandering. From working in the shop, tailoring clothes, to walks on the beach, and making their own oat milk at home (Rosie hadn't even known it was possible). The week had flown by and Rosie hadn't had time to think about Matt or Oliver. It was now Friday night, and they were sitting in the pub with Rosie's friends. Rosie's father, Michael, was due to arrive at any moment.

"Can we not tempt you to retire to Ives-On-Sea?" Aisha asked Lisa, handing round a packet of bonbons she had brought from the sweetshop.

"I'd love to, but my husband is still working.

Although, I would like to take a few more holidays." Rosie tuned out of the conversation as she felt her phone vibrate from her pocket. She chuckled inwardly as she saw that two messages had come through at the same time; one from Matt and one from Oliver.

Rosie felt torn. Which one should she open first? Her finger hovered over Matt's name. Pushing her emotions away, Rosie forced herself to open Oliver's text first. She took a deep breath before reading it.

I meant what I said about not signing the divorce papers until I speak to you. I won't turn up on your doorstep, but I hope you'll get in touch soon so we can meet and talk. Don't we owe ourselves some closure?

Rosie scoffed. Closure? Where had the offer of closure been when he took his secretary on a dirty weekend away whilst she packed her bags? At first he had begged her to stay, said they could salvage their relationship. When he realised she had made up her mind, he went back to the woman he had cheated on her with. Rosie skimmed over the rest of the message. She noticed he had left his address at the bottom. He'd moved into an apartment near to where they had been living together. At some point, she would have to talk to him to move on with the divorce. However, right now, she really did not feel like speaking to him. It also angered her that he thought she owed him anything. Rosie needed some time to calm down before she could speak to Oliver.

By now, Rosie was dreading opening Matt's text. Her mood had plummeted and the last thing she felt like was reading a message from another man who wanted something from her. However, she had to know what he had to say, and so she steeled herself and opened it.

Can't stop thinking of you. I've missed you so much this week. Looking forward to next weekend. xxx

"Rosie?" Someone was calling her name. Rosie put her phone back in her pocket and looked around the busy pub. She had completely forgotten where she was. Rosie noticed her mother calling her name.

"Sorry mum, I just got distracted."

"Your father's here." She pointed to Rosie's other side where her father was standing, staring down at her.

"Dad!" Rosie exclaimed. She jumped up and hugged him.

"You were a million miles away," her dad observed as he took the seat next to her. Rosie's friends had quietly departed and her mother had gone to get a fresh round of drinks.

"Sorry. My phone distracted me."

"Are you okay?" Her father was perceptive. Rosie was close to both of her parents. She knew she could go to either of them with her problems and both would be supportive.

"Just boy problems." Rosie laughed to take the edge off of her comment.

"Come on, tell me."

"Matt texted me, saying he'll be down next weekend. I really miss him, dad, but I'm scared of missing him. What if he breaks my heart? That's not something I could go through again." Rosie bit her lip.

"Oh, Rosie. I know Oliver broke your heart, but you can't hide away for the rest of your life. Don't be lonely." Her dad wrapped an arm around her shoulders and pulled her in for a hug.

"Why do you make so much sense?" Rosie let out a brief chuckle.

"It's part of being a dad. Anyway, what have you and your mother been up to?" Rosie appreciated her father's attempts at steering the conversation away from her disastrous love life.

"We've been working mostly, but mum has made sure I've been constantly busy!" Rosie chuckled to herself as she remembered Thursday evening. They had been sitting sketching when Rosie's mind had wandered to her love life. Her mother had immediately noticed the drop in her mood and had insisted they walk down to the harbour to watch the moon above the sea. She had declared that their creativity needed it. Rosie had sighed and agreed to accompany her mother. Despite being a twenty-nine-year-old, almost divorced, woman, she still wouldn't dare defy her mother.

"I've had a rather nice, peaceful week with your mother gone." Rosie's father joked.

Her mother returned with the drinks and asked her father how his journey had been. He had taken the train and got a taxi from the station. Rosie looked around the pub. There were so many happy couples surrounding her. It reminded her of when she and Oliver would visit her parents. They would always go for dinner at the pub on the day they arrived. Before leaving the pub, they would have tears of laughter streaming down their faces as Oliver unleashed his dry sense of humour. Rosie missed their past and the relationship they had once shared. He had been her world.

"You've zoned out again." Rosie's mother pushed her drink in front of her. "Enjoy tonight and forget your worries."

"Thanks. They've both texted me."

"Ignore them both. Oliver doesn't deserve a second of your time. As for Matt, if he deserves you, he'll understand you're with your parents and need some time to clear your head." Rosie felt taken aback by her father's advice. He really knew what he was talking about.

"Thank you, dad. I'm going to turn my phone off."

Rosie enjoyed her first evening with both of her parents. The last time they were in Ives-On-Sea, they had been helping her move in and so they hadn't had any time to just relax and take in her new home.

"How are you finding life here?" asked her father. Rosie rolled her eyes. Her mother had already asked her these questions, and now it was her father's turn. Apparently, they only communicated about her love life, not how well she had settled into her new life.

"I love it here. I can't wait to show you the shop. You won't recognise it."

"Wait until your father sees the dress you're working on. The one for the girl who is going to be her mother's bridesmaid. It's exquisite." Rosie's father was used to being shown items of clothing that her mother had created.

"I'll show you it when we get back." Rosie smiled. She knew her mother was trying to boost her confidence. She also knew her father would never say anything negative about a piece she was working on.

"Rosie, you seem different. I think, despite everything, you're happy here." Her father took her hand in his and squeezed.

"Thank you, dad. I am happy. Just a few loose ends still to tidy up." It was true. At the heart of her life in Ives-On-Sea, she was happy.

CHAPTER
TWENTY TWO

The following morning was a Saturday and Rosie treated herself to a lie-in since she didn't have to be in the shop. She needed to make the most of her Saturdays off. Once the tourist season picked up, Lily would need her help. Her parents had moved to a holiday cottage on the edge of the village and so she had her flat to herself again. It was nice to have her space back. Having gone from living with her parents, straight to moving in with Oliver, Rosie had never had the chance to enjoy some time on her own. Moving into the flat had been amazing. She no longer had to answer to anyone. She could stock the fridge with all her favourite foods. There were no more smelly half-opened tins of tuna that Oliver used to leave hanging around. If she wanted toast for dinner, she could. She didn't have to consult anyone else. Friday night drinks at the pub were her favourite. It didn't matter what time she got home, since nobody was waiting for her. Occasionally, the loneliness set in. However, right now, the joy of being in her own company lazing around in bed trumped anything else.

Her phone buzzed from the bedside table, and Rosie rubbed her eyes before picking it up to read the message. It was from her mum suggesting they went out for breakfast at the harbour cafe. Calling it a cafe was a bit of a stretch. The posh harbour restaurant transformed at the weekend to serve brunches. Rosie quickly sent a reply saying she would meet them in an hour. As she went to put her phone back down, she remembered she had ignored Matt's message from last night. She stared at the screen, wondering what to say. Eventually, she tapped out a message without thinking too much into it and hit send.

I miss you too. Although I wish I didn't. My mum's been staying all week and has been keeping me busy! Had a therapy session on Monday and she thinks I should trust you and open myself up to heartbreak. xxx

Rosie also spotted a message from Sofia saying how much they had enjoyed their stay in Cornwall and they hoped to see her in London soon. Rosie rolled her eyes, muted her phone, and went to get ready to meet her parents for breakfast. She wouldn't put it past Sofia to throw her and Oliver together. Ignoring the message seemed to be the best option. They had outgrown their friendship, there really was no point in making the effort.

An hour later, she walked into the harbour cafe. She had dressed in a chunky knit orange jumper with a pair of vintage denim dungarees over the top. She tied her hair up in a bun with a matching orange silk scarf. It only clashed a little. Rosie smiled to herself as she spotted her parents and realised her mother was also wearing a pair of denim overalls. They'd always had a very similar taste in fashion. Teenage Rosie would have turned around, run home, and changed. Thankfully, Rosie was now mature enough to see the funny side.

"Sorry, I forgot the memo and didn't pack my dungarees," joked her father, as he got up to kiss her on the cheek.

"I'm sure I've got a pair in the shop if you want to change after breakfast?" Rosie teased.

"Your father isn't as slim as he once was, darling. I don't think they'd fit him." Rosie laughed at her mother's comment and took a seat at the table. She ignored the empty fourth seat where her husband should be sitting. Spending time with her parents made her realise just how lucky she was. They had a great relationship.

They ordered their breakfasts and coffees and stared out at the sea. It was a dull day, and the sea was thundering in. Enormous waves threatening to splash over the harbour wall. It was a foreboding sight.

"Your brother called in the week. He wants to arrange a family meal." Rosie hadn't known her mother had spoken to her brother whilst staying with her.

"A family meal?" she questioned, wondering why Will wanted to get everyone together. They were a close family, but they normally limited family dinners to birthdays and Christmas. "Have I missed his birthday?"

"No. I think he's got some news he wants to share with us." Rosie noticed her mother glance nervously over at her father.

"What's going on, mum? Dad?" Rosie looked at her parents. Neither of them wanted to speak.

"We think he's proposed to his girlfriend." Her father refused to make eye contact as he spoke. Rosie breathed a sigh of relief. She was worried Will was ill.

"Why are you two acting strange? It's great news!"

"Are you sure, darling? You're okay with it?" Her mother's face was filled with pity as she anticipated Rosie's reaction.

"Mum, just because my husband turned out to be a cheating waste of space doesn't mean Will doesn't deserve happiness."

"He seems very happy with his girlfriend. I know they haven't been together very long, but I hope things work out for them. We might even get to meet her if he proposes."

"Being together for a long time doesn't

guarantee happiness. Just look at my marriage."

Rosie's mother looked embarrassed.

"Oh darling, I'm so sorry."

"No, mum. I didn't mean it like that. Look, let's just forget about it. I'm happy for Will. I promise not to have an emotional breakdown when we meet her for the first time. My therapy has been going really well. Last week's session, we discussed how I might trust someone again. I feel a lot more positive about things. Now, let's change the subject. What are our plans for today?" Rosie was excited to explore the area with her parents. The streets were filled with memories from her childhood. She had spent all week trying to avoid talking about Matt with her mother. It was something she needed to work through in her own head, not something her mother could help her with.

Once they had finished their breakfast and had caffeine in their systems, they walked along the harbour wall. There were a handful of shops, one of which was Aisha's sweetshop. As they stepped inside, the sweet scent of confectionary overpowered their senses. Aisha had merged the interior of a vintage sweet shop with a nautical theme. Jars of sweets filled the shelves from floor to ceiling and a ladder made from driftwood hung from a rail, allowing all the sweets to be accessed. It was sweet heaven.

"Morning!" Aisha called from behind the counter. She was wearing all black with a blue and white striped apron on top. Sweets By the Harbour lit up in blue LED lights behind the counter - the only wall not covered in sweets.

"Morning, Aisha. I really should pop in here more often." Rosie's eyes strained as she spun around looking at the sweets. She had always had a sweet tooth.

"Only on days you're not hungover. I know what a sweet tooth you have with a hangover." Aisha winked at her as she weighed out a bag of strawberry fizzes for a customer.

"That'll be every day then," teased Rosie's father.

"Dad! I'm reliving my early twenties. I was too busy keeping house to go out partying, so now I'm making up for it."

"And we do it so well." Aisha laughed. She had also recently left a long-term relationship and the two women had spent many nights in the pub discussing their love lives over a bottle or wine. Rosie had been much more forthcoming about her breakup. However, she could tell from the pain behind Aisha's eyes that she had suffered just as much.

They each picked out a bag of sweets and said goodbye to Aisha.

"Where are we going now?" Lisa asked, popping a pink shrimp in her mouth.

"I thought we could visit Rose Hill. I've checked and the cafe we used to visit is still there. We can have hot chocolates and a walk along the beach." Rose Hill was a village they used to visit.

It was only a fifteen minute drive away and by the sea. Rosie and her brother loved visiting there as the cafe sold huge hot chocolates covered in marshmallow and cream. With everything she had been through lately, she was keen to emulate those happy childhood memories.

They had a wonderful day together. The little cafe still sold those amazing hot chocolates, and they each had one with a slice of chocolate cake. Rosie even took a photo of the three of them in the cafe and sent it to Will. As she pulled her phone out, she noticed she had a reply from Matt; she ignored it. She was having a wonderful day with her parents and didn't want to ruin the day worrying about their on-off relationship. Rosie had deleted the notification for his message and pushed it from her mind. Will had immediately replied, saying he was jealous and wished he was with them. Rosie was excited to see him soon. She hoped he had a happy announcement to make. Although they didn't talk often, they were close, and she wished nothing but happiness for her little brother.

Her parents dropped her off at home to get ready for their evening meal. Once inside her flat, Rosie pulled out her phone to read Matt's message. She had intended to leave it until she was home from dinner, but she couldn't wait any longer.

Have a lovely time with your parents. I'm hoping to come down on Friday night and stay until Monday morning. If you would rather not see me, then let me know and I won't come. I promise you, Rosie, I have no intention of breaking your heart. xxx

Rosie finished reading the text and realised she had a big, soppy smile on her face. She could just imagine Matt sat at his desk, his crisp white shirt and expensive suit, rubbing a hand against his stubble as he composed the message to her. Despite the mix-up with his ex, and their problems with distance, she honestly believed he had no intention of hurting her.

Ignoring the message for a little longer, Rosie jumped in the shower to consider her reply. She washed her hair and allowed it to dry naturally into its ringlets as she applied her makeup. Rosie dressed in a milkmaid style dress her mother had made for her. She had crafted it from silk in an emerald green. They were only going to the pub for dinner, but Rosie wanted to make the effort. As she looked in the mirror, she smiled at herself. Despite the heartbreak and turbulent last year, her eyes were shining back at her. Her heart might be causing her problems, but she knew she was strong enough to get through it. Whatever happened, she was Rosemary Witham and nobody would ever take that from her. Oliver's betrayal had taught her how to be strong and comfortable in her own skin.

Before leaving for dinner, Rosie grabbed her phone and quickly sent a reply to Matt.

I look forward to seeing you on Friday. xxx

Spending time with her parents had reminded her just how much she craved a relationship like theirs. She felt that spark with Matt and she wanted to explore it. Although heartbreak terrified her, she knew avoiding it was not an option.

CHAPTER TWENTY THREE

The week with Rosie's parents whizzed past. They had spent each day in the shop with Rosie. Occasionally escaping for the odd hour to have some time by themselves. They were still very much in love and enjoyed each other's company. It was Friday morning and her parents were packing up the car, ready to drive home.

"You're sure you're okay? I can stay for longer. Especially since Lilly is ill and can't work tomorrow." Her mother was reluctant to get in the car.

"I'm fine. Honestly. I will miss you both, but I think it's time we all got back to normality." It had been lovely to have the constant distraction of her parents around, but Rosie knew she needed time on her own to explore her feelings.

"Come on. Matt will be arriving soon and I'm sure Rosie isn't ready to introduce us." Rosie's father opened the car door, encouraging her mother to hurry. Rosie had told them about Matt's plans to visit, and so they had decided to leave early to allow her some time alone before her next guest arrived.

Rosie waved her parents off. She would see them soon in London if Will had some news to share. Her phone bleeped with a text from Matt saying he was ten minutes away. He was earlier than expected. She was still in her pyjamas. Rosie ran back indoors, put her coffee cup in the dishwasher, brushed her teeth, and put her hair up into what was now her signature bun. However hard she tried, hair was sticking out everywhere. She sighed as she looked in the mirror. Dishevelled was the look she was going for today. It would be a boring couple of days for Matt as she was covering Lily while she was off ill.

Even though she was expecting it, the knock on the door made Rosie jump. It was only eight in the morning. Matt must have left at a ridiculous time. Was he eager to see her or did he just have lots to do here? Shaking her head, Rosie opened the door.

"Hello." Her breath escaped her as she saw him standing in front of her. Rosie had to remind herself to breathe. Yet again, he was wearing a suit. Stubble peppered his face and his eyes remained focused on her.

"Morning. Sorry, am I too early? I can come back later." He ran a hand through his hair. It had grown since Rosie had last seen him. He had probably been too busy working to fit in a haircut.

"No, it's fine. I have to work today, so I need to get ready. You're welcome to wait for me or I understand if you'd rather come back."

"I'd rather stay with you. Could I use your shower?" Rosie nodded and led Matt into her flat. It was awkward, they were being so polite to each other. He was wearing a suit and Rosie wondered whether he'd come straight to Ives-On-Sea from work.

"You jump in the shower first, I'll grab a coffee. Do you want anything?" asked Matt. Rosie wanted to ask for a kiss, but she felt shy around him. Pushing the thoughts aside, Rosie jumped in the shower. She dressed and got herself ready for work while Matt was showering.

"Did you come straight from the office?" Rosie asked.

"Yeah. I've been working late all week." He sighed, staring down at his coffee cup. Matt was sitting in her kitchen with his wet hair dripping down his long-sleeved polo shirt. He was finally wearing something other than a suit.

"You should take a break." Rosie sat opposite him and took his hands in hers. Now she was close she could see the dark circles under his eyes. He looked as though he hadn't slept since he had last seen her.

"I've been staying late at work on purpose." He was still refusing to meet her eyes.

"Matt, what's wrong?"

"When I was here with you, I felt as though I could tackle anything. Going back to London made me realise how alone I am. I miss my mum." Tears were pooling in his eyes and Rosie got up to hug him.

"Of course you miss her, Matt. It's okay." She held him as silent tears trickled down his face. Rosie had been expecting this last time. Instead, he had pushed aside his feelings until he was alone.

"I'm sorry. I didn't mean to turn up at your door and start crying. You've got enough to worry about without me unloading my grief on you." He rubbed the palms of his hands against his eyes and stepped back. His walls had sprung up again, and he was back to being the Matt she had first met. Truthfully, Rosie felt relieved to see this show of emotion from Matt. She had worried about how much he was suppressing his grief. Her mum had been right. They were both grieving.

"Please, don't apologise. I'm always here for you." She meant it. Despite their short time together, she really did care for him. Whatever happened between them, she wanted to make sure he was okay.

"Thank you, Rosie. Thank you for allowing me to be me around you and not trying to change me." His voice wobbled. Rosie felt her heart yearn for him as he opened up to her.

"I would never change you."

*****

By the time Rosie opened up the shop, she was half an hour late. She only hoped nobody would realise. Rosie had left Matt upstairs, making himself some toast. Alone in the shop, she had some time to think. Seeing his vulnerable side had only added to her confusion. She was falling for him and yet she still couldn't see a future where they could be together. Either way, one of them would have to give something up. Then there was the ultimate question; could she ever truly trust him?

Being in the shop was calming. Silence filled the air, and yet Rosie knew endless memories surrounded her. People's lives had played out in the clothes around her. Today, Rosie had dressed in a simple green and black pinafore dress, thick tights, and a black jumper underneath. It was chilly in the shop. Rosie made two cups of coffee, ready for Matt to join her once he had finished his breakfast.

Rosie's phone buzzed with a text from Aisha asking if she wanted to go to the pub tonight. Rosie thought about it. Perhaps the pub was just what she and Matt needed. Some time together where they couldn't think about the future. Her friends would keep them distracted. She texted back, saying she and Matt would love to join them.

"Sorry about my little outburst this morning," apologised Matt as he entered the shop.

"Please, don't apologise. I'm just glad I can

173

be there for you." Rosie smiled and handed him his coffee. Matt took the coffee and sat on the stool beside where she was sewing a new dress.

"Have you been busy this morning?" he asked.

"No. Not a single person. It'll get busy again next weekend. The first weekend of December is always busy. Everyone remembers they have Christmas presents to buy and outfits to be made." It excited Rosie. She loved helping people choose gifts. The person would tell her about the recipient, and Rosie would consider the history of each piece before she made a suggestion.

"How do you know all this?" Matt was staring at her, his eyes wide.

"My mum ran a haberdashery shop. I spent many weekends and school holidays working there."

"I imagine you had lots of fun."

"It was wonderful." Rosie had longed to take over the shop when her mother retired. However, Oliver had pointed out that their lives were in London.

"What are your plans for Christmas?" Matt's change of subject was quick and Rosie noticed he was refusing to meet her eyes.

"I haven't even thought about it. Why?"

"I was hoping I could spend it with you." Rosie took a sharp intake of breath. She had not been expecting Matt to say that.

"Do you not have any friends in London?" As the question left her lips, Rosie realised how it sounded. His face dropped.

"I could ask them. Most of them have young families, so I'd feel I was intruding."

"Sorry, I didn't mean it how it sounded. I just thought you might have someone you know better than me who you would like to spend the time with."

"There's nobody I'd rather spend time with." He looked up and his eyes met hers. Rosie could see the sincerity in his words.

"Of course you can spend it with me. I'll probably be seeing my family, but you're welcome to come too."

"Thank you, Rosie."

Matt leaned over to kiss her but the first customer of the day interrupted them. Once the customer had been and gone, there was a slow trickle after. Rosie was busy all day with dress fittings and general customer enquiries. Matt did his best to help where he could, but that mostly comprised of folding items and putting them into bags. It was fun having him with her, and she knew he was grateful for the distraction. She was seeing a softer side to him, one that was not so career driven. Perhaps even one she could see settling in Ives-On-Sea. Rosie pushed the thought away as soon as it came. She could not allow herself to get her hopes up; it would only break her heart.

*****

They closed the shop at four and had an hour before they had to be at the pub.

"Are you sure you don't mind us going to the pub? I know we need to talk, but honestly, I just want to put it off."

Matt reached out for Rosie's hand and gave it a small squeeze.

"It's fine, honestly. I'm looking forward to it. Let's just agree to have fun this evening and forget about the serious side of life. We can talk tomorrow. There's no rush here, Rosie."

"That sounds perfect." Rosie smiled and reached up on her tiptoes to press her lips to Matt's. She pulled away before he could deepen the kiss. "I need to get ready."

They were late to the pub and everyone was sitting waiting with menus open in front of them.

"Finally! We're starving." Chloe cried as they sat down. Aisha was sitting beside Chloe with a glass of white wine on the table in front. Milo and Craig were also there. They were sharing a bottle of red.

"Sorry." Rosie apologised.

"I'll go get the drinks." Matt wandered off.

"So, tell us the gossip. How's it going?" Aisha leaned across the table.

"The problem is, he's perfect." The words hung in the air and Rosie sighed.

"He does look perfect." Craig was looking across to the bar where Matt stood ordering the drinks. He had opted for another suit. This one was navy and tailored perfectly to him.

"The other problem is our lives are worlds apart." Rosie felt the familiar bubble of anxiety in the pit of her stomach.

"We could have a stern chat with him. Find out what his intentions are?" offered Milo.

"Please don't. I'm trying to just live in the moment."

"Rosie, you own a vintage dress shop and you want to live in the moment?" The entire table erupted into laughter at Aisha's comment.

"This is going to end terribly, isn't it?" groaned Rosie.

"We'll still be here." Chloe reassured her.

Matt interrupted the conversation as he returned to the table and placed a gin and tonic down in front of Rosie.

"Thank you."

The night was a success, and Matt charmed all of her friends. Rosie pushed her worries aside and allowed herself to relax and enjoy the evening.

CHAPTER TWENTY FOUR

Saturday morning, Rosie awoke alone in her bed. Last night, Matt had kissed her goodbye on her doorstep and gone back to his parents' house. It had been a lovely evening spent in the company of friends, but Rosie was determined to talk to Matt today. They had to know where they both stood and what their thoughts for the future were. If this was just a fun fling, she needed to know.

There was a knock on the door as Rosie was getting ready. She wandered over to the window to see who it was. Matt was standing looking up at her, a grin on his face. Rosie rushed to let him in. The last thing she needed was the neighbours gossiping about a handsome man on her doorstep early in the morning. She'd have lots of locals in the shop today trying to glimpse her mystery guest.

"Morning." He beamed at her as she let him in.

"Hello." Rosie blushed as she realised she was still in her dressing gown.

"You finish getting ready. I'll put the kettle on."

Once Rosie was ready, she had a few minutes before she needed to open the shop and so she took her coffee and sat opposite Matt at the kitchen table.

"Is it a full day in the shop for you?" Matt asked.

"Yeah, I'm afraid so." She wished she could spend all day with him, but with Lily ill, she had nobody else to open the shop.

"That's fine. I'd love to spend the day with you, but I'm going to get something ready for this evening. I thought I'd take you somewhere special, with no distractions, so we can speak properly." He glanced at her, waiting for her reaction.

"That sounds like a good idea." Rosie's hand shook as she clutched her cup. She thought she knew what she wanted to say to him, but now they had a plan, her mind was blank. At least she had the day in the shop to find the words. Was she truly ready to open up to him and tell him how much he already meant to her? Rosie wouldn't know until the moment.

*****

"I'm freezing!" Rosie exclaimed as stepped out onto the cold streets of Ives-On-Sea. Matt had told her to pack an overnight bag and to come with him.

"Sorry, I didn't think it was worth driving. We're heading down to the harbour, to the little blue cottage. I remember you telling me you stayed there with your family." He paused for a moment. "I thought it was secluded enough for us to talk with no distractions."

"That sounds wonderful." Rosie beamed back at him. She hadn't been to the little cottage for over ten years now. It held so many fond memories for her. She only hoped that their impending conversation wouldn't tar those memories.

"Don't forget, I need to be up early." Rosie reminded him. For the first time, she resented having to get up early for the market.

"How early is early?"

"I need to be leaving by seven."

"We'll set some alarms! Who's opening the shop for you?"

"Lily's feeling better, so she said she was fine to open. I told her to call me if she struggles and I'll take over in the afternoon."

They had reached the blue door to the cottage. Matt pulled a key from his coat pocket and opened it, holding it open for her to walk ahead of him.

Matt followed her, carrying both of their overnight bags. The cottage had enjoyed a makeover since Rosie had last visited. They had painted the living space white with powder blue furnishings.

"It's beautiful." Rosie sighed as she spun around, taking in the space. It looked nothing like the old-fashioned little cottage she remembered from her childhood.

"Thank you. After my father passed away two years ago, my mother threw herself into renovating the cottage. Nothing could help her heartbreak, but it gave her a distraction. She poured all of her pain into this." Matt's eyes were glassy as he looked around at the space.

"We don't have to stay here." Rosie walked over to him and slipped her hand into his, weaving their fingers together.

"No. I want to and I can't think of anyone else I'd rather be here with. Come on, I want to show you upstairs." He kept hold of her hand as he led her up the narrow stairway. Rosie gasped as they walked into the main bedroom. A copper bath sat in front of floor to ceiling windows, looking out to the grey stormy sea.

"The glass is one way. It's a mirror on the outside," Matt explained as he saw her looking over.

"Wow. Are you sure this is the same cottage? I remember this room with its pine furniture and frilly bedsheets."

"It's a little nicer now." Matt led her over to the windows to look out at the view. "I love it here. Seeing the sea stretch out below. It really puts life into perspective." He let go of her hand and traced a finger across her cheek.

"Thank you for bringing me here." Rosie was finding it difficult to get her words out as he stepped forward, closing the gap between them. He kissed her until Rosie's senses returned and she stepped back from him. "We need to talk." She reminded him.

"Come on." He led her back down the stairs to the kitchen. "I stocked the fridge with picky food."

Together, they pulled the food out of the fridge and Matt poured them both a glass of wine. Despite feeling sick, Rosie was grateful for the distraction of the food. She opened a bag of crisps and nibbled on one as she waited for Matt to begin the conversation.

"I don't know where to start, Rosie. I'm worried I'll scare you if I tell you how I'm feeling." He was staring down at the cracker he'd just covered in hummus.

"As hard as it may be for me to hear certain things, we have to be honest with each other."

"Why don't you tell me what you're thinking and feeling?" Matt put the cracker in his mouth and chewed, leaving him unable to speak. Rosie put down the crisp she was holding and wiped the salt off of her fingers with a napkin.

"Matt, I really do like you. Am I ready to trust someone again? I'm not sure. I don't know if I'll ever be sure. All I can do is keep pushing myself and continue to get to know you. I'm scared, Matt. Our lives are worlds apart. Seeing Sofia made me realise how much I love it here. The person I was in London is dead. I don't think I could ever go back. It just feels as though everything is against us being together, and yet there's nobody else I'd rather be with. When I'm with you, I feel so happy. You understand me and you know what I need before even I know it. I want nothing more than to be with you, but I don't know if we can make it work. If there's no chance of us ever being together, then I think we need to end whatever this is between us before we hurt each other." She took a deep breath to still her thumping heart. Had she said too much? Rosie picked up her wine and took a gulp of it as she watched Matt's face as he processed everything she had said.

"Rosie, I want nothing more than to be with you. I've never felt this way about anyone before." He leant forward and took a hold of her hand as Rosie felt her pulse racing. "I know the distance is a problem, but we'll work it out. My heart was always set on London. Coming back to Ives-On-Sea has made me realise I ran away to London to avoid the pain of my childhood. I'm not as opposed to moving back home as I once was. My heart isn't in London anymore. As for trusting me, I want to spend every day with you, showing you that you can trust me. I know I need to earn your trust. Rosie, I'm prepared to spend my life earning your trust." Matt stood and pulled Rosie into his arms. "I'm not saying I love you, Rosie, but I can see myself falling for you." His eyes were bore into hers. Rosie tried to tell him she felt the same way, but her mouth was too dry to form words. Her body trembled as he put his finger under her chin and tilted her lips up to meet his. She relaxed against him as he kissed her. They pulled apart and Matt took her hand and led her towards the stairs up to the bedroom.

CHAPTER TWENTY FIVE

Rosie's alarm filtered through her peaceful sleep. Her eyes fluttered open, and she was immediately aware of the body lying next to her. Matt's arm was wrapped around her waist, his bare chest pressed against her back. They had forgotten to close the curtains last night, and it was still dark outside. Rosie wanted to snuggle into his embrace and close her eyes, but she couldn't. It was Sunday, and she had to get to the market.

"Do we have to get up?" Matt groaned.

"You don't have to come with me." Rosie pulled his arm away from her waist and wriggled away from him before he convinced her to stay in bed.

"I'm coming with you." He sat up in bed and

ran a hand through his dishevelled hair. Rosie felt her cheeks flush as memories of last night flashed in front of her eyes.

"I'm going to jump in the shower." She grabbed a towel and quickly made her way across to the bathroom.

"Shall I join you?" Matt called after her.

"We don't have enough time!"

Rosie threw together an outfit from the clothes she packed in a haste yesterday. They arrived at the market and set up quickly. Matt was already getting used to how the bus worked. He bought them coffees, and they set about chatting to customers. It was a gloomy November day and sales were slow. However, Matt made sure she had a smile on her face. He smiled and joked with everybody, and Rosie couldn't help but join in. His enthusiasm was contagious, and not even the weather could dampen it. Their eyes kept meeting, and each time Rosie felt a huge smile spread across her face. She couldn't help but feel it was too good to be true.

"What time do you have to leave?" Rosie asked as she packed up the bus ready to drive back to Ives-On-Sea. Matt had received a call from his boss to say there had been a crisis at work and they needed him in the office tomorrow.

"I thought I could cook us dinner, then I have to leave."

They travelled back in silence and dropped off the bus before grabbing coffees and walking along the seafront. Rosie slipped her hand into Matt's, partly for warmth but also for the comforting feel of his skin touching hers.

"What are we going to do, Matt?" her voice wobbled. The thought of not seeing him for another week hurt.

"Don't cry, Rosie." He wiped the tears from her cheeks and took her hand in his.

"We're in an impossible situation." She angrily swiped at the tears Matt had missed.

"It's not impossible. Being with you is making me open up and confront emotions I'd buried. What I want is changing. There's lots of repressed memories that I have from living here. But being with you is helping. I want to be here more than I want to be in London. It's a big decision, and I need to know we're both ready if I decide to walk away from my life."

"I can't ask you to walk away from your life in London." Rosie stepped back to leave some space between them. It was unreasonable to expect him to give up his modern life in the city and move back to the sleepy village just for her. London and Cornwall were worlds apart. Rosie knew she couldn't give up her life in Ives-On-Sea and move back to London. Her little shop meant too much to her. It symbolised her independence and everything she had achieved since leaving Oliver.

"We're both damaged people, Rosie. This probably won't be easy, but I'm not giving up. We'll find something that works for us. I promise." He moved his free hand to cup the side of her face and

Rosie leaned in to his touch.

"What worries me is that I don't want you to go." The words slipped out before Rosie could stop herself.

"What worries me is that I don't want to leave." Rosie could see the change in Matt's face as he opened up to her.

"You could call in sick." She knew he wouldn't, but she still tried.

"I've never taken a day off sick." Rosie rolled her eyes at his reply. It was obvious work had consumed Matt's life.

"I'll see you soon?"

"I'm not sure about next weekend, but I'll be down the following." His words echoed in the wind as Rosie tried to calm her breathing. Two weeks without him. She shouldn't feel as though her world was caving in just because she wouldn't see him next weekend.

They walked in silence for a while, both processing their thoughts and emotions. Something had shifted between them after their night together. They had allowed each other in and shared their emotions. It was scary. They were on the verge of falling, and yet they didn't know whether they had a future together. Rosie squeezed Matt's hand. He was still real, and he was still by her side.

"I meant it when I asked if I could spend Christmas with you."

"I meant it when I said you could."

"I'm looking forward to spending the time

with you."

"What about work?" Rosie was trying to ignore the niggling worries about Matt's approach to work. It was his life. Did he know who he was without it? She suspected he didn't.

"I'm going to take the Christmas period off. I've never done it before, so I'm sure I'm owed it."

"You've never taken Christmas off? What about spending Christmas with your parents?"

"I drove down on Christmas Eve, after work, then I always returned late Christmas Day."

"You didn't even stay for the full festivities?"

"No. I was an only child, so the holidays were quite short-lived." He shrugged his shoulders and turned to look out to sea. From the rigid stance of his back, Rosie could tell he didn't want to speak about his childhood any more.

"I'm sorry. I ask too many questions. My brother would say it's the result of being the spoilt older sister." Rosie sighed. The differences in their childhoods were plain to see.

"It's okay. I want you to ask questions. I'm not very good at just telling people things, so your questions are good. Christmas isn't the easiest time for me, but I'm looking forward to experiencing something different with you." His face lit up as he turned to look at her again. "I really meant it, Rosie. There's something inside of me that's changing for the better. I'm realising that there's so much more I want from life. For years, I had convinced myself my work was all I wanted and needed. Meeting you has changed everything. I want so much more, and I want so much more with you."

They walked back to Rosie's flat, hand in hand, as the drizzly weather continued. Neither wanted to say goodbye, but they had to. As promised, Matt cooked dinner. They kept the conversation light as they ate. Neither wanted to address his impending departure. Eventually, the time came, and he said his goodbye. Rosie watched from the window as his car pulled away. She promised herself she wouldn't cry. Despite him promising he'd be back in two weeks, the thought that she might never see him again scared her. Oliver had decided he no longer wanted her. What was stopping Matt from doing the same?

After Matt left, Rosie busied herself catching up on some tailoring projects. The sound of her phone ringing echoed through the empty flat, making Rosie jump. She'd barely thought about her phone since Matt had arrived. Eventually, she found it under one of the sofa cushions. She answered it just before it went to voicemail.

"Hello?" Rosie was out of breath. She hadn't even had the chance to check who was calling.

"Rose, it's me, Will." Rosie relaxed as she heard her brother's voice.

"Hi Will. Sorry, I couldn't find my phone."

"Mum said you might not answer. Something to do with a man." He was teasing her.

"Grow up." Rosie rolled her eyes. Age hadn't changed them much.

"Sorry, Rosie. I didn't mean to tease. I want you to be happy. You deserve it." It meant a lot coming from her brother. He had been there for her the day she had discovered Oliver's affair. She had only had to ring him and within half an hour, he was at the door.

"Thank you. Anyway, what did you want? You don't normally just call me for a chat."

"I was hoping you might come down to London for dinner next Saturday evening? You're obviously welcome to stay at mine rather than booking a hotel. Mum and dad are having the spare room but there's always the sofa." Rosie had never slept on Will's sofa. He had only lived fifteen minutes away, and so there had never been a reason to.

"I'd love to. I'll get the train down." Rosie's mind was whirling. Perhaps she could get the train down on Friday and surprise Matt. He had said he was busy, but hopefully he could spare Friday evening. She didn't have his address, but she knew where he worked. Rosie put the phone down and felt a huge smile spread across her face. Excitement fizzed inside of her at the thought of seeing Matt again. She hoped he would like the surprise. Before Rosie could worry, she pushed the thoughts to the back of her mind. His life revolved around work. Surely he was lonely in London. He would love seeing her.

Rosie was too restless to go to sleep, so she slipped downstairs to the shop. There was something relaxing about being surrounded by so many silent memories. They were each sat there, waiting for her to pick them up. She needed two new outfits; one for surprising Matt and the other for dinner with her family. Rosie needed something flattering, but comfortable for Friday. She wanted to wow Matt, but she was also aware she would be sitting on a train for hours. In the corner was a pile of donations that needed altering. Some fabric shimmering in the moonlight caught Rosie's eye. It was a beige silk slip dress. The top was moth eaten but Rosie knew she could make something from it. As she looked at the fabric, she immediately knew it would look beautiful as a skirt. She would alter it, perhaps with a split up the side. That was one outfit decided. Rosie looked back over at the rows of dresses. She could indulge her love of vintage for her family meal. Rosie had been pining over a gorgeous 1920s dress which she had bought at auction last month. She couldn't justify buying it, but she could always rent it from the shop. Rosie rolled her eyes at her attempts to justify the dress. It was beautiful. The dress was full length and black, with a sweetheart neckline and cap sleeves with beading. As Rosie slipped it on, she realised it fitted her perfectly. Fringing covered the skirt from the waist to the ground. She spun, and it moved with her. It was breathtakingly beautiful. Rosie only wished Matt would be there to see her in it. She didn't know his plans for the weekend, but perhaps he'd invite her back to stay on Saturday night. Only an hour ago, Rosie had been dreading the weekend, and now she was excited about it.

She took the dress back upstairs with her and hung it in her wardrobe, ready for the weekend. Rosie got ready for bed and checked her phone. There was a text from Matt saying he was halfway home. She wanted to stay up and wait to check he got home safely, but her eyes were heavy. Giving in to sleep, Rosie ignored her thoughts of everything she had to do before she went away.

CHAPTER TWENTY SIX

"How was your weekend?" Chloe bounced into the shop as Rosie turned the sign to open. She was holding two takeaway cups and a bag of pastries.

"Confusing. What are you doing here?" Rosie fetched the spare stool from the storeroom so they could sit together behind the counter.

"I thought you might need a friendly face. I saw Matt's car leaving Ives-On-Sea last night. Well, actually I heard him on the phone. You know how when you call someone through your car it's so loud?" Chloe's eyes grew dark and she picked at the croissant on her lap.

"Chloe, what's going on?"

"I think he was on the phone to Mimi." Chloe's voice was just above a whisper.

"What made you think that?" Rosie's tone was hard.

"I heard him say her name." Chloe let out a sigh. She knew she couldn't hide the truth from her any longer.

"Oh." Rosie rubbed the heels of her hands against her eyes. Was that why had been so eager to go home yesterday? Was he going back to Mimi?

"Are you okay?" Chloe's brow was furrowed as she stared at her friend.

"We had such a lovely weekend, Chloe. He promised me I could trust him and said he'd spend the rest of his life proving it to me."

"It was just a phone call, Rosie."

"Was it though? What if he was going home to her?"

"Maybe I shouldn't have told you." Chloe took the untouched cup from Rosie's hand and pulled her into a hug.

"No. Please, always tell me."

Chloe kept reminding Rosie that it was just a phone call and there was nothing suspicious about it. She had only heard Mimi's name before the car sped off.

"I need to get back to the cafe. Speak to him, Rosie. Don't just shut him out." Chloe squeezed her hand and left without another word.

Before she changed her mind, Rosie pulled out her phone and texted Matt to ask him if they could chat on the phone later. He immediately replied, saying he'd call her after her therapy session.

The day passed slowly, and Rosie was grateful for the session with her therapist. Together they talked through Rosie's fears and her therapist reminded her not to jump to conclusions. It disappointed Rosie when the session ended. For the first time that day, she felt as though she was thinking rationally. It had just been a phone call. Matt told her about Mimi's constant attempts to contact him, so a phone call wasn't unusual.

With trembling hands, Rosie accepted Matt's call.

"Hello?" Her voice wobbled as she greeted him.

"Rosie, it's nice to hear your voice." His reply sent shivers down Rosie's body. She missed him.

"I need to speak to you about something." There was no point trying to put it off.

"Is everything okay?" Matt's voice filled with concern.

"Chloe popped into the shop this morning because she'd heard you on the phone as you drove out of Ives-On-Sea." Rosie held her breath as she waited for his reply. Would he be honest with her, or would he try telling her that Chloe had got it wrong?

"I turned my phone on when I left yours to find lots of texts and missed calls from Mimi. Ignoring her hasn't been working, so I called her. I wanted to tell her I'd met someone new and to stop harassing me."

"How did she take it?" It surprised Rosie to

realise she believed him. The doubt that had been plaguing her had vanished.

"Not well." Matt sighed.

"Do you want me to talk to her?" The words were out of her mouth before Rosie had thought through her offer, and so it was with relief when Matt refused her help.

"I think it's best if we leave her alone. Anyway, enough about her. How's your day been?"

As Rosie put the phone down, she realised her cheeks hurt from smiling. They'd been on the phone for two hours talking about their days. She worried all day for nothing. The second she heard his voice, she knew he was telling her the truth. With a jolt, Rosie realised she was starting to trust him.

CHAPTER TWENTY SEVEN

Friday morning finally arrived. It had been a long week, but Rosie had spoken to Matt every evening. Somehow, she'd kept her visit to London a secret, determined to surprise him. Aisha had offered to give Rosie a lift to the station. It would be a long day of travelling. She had packed a new sketchbook and a portable charger for her phone. Rosie knew where Matt worked and so she was going to go straight there. If her plan failed, she would just simply call him and tell him she was in London and hoped to see him. Hopefully, it wouldn't come to that, but at least she had a back-up plan.

In the car on the way there, Rosie noticed Aisha's puffy eyes. She was also quieter than normal. Usually, Aisha could fill a silence with endless chatter. "What's wrong with you?" Rosie asked.

"It's nothing." Aisha sighed and kept her eyes studiously on the road ahead.

"Aisha, don't lie to me." Rosie insisted. Aisha's response worried her. Although Aisha was quiet, she wasn't often one to hide things.

"It's just my ex. I had an email from him. Can we talk about it when you're home? I just don't feel ready yet." Rosie nodded and allowed them to fall into a comfortable silence for the rest of the journey.

"Are you going to be okay?" Aisha asked as she opened the boot of her car for Rosie to get her suitcase out.

"Aisha, I'm going to London! I lived there for years. I'll be fine."

"Sorry. I've never been and you hear so much on the news." Aisha looked down at her feet.

"Thank you for caring, Aisha. Perhaps we could plan a London trip so you can experience it?" Rosie liked the idea. It would be nice to show her friends around London, and she wanted to prove to herself that she was no longer the same Rosie from London.

"I'd love that." Aisha's face immediately brightened with a smile. They both needed something to look forward to.

"We'll start planning when I'm home. I better go or else I'll miss my train. Thank you for the lift." She briefly hugged her friend and waved goodbye before running to the ticket office.

With her suitcase stowed, Rosie sat in a

window seat and pulled out her phone. She had a message from Matt wishing her a good day. Rosie quickly typed a response, asking him what his plans were for that evening. As she waited for his reply, she smoothed down her skirt. She had repurposed the silk dress into a lovely midi skirt and paired it with a black soft knit jumper. The scenery whizzed past as the train hurtled towards London. Rosie settled down in her seat and enjoyed the quietness of travelling alone. It was a beautiful crisp day, and the train was empty. Excitement fizzed away inside her at the thought of seeing Matt. He would be so surprised to see her outside his office. At least, she hoped he would be. Doubts were creeping in, but she resolutely pushed them away. Matt had spent hours on the phone with her every night this week. Of course he'd be happy to see her.

The journey dragged as the train pulled into each station along the route. It was a five and a half hour journey from Cornwall to London, but Rosie kept herself busy. She watched the people getting on and off the train, wondering where life was taking them. After a while, she pulled out her sketchbook and started working on some new designs. Her newfound happiness with Matt had put a spring in her step. Rosie was brimming with creativity, so much so that she couldn't keep up with all the designs floating around her head. At least the journey would give her time to draw.

Eventually, the train pulled into Paddington Station. Rosie packed up her sketchbook and retrieved her suitcase. It was four o'clock and rush hour was only just beginning. She knew Matt would be working for a little while longer. He had texted her back saying he had no plans; he was going to stay late at work. Rosie walked outside the station and made her way to the nearest Starbucks. After ordering a coffee and panini, she took one of the few spare seats. Now she had to decide how to surprise Matt. In her head, she would turn up and he would magically walk out of the building at the same time. However, she knew that scenario was highly unlikely. As she sipped her coffee, she decided to go to his office and then call him from outside. It might not be the big surprise she had hoped for, but all that mattered was seeing him. With a plan in mind, Rosie took a bite of her cheesy panini. It was nice enough, but bland compared to her cheese and chutney doorstop from Chloe's.

Once she had finished her food, Rosie went outside and hailed a taxi. She reeled off the address and tried to sit still for the drive. It took around forty-five minutes to get to Canary Wharf. Rosie knew it would have been much quicker to get the tube, however her time away from London hadn't dulled her memories of rush hour. She loathed the idea of squishing herself on to an over-packed tube carriage. Her height meant she always found herself underneath somebody's armpit as they reached for a handle to steady themselves. It was now almost half-five. She only hoped he wasn't so busy he couldn't leave work with her. Nerves were building inside her. Was she really doing the right thing by surprising him? It was too late for that. As they trundled along the busy streets, Rosie looked out at the sea of people. All with their heads down, staring at mobile phones, and marching towards unknown places. Were these people really happy? Rosie thought back to her stroll up the cobbled path to the pub with the sea air filling her nostrils. That was happiness, not this pollution filled city.

"Here you go, love." The taxi driver announced as he pulled up outside a building. Rosie glanced out and saw the name of Matt's workplace in big letters above a revolving door.

"Thank you." Rosie handed over the money and, with shaking legs, got out of the taxi. There was a bench to the right and so she wheeled her suitcase over to it. Once sat, and without her legs shaking beneath her, Rosie felt more able to gather her thoughts. Doubt was creeping in. What if Matt wasn't happy to see her? She pushed her thoughts to the side and grabbed her phone, pressing call on his number before she could give it a second thought. It rang twice before he answered.

"Rosie, could I call you back in an hour? I'm just going into a meeting." He didn't even give her the chance to respond before putting the phone down. Rosie felt herself blush with embarrassment.

"I'm so stupid," she whispered to herself. "How could I ever think he'd just drop everything for me?" Now what was she supposed to do? She had always known surprising him would be a risk, but she hadn't expected him to be so blunt on the phone. She could drop her suitcase at Will's and then come back in an hour.

Rosie wiped her eyes as a figure emerged from the building. It was Matt. Had he already seen her? Was he trying to surprise her? A smile spread across her face and she went to jump up and run to him. However, before she could instruct her legs to move, she spotted a figure beside him. A gorgeous leggy blonde with her hair tied back into a ballerina bun. A light smattering of makeup emphasised her petite features. She was gorgeous. Rosie couldn't help but notice the way the woman's suit matched Matt's. Both were expensive and perfectly tailored to their figures. Rosie felt a sickening feeling in the pit of her stomach as she watched the woman link her arm through Matt's. Jealously boiled within her. Angry tears threatened to fall from Rosie's eyes. She couldn't be jealous of Matt just walking out of work with a female colleague. He had told her he was about to go into a meeting. Perhaps they were travelling to another office.

"Mimi!" Someone came running out of the office and over to the blonde woman. As Rosie heard the name, she felt her heart shatter. It wasn't just a colleague, it was Matt's ex. Hurt and anger encompassed Rosie and she looked away from the pair. Matt had been stringing her along. She wasn't his type. He just wanted a distraction for when he was in Ives-On-Sea dealing with his parents' estate. Her breath came in frantic waves as she tried to gain control of herself. She couldn't succumb to her emotions here.

Rosie frantically looked around. She felt exposed in Central London, with home a six-hour journey away. Her eyes wandered, looking for somewhere to go. She noticed Matt and Mimi had left. Probably for a lovely meal out before going back to Matt's for a passionate evening. Rosie knew Will would let her stay tonight if she asked. However, she didn't want to tell him about Matt. It was embarrassing to know that yet another man didn't want her. She sucked in a deep breath. Rosie knew where she would go. She pulled out her phone and scrolled down her messages, looking for the address. If all men were cheats, perhaps she should stick to the one she knew so well.

CHAPTER TWENTY EIGHT

Rosie took a deep breath as she looked at the buzzers for the flats. She knew what she was doing was stupid, but she couldn't stop herself. With a deep breath, she pushed the buzzer for flat three. It wasn't long before a familiar voice drifted through the intercom, bringing with it a flood of emotions.

"Hello?"

"It's me. Let me in." There was silence, but the buzzer turned green, indicating the front door had been unlocked. With trembling hands, Rosie pushed open the door and wheeled her suitcase behind her. Her head and her heart were screaming at her to run. This was the last place she should be, and yet here she was. She had nothing left to lose. The sound of his voice had brought back all the heartbreak again. He had been the one person she thought she could rely on. The person she thought she was going to spend the rest of her life with.

Rosie walked into the hallway and realised she had no clue where to go now. Set over three floors, the building had no signs showing where each flat was. She spun around, looking for numbers on doors. Was this a sign telling her to leave?

"Rosie?" a voice called from the top of a flight of stairs. Her head snapped up at the noise and she stared into the eyes of her almost-ex-husband. Her stomach did a little flip as she took in his appearance. He looked exactly the same as he always had. His dark hair skimmed his forehead and his piercing green eyes appraised her. She was still attracted to him.

"Hi." He stood opposite her. She didn't know what to say. Rosie had only thought as far as seeing him. Now he was standing in front of her, she realised what an awful idea this was.

"Are you okay?" he asked, glancing at her suitcase.

"I didn't know where else to go." Rosie stopped a sob from escaping her. She felt embarrassed at the impulsive decision she had made, thinking if Matt could spend the evening with his ex, then so could she.

"Come on." Oliver came over and grabbed her suitcase for her. Rosie didn't argue. She followed Oliver into his new flat. A gasp escaped her lips as she walked into the hallway. It was a replica of the home they had once shared. When they had sold their home, Rosie had told Oliver she didn't want to keep any of the furniture. She didn't want any reminders of their life together. It looked as though he had moved it from their shared home to his new place. He hadn't even bothered to rearrange the layout.

"It reminds me of you." he admitted, seeing the look on her face. His head turned to hide the blush on his cheeks. That was new. He had always been confident around her. Rosie balled her fists. She didn't care how he acted around her.

"You should move on, Oliver." Her tone was stony to hide the emotional turmoil within. Why had he broken her heart? They could have been happy together.

"I can't move on, Rosie. I love you." He stepped towards her. Rosie's heartbeat picked up and her breath caught in her throat. Oliver was within touching distance. He reached forward and took her hand in his. "I miss you."

"I miss you." The words were barely audible as she whispered them.

"Come home, Rosie." Oliver's hand trailed down the side of her face until it came to cup her cheek.

"I can't." Rosie shook her head, let go of his hand, and stepped back, out of Oliver's reach. It wasn't him she missed. She missed his familiarity. She missed the security of being one half a partnership.

"Can I get you anything?" he asked, ignoring her reaction.

"Could I have a cup of tea, please?" Rosie needed a distraction. A part of her still wanted him. Oliver left her alone in the hallway to put the kettle on. Rosie glanced at the pictures on the wall before following him. They were all photographs from their wedding.

"Why do you have the photographs up?" Rosie had to know why he kept these reminders on show. Relief flooded through her as she discovered the pale blue kitchen was nothing like the one they had shared. Rosie had spent hours designing that kitchen. Oliver enjoyed cooking and so she had invested in all the high-end gadgets for him. They had dreamed of hosting endless dinner parties and Christmases in that kitchen. Instead of those joyous memories, all Rosie was left with was the memory of sitting at the breakfast bar and confronting Oliver about his affair.

"I still care, Rosie. I know I made the biggest mistake of my life and I'm not ready to move on from it yet." Rosie knew him well enough to know when he was telling the truth. His brow furrowed as he refocused his attention on the drinks. Rosie didn't know how to respond. Although he felt remorse over his actions, that didn't change what he had done. Neither of them could go back and rewrite history.

"You didn't care when you were sleeping with

your secretary, or when you took her away for a dirty weekend while I was packing up my things. That was our chance to talk, Oliver." It was a cheap shot, but Rosie couldn't help it. He'd shattered her heart for nothing, and here he was, acting as if she had turned her back on him. There had been many occasions where Rosie had envisioned seeing Oliver again, and yet none of them had played out like this in her head. Truthfully, she had expected him to have moved on. She had assumed his messages were just him trying to be awkward and make her life difficult. However, now she was face-to-face with him, she could see he still loved her.

"I can't apologise enough, Rosie. It was stupid. I love you so much and I hate myself for being so stupid and throwing away everything we had together."

"It's a shame you had to ruin our relationship before you realised how much it meant to you." Rosie could hear the bitter words spewing from her mouth, but she couldn't stop herself. It was easier to take her anger out on him rather than admit how much it hurt to see him still in love with her. A part of her would always love him, but there was no future for them. She had to push him away, even though it hurt to do so.

"I can't apologise anymore, Rosie."

"I'm sorry, I'm just still so hurt. I should go."

She went to turn around but Oliver grabbed her arm. "Please, don't go yet." His eyes bore into hers. Begging her to stay. Those eyes that Rosie had lost herself in so many times before. She allowed herself a moment to sink into them. To turn the clock back a couple of years and pretend everything was fine again.

"How could you hurt me like that?" she whispered.

"I didn't mean to, Rosie. It's just we'd been together from such a young age that I suppose I wondered how life would feel with someone else." He was still holding onto her.

"Life with me wasn't good enough?"

"That's not what I said, Rosie." His eyes hadn't left hers. Rosie's entire body was shaking under his gaze. It was as though she could just step back into her old life. Slowly, she felt herself reaching up on her tiptoes, seeking Oliver's lips. Her eyes fluttered closed, and she waited for the touch of his soft lip against hers. As soon as her eyes were closed, images of Oliver with his secretary flooded her mind. She pulled back before his lips met hers.

"I'm sorry, I shouldn't have done that. It's just so strange being here with you."

"It's okay." Oliver let go of her.

"Shall we sit down?" Rosie took her drink and gestured to Oliver to show her towards the living room. He took her through to a room which mirrored the living room she had painstakingly designed. On the far wall was the vintage mirror they had brought home from a day-date at Camden Market. He had hated the mirror, so Rosie wasn't sure why he still had it up. The scatter cushions she had bought from a charity shop still adorned the sofa. It was like stepping back in time. Back to her old life. Despite the pain, Rosie knew she had done the right thing in leaving. Her life had changed so much and yet she was happy. Well, she was happy when she wasn't getting her heart broken.

"Rosie, I needed to speak to you. I had to see you face-to-face to know there was no chance of us rekindling anything. I couldn't sign the divorce papers until I'd seen for myself. Rosie, you look amazing. Life without me suits you. Seeing you now, I know we could never go back to how things were. That spark hasn't gone, but I've hurt you too much." Oliver let out a dark chuckle.

"My life is unrecognisable from the one we shared, but it's everything I've ever wanted. I love everything I've built for myself." The image of Matt leaving the office with his ex crept into her mind, bringing it all into doubt. Rosie pushed the thoughts from her mind. Now was not the time to think of Matt. She had come here to take her mind off of things and close the door on her past.

"I'm glad you're happy. You deserve it."

"Thank you. How are you?" It surprised Rosie to discover she really wanted to know how he was. Seeing him made her realise her feelings for him had shifted. There was still love there, but it wasn't romantic. She cared for him, but only because they shared so much history.

"It's been rough, but I'll be okay. Seeing you has really helped. It's made me realise perhaps one day I can be as happy as you are now." He gave her a weak smile.

"You will, Oliver. We went through a lot together. Perhaps we were never meant to last." The words hung in the air as they both considered it.

"I'll always love you," his voice was a whisper.

"I'll always love you, Oliver, but I'm no longer in love with you."

"I can see that. Let me get the papers and I'll sign them." He left the room and Rosie sat back, sinking into the sofa. She felt awful for ignoring his messages. He really had just wanted to speak to her in person before signing the papers. He hadn't meant to be awkward. There was something cathartic about seeing him. The hurt was easing and Rosie felt as though she was getting the closure she didn't know she needed.

It wasn't long before he walked back into the room and handed her the documents.

"I wish things had been different." He brushed her hand.

"So do I, but let's not dwell on that."

"I saw Sofia and Harry a few days ago. They told me you were dreadfully unhappy in Cornwall and that I should go and sweep you off your feet."

Rosie's mouth dropped open at the revelation.

"Why did they say that?" she asked, trying to hide her anger.

"They felt you had changed and were no longer the person they once knew." He shrugged his shoulders.

"I have changed, Oliver. For the better."

"I can see that. I'm sorry. I didn't mean to upset you."

"No, thank you for telling me what they said. I think it's a friendship I'll be happy to leave in the past. Oliver, do you still have that bottle of champagne your parents got us for our last anniversary?"

"I do."

"Shall we toast to all the wonderful years we've had together?" Rosie really needed a drink.

Sharing a drink with Oliver felt strange. It felt so right, and yet so much had changed since they had last raised a glass together.

"To our futures." Oliver sat down next to her and lifted his glass to hers.

"And our happiness." Rosie added. She reached out and took Oliver's hand in hers. "You'll find someone, Oli."

"Have you found someone?" he asked. She heard him take a deep breath, steeling himself for her answer.

"I thought I had, but I'm not sure."

"I'll wait for you. Be with someone else for a while. Experience life without me. I'll wait." Oliver's words hung in the air as Rosie tried to digest them.

"Oliver... I..." She didn't know what to say. The offer was tempting. It would be a comfort to know that whatever happened, Oliver would always be there to go back to. If she tried hard enough, she could fall back in love with him.

Before either of them could say anything more, Rosie heard a key in the door.

"Hello? Oli, it's me." A high pitch voice sounded throughout the hallway. Rosie didn't need to see the person to know who it was.

"Everything you said. The decor of your flat. It was all a lie." Rosie shook her head in disbelief. She'd almost fallen for it.

"Rosie?" Oliver's secretary walked into the room, her face mirroring the shock Rosie was feeling.

"You're welcome to him." Rosie finished her drink and stood up with the divorce papers tucked under her arm. Staying wasn't an option.

"I thought you had nowhere to stay?" Oliver's face fell as he watched her gather her belongings.

"I'll call Will. I don't want anything more to do with you, Oliver. Best of luck for your future together."

Without looking back, Rosie wheeled her suitcase out of the flat and back down to the street. It had been a very confusing evening.

Rosie pulled out her phone and dialled Will's number.

"Hello?" he answered quickly. Rosie strained to hear him through the background noise.

"Will, are you home?"

"No, I'm having a few drinks after work. Are you okay?" Rosie could hear him walking away from the crowd so he could hear her better.

"I need somewhere to sleep tonight." She

hoped he wouldn't ask questions.

"There's a spare key in the hanging basket. I'll be home soon. Put the kettle on." Rosie smiled as she put the phone down. She could always count on her brother having her back.

CHAPTER TWENTY NINE

Rosie's taxi dropped her outside Will's house before he arrived home. The drive hadn't been too bad. For once, Rosie was entirely grateful for the driver's attempt at small talk. The few comments that had passed about why she was in London stopped her mind from wandering. She had erased the last few hours from her explanation. Now, she was alone standing on Will's front drive, looking at some very sorry looking hanging baskets containing soil and the remains of plants. Cringing, she reached up and put her hand into the basket, looking for the spare key. She squealed and pulled her hand back. Something had wriggled against her hand.

"Evening!" Will called as he climbed out of the taxi. He was waving joyously at her, having obviously just witnessed her searching for the key.

"There better not be slugs in these baskets!" she called back.

"You should be used to slugs. You were married to one!" Will had obviously made time for a few after-work drinks. She rolled her eyes and waited for him to pay for his taxi. Despite Will's years of living in the city, he still insisted on using cash for everything. He stumbled down the pathway towards her and Rosie wrapped her arms around herself. She hadn't worn a coat, and it was freezing. Tonight was far from what she had been expecting. She had so many emotions to process, but she didn't know where to start.

"Sorry." Will hiccuped as he fumbled for his keys.

"No, I'm sorry for ruining your evening." It seemed she was ruining everyone's evening.

"You didn't. In fact, you probably did me a favour. I'd be in a dreadful state tomorrow if I stayed out any longer." Will unlocked the front door and held it open for Rosie.

"Thank you, Will."

"Have the spare room tonight. I'm just going to have a quick shower. Why don't you make yourself at home and put the kettle on?"

Rosie put her suitcase in the spare room and changed into her pyjamas. As she wiped off her makeup, she allowed her tears to fall. Seeing Oliver had forced her to bury the hurt of seeing Matt with his ex. Now she was alone, the pain was washing over her. How could he have been so heartless? Rosie could feel her emotions threatening to consume her. Her phone bleeped from her handbag. It was a text from Matt. She opened the message.

Sorry I haven't called you back. Meeting ran on. Just leaving the office now. Miss you xxx

Rosie felt anger rise within her. How dare he lie to her? She knew better than to reply when her emotions were so erratic. With a sigh, she put her phone back in her bag and went to put the kettle on.

It was strange being in Will's home by herself. She had visited plenty of times, but always with Oliver. Rosie's mind wandered to the signed divorce papers in her handbag. She finally had what she wanted, and yet there was no sense of relief or happiness. A chapter of her life had been closed tonight. Perhaps even two chapters. Her move to Ives-On-Sea was to start a new life. A life for her. Yet, here she was still missing the familiarity of Oliver and with a freshly broken heart.

"Is the tea ready?" Will walked into the kitchen. He looked as though he had sobered up a little.

"It's just brewing." Rosie replied. She was trying to pull herself back from her thoughts and focus on the moment.

"Do you want to talk?" Will asked.

"Yes, please." Rosie finished making the drinks and followed Will into the living room.

They sat on the sofa and Rosie took a sip of

her tea as she organised her thoughts. Where did she start?

"Start from the beginning." Will could see the confusion on her face.

"I came down early to surprise Matt. I'm not sure what his address is, so I went straight to his office." Rosie paused as her voice wobbled. She took a moment to compose all the jumbled thoughts in her head before telling Will what had happened outside Matt's workplace.

"You're sure it was his ex?"

"Yes, I heard someone call her name." Saying it out loud only worsened the pain.

"You say her body language suggested they were a couple? What about his?" Will always knew the right questions to ask. Rosie thought about it for a moment. She recalled the painful memories. Matt's face had been neutral, and he had shown no affection towards Mimi. Rosie's mind was blank as she tried to conjure up a memory of how he acted around her. Did he have the same neutral look on his face when he was around her? She didn't know. The pain was engulfing all of her memories, making it impossible to think straight.

"I'm not sure."

"I hate to say this, Rosie, but I think you need to speak to him."

"I know I can't ignore him forever, but I need some time."

"You're entitled to as much time as you need." Will got up and picked up a chocolate from a box of Quality Streets on the coffee table. Rosie saw him think for a moment before he handed the chocolate to her. It was her favourite, a toffee penny.

"Thank you." She smiled and unwrapped the sweet.

"So what happened after that? You obviously didn't come straight here."

"I went to see Oliver." Rosie popped the sweet into her mouth. She knew Will would send a barrage of questions her way and so it would buy her some time as she chewed.

"You did what?" Will jumped up from his chair and spilt his tea. Rosie nodded her head, still chewing. She'd known what Will's response would be.

"Rosie, why would you? He's been blackmailing you over those divorce papers. You've just played into his hands."

"It wasn't like that, Will. I'm glad I saw him. It was the closure I didn't know I needed. I also have the signed papers upstairs in my handbag."

"Are you okay?" Will asked. Her face had fallen at the mention of the papers.

"I was expecting to feel relieved, but I just feel sad. He asked me to go back to him and I came so close to saying yes. Then his secretary let herself in." Rosie felt such a fool for almost accepting his offer.

"Oh, Rosie. At least you know he hasn't changed. He wasn't the person you thought he was. You can close the book on that part of your life and move on."

Will was right. Despite how the relationship had ended, Rosie and Oliver had experienced years of happy memories together, but now that was lost and the memories tarnished by Oliver's actions. With the divorce papers signed, she felt as though she could properly grieve the loss of her marriage.

"Thank you, Will." Rosie meant it. Her chat with her brother had put a new perspective on her evening. "I think the chat with Oliver was inevitable. Out of respect for our years together, we needed to sit down and talk. When I moved to Ives-On-Sea, I thought that part of my life was over, but it's only now that I realise it's truly behind me. I can finally move on with my life, knowing there was no hope of a future together."

"And will you be moving on with Matt?"

"I'm not sure. Even if there's nothing between him and his ex, can it work if I obviously don't trust him?" Rosie didn't know if she could ever trust anyone again, or if she even wanted to.

"Rosie, after how Oliver treated you, do you really feel as though you could trust someone straight away? Sometimes trust has to be earned. Although you might have a connection with Matt, you hardly know him. I don't think it's unreasonable for you to have some reservations. If he cares about you, he'll understand. First, you need to talk to him about what's going on with his ex. Decide whether there's something going on between them or if he's just being amicable because they have to work together."

"When did you become so grown up?" Rosie joked, trying to move the conversation on to a less serious topic. She'd done enough talking for one night.

"I've always been this grown up. Sleep on it and speak to Matt tomorrow."

Rosie nodded in agreement, and the pair slipped into silence as they sipped their tea.

"Anyway, enough about me. What's this family meal about?" Although Rosie's intention was to shift the attention from her, she was also interested in why Will had summoned everyone to London.

"I have someone I want you all to meet." He blushed as he looked down at his cup.

"Have you proposed to her?" Rosie couldn't resist teasing him.

"No, I haven't proposed to *him*."

"Oh!" Rosie squealed as she realised exactly what he had just said. "Do mum and dad know?"

"No. I felt I should tell you all together, but I'm scared. Telling you first seems a lot easier."

"Oh, Will. They're going to be so incredibly happy for you. We could all see something was missing with the women you've dated."

"Do you really think they'll be okay?" Will's brow furrowed.

"Will, all mum and dad have ever wanted is for us to be happy."

"Thank you, Rosie. For a sister, you're pretty cool." They both chuckled at Will's attempt at humour.

"Is he coming to dinner tomorrow evening?"

"No, I thought it might be best if he wasn't there when I told mum and dad."

Rosie was disappointed. She wanted to meet the man who had made her brother so happy and comfortable in his own skin.

"Why don't we meet him for a drink after? I know mum and dad will be fine with it, but if you're worried, it can just be us two."

"I'd like that and I think he would, too. I'll tell him it's just us and then if mum and dad come, it'll be a bonus."

"Perfect! You message him and I'll pick a film for us to watch."

Will groaned, knowing how different their taste in films was. For a little brother, he was alright. Rosie knew how lucky she was to have such a supportive family. Without them, she didn't know how she would have made it through the last couple of years.

CHAPTER THIRTY

When Rosie woke the next morning, she had a new outlook on life. At least, she was trying to convince herself she had a new outlook on life. It had taken her a while to fall asleep, and as she lay in the darkness, she realised she needed to change how she approached things. Before she even had time to rub her weary eyes, she picked her phone up from the bedside table and quickly typed a message to Matt. It read,

At my brother's. Need to speak to you about something, but now's not the time. Will message you when I'm back home xxx.

Rosie had tossed and turned in the night, trying to decide what to say to Matt. She didn't want to make him fret until she contacted him. However, she couldn't pretend nothing had happened. Rosie shook her head. That way of thinking was not akin to her new outlook on life. She would not make excuses for other people's actions anymore. Rosie was soon to be a divorcee, and she intended to make the most of her life from now on. Despite the bad times, there were many happy memories, and those were what she was going to focus on. Well, those and the gorgeous vintage dress shop she was already pining for. Rosie hit send on the message and left her phone in the bedroom. Today was about Will. He didn't need her checking her phone every five minutes. For now, she could put those worries to the back of her mind and enjoy her time with her family.

Will was already awake and eating breakfast in the kitchen.

"Morning!" Rosie called, walking straight over to the coffee machine.

"Sleep well?" Will asked around a mouthful of toast.

"Yes, thank you. I'll grab a shower after breakfast then I'll move my stuff out of the spare room for mum and dad."

"Thanks! Mum said they're going to meet us at the restaurant as dad has had to go into work this morning."

"Does that mean we have all day to ourselves?" Rosie was almost jumping with excitement.

"Yes. Why?" Will looked nervous.

"So we can trail London's vintage shops for stock?"

"I love how you can now justify it by referring

to it as buying stock." Will rolled his eyes. He knew his sister too well.

"Will you come with me? It's been ages since we had some sibling bonding time."

"You just want me to come with you so I can reach the higher racks of clothing."

"They hide some of the best stuff up high!"

"Okay, but you can buy me lunch."

"Deal!" Rosie grabbed her coffee and went back upstairs with it to get ready. She didn't want to waste a single minute of snooping around London's vintage offerings. There was nothing better than hiding a broken heart under a heap of shopping bags.

*****

Rosie's feet were aching by the time they returned, laden down with bags.

"How are you going to get all this home?" Will asked, staring at the pile of bags now in his hallway.

"I'm not sure. I didn't really think of that." Rosie laughed. It had been fun walking around London with her brother, forgetting about all of her problems and indulging herself in her love of vintage clothes.

They had sauntered around Notting Hill and then made their way over to Camden and stopped at every second hand shop in between. It had been Rosie's idea of the perfect day. Will hadn't moaned once, despite being bored. Instead, he reached up to the top shelves and carried bags while Rosie inspected rows of clothes.

"I've got some boxes in the loft. I'll arrange a courier to drop it to you next week."

"You're the best!" Rosie called, running up the stairs. They were running late, and she needed to get ready.

"You're not leaving all of this here!" Will called after her. It was useless. She couldn't hear him.

*****

An hour later, Rosie was ready to leave. She had tamed her unruly hair into a pretty up-do. A light smattering of makeup covered her face, and she was wearing the gorgeous 1920s fringed dress that she had borrowed from the shop. She didn't need a man to tell her she looked beautiful. She felt beautiful.

"Are you ready?" Will called from the bottom of the stairs.

"Coming!" She grabbed her clutch on the way out, leaving her phone stowed in her suitcase. Will had ordered a taxi, which was already waiting for them.

"You look lovely. I'm so proud of you, Rosie. You've been through so much. Tonight, you look happy." Will opened the door for her, allowing her to walk ahead.

"Thank you, Will. I feel happy. Anyway,

tonight's about you! Let's go tell mum and dad about your boyfriend."

They arrived at the restaurant a few minutes late and their parents were already waiting. Rosie breathed a sigh of relief as she saw her mum had made a similar effort. She wore a burnt orange silky jumpsuit with a matching hair scarf.

"Mum, you look amazing!" Rosie hugged her. It had only been two weeks since they had last seen each other and yet so much had happened.

"So do you, Rosie."

Everybody said their hellos and took their seats.

"Is the lucky lady not joining us?" Rosie's father asked.

"Actually, that's what I wanted to speak to you about." Will glanced over at Rosie and she gave him a reassuring smile. There was not one doubt in her mind that their parents would be happy for him.

"What is it, Will?" Their mother had caught the glance between them.

"There is a lucky person in my life. But it's not her. It's him." There was silence as her parents understood what Will was saying. Rosie could see Will's face contort as concern crossed it.

"Oh, Will! Darling, why didn't you tell us?" Within seconds, their mother was up from her seat and had come round to hug him.

"I didn't know myself until recently," he admitted, hugging her back. His whole body sagged with relief.

"So when do we get to meet the lucky man?" asked their dad.

"Rosie suggested we all meet for drinks after dinner. I thought dinner might be a little formal." Will gave Rosie a quick smile.

"Wonderful. I'm looking forward to it. Will Matt be joining us, Rosie?" Just like that, her mother had moved the attention away from Will and back on to her love life.

"No, he won't. Things are a little complicated between us at the moment." The last thing Rosie wanted to do was explain what had happened. Tonight was all about Will.

"What's happened?" asked her mother.

"Mum, tonight's about Will."

"Rosie, what did he do?" Even her dad was getting involved.

"It's okay, Rosie. I've been so worried about tonight. It's quite nice to have the attention shifted from me." Will encouraged her to speak. Rosie took a deep breath before retelling the story of coming down to London on Friday.

"At least you got to speak to Oliver and finalise things with him. Let's hope that Matt has a reasonable explanation when you speak to him. I know you, Rosie. This won't break you." Her mother's words were encouraging.

"It's different this time. I have too many other loves in my life to allow a man to ruin it all."

The food arrived, which naturally moved the conversation in another direction. Rosie was grateful to have the attention off of her.

"Where are we meeting him?" Rosie asked, as her father paid the bill for dinner.

"There's a bar round the corner from here in the style of a speakeasy, so we've arranged to meet there." Will smiled as he watched Rosie's face light up.

"Thank you, all of you. I know I've not been the easiest person over the last year, but it means so much to know my family loves and supports me." Rosie felt her heart swell with happiness. She blinked back tears. The last thing she wanted was to meet Will's boyfriend with a tear-stained face.

"We love you. Now, what's this boyfriend's name?" Her mother squeezed her hand across the table.

"His name is Niall."

"Let's meet Niall!" Their father pushed his credit card back into his wallet and stood up, ready for everyone to follow him.

It was a chilly night, but Will promised the bar was around the corner and so they walked. As they made their way, Will told them all about how he had met Niall at work and the pair had soon realised there was a spark between them. Eventually, they arrived outside an unassuming door and Will knocked three times. A doorman answered and led them down a windowless hallway, lit only with a few candles. The sound of jazz filled Rosie's ears, and she already knew she was going to love this place.

The hallway opened out into a dimly lit room where a jazz band played and the buzz of conversation could be heard in the background. Exposed brick was lit with old-fashioned candelabras. The bar was on the far back wall, filled with vintage spirits. It drew Rosie towards it and she left her family behind as she went to explore.

"I love your dress!" The woman behind the bar exclaimed. She was wearing a 1940s maroon tea dress with her hair in pin curls.

"Thank you! This is amazing." Rosie's head was spinning as she took everything in. The dark wood flooring shone in the dim lighting. There were leather barstools adorning the bar. On the other side of the room were bright pink velvet booths. It was a truly beautiful collection of vintage items.

"Rosie, are you okay?" Will asked, approaching the bar.

"Yes, sorry. I got a little carried away." Rosie forced herself to focus on Will's face. As she tuned out the surrounding bar, she noticed someone stood beside Will.

"This is Niall. Niall, this is my sister, Rosie. As you can probably tell, she's a little obsessed with all things vintage."

"Niall, it's lovely to meet you!" Rosie leant forward and enveloped Niall in a hug.

"It's lovely to meet you! Will's told me lots about you."

"Forget everything he's told you!" Rosie joked.

"Why don't you two sit down and I'll get the

drinks in? Rosie, what would you like?" Will was trying to keep Rosie's attention.

Rosie asked for a martini and followed Niall back to the table where her parents were sitting.

"Isn't this gorgeous?" her mum asked as she took a seat next to her.

"It's amazing." Rosie was in awe.

"Will told me you have a vintage dress shop?" Niall asked. Rosie smiled at his attempts to make conversation.

"I do. It's not just dresses, we stock all vintage clothes. I love your suit." As Rosie properly took in Niall's appearance, she realised his handsome looks had distracted her from his clothing. He was wearing what looked to be a vintage herringbone tweed suit.

"Thank you. A friend of mine's wife owns an auction house, so whenever I'm visiting, I buy a lot!"

"Oh, you're going to fit in well." Rosie laughed at her mother's comment. It seemed Niall was the perfect fit for their family.

The evening was a success, and Rosie enjoyed every moment of seeing her brother happy. For the first time since her teenage years, Rosie felt happy being on her own. She was embracing everything she loved with people around her who loved her. Despite having nobody beside her, she felt whole for the first time in a long while. She would eventually speak to Matt and ask him to tell her the truth. Rosie knew she would be heartbroken if he admitted to cheating on her. However, she also knew she would be okay. Even if it was a misunderstanding, it still needed to be spoken about, and Rosie had to express her insecurities and trust issues. Either way, it wouldn't be easy.

CHAPTER
THIRTY ONE

Sunday's journey home felt endless. As Rosie watched the scenery roll past the window, she kept replaying the weekend's events. A text from Chloe interrupted her thoughts. She was inviting her to dinner. Dinner with her friends sounded perfect. Rosie could talk to them about Matt and try to decipher the jumble of emotions she was experiencing. She texted Chloe back and turned to stare out of the window. As the familiar seascape came into view, Rosie felt herself relax. It felt as though she was coming home.

Chloe and Aisha picked Rosie up from the station. They were going to drive her home so she could unpack and freshen up before dinner.

"How was it? Was Matt surprised?" Chloe

threw a barrage of questions at Rosie as she climbed into the car. Aisha was sitting in the back, eagerly awaiting Rosie's answers.

"I had a lovely time, but I didn't spend any time with Matt." Rosie explained what had happened and watched as Chloe and Aisha became angrier and angrier.

"If he dares come anywhere near you." Chloe was gripping the steering wheel so hard her knuckles had turned white.

"Want me to jump on a train to London and tell him exactly what we think of him?" offered Aisha. Her hand reached for the door handle, despite the moving car.

"Girls, please. I haven't even spoken to him properly. There might be a perfectly innocent explanation." Rosie wanted to calm them both down.

"Are you trying to convince me or yourself?" demanded Aisha.

"I knew he was too good to be true," commented Chloe.

"Oh, I don't know. All I know is visiting London made me realise just how happy I am here. Yes, I enjoyed being back in the city, but the entire time I was yearning for my little shop. If things with Matt are over, I'll be heartbroken, but I know I'll be okay. My life here is wonderful and I now have my divorce papers signed. Honestly, I don't think I truly realised how much I've changed until this trip. I'm enough on my own. I don't need anyone by my side."

Rosie was rambling. "Everything will be fine. I'll get through it." She promised her two best friends.

Rosie went home and unpacked before having a quick shower. She unpacked her phone and put it on charge. There was a missed call from Matt and a couple of texts. She let him know she was home and going out with her friends. Although they needed to talk, she didn't want to just jump into it. With her hair still wet, Rosie left for Chloe's. They had agreed not to mention Matt again. Rosie knocked on Chloe's door, hoping she would be home. The girls had gone for a drink after dropping Rosie off, agreeing to meet again in a couple of hours.

"Where's Aisha?" Rosie asked as she poured a glass of wine. Chloe was standing by the cooker stirring dinner.

"Someone turned up at the pub looking for her. Aisha said she'd have to miss dinner, but she'd message us either later or tomorrow to explain." Chloe shrugged her shoulders.

"Who turned up?" asked Rosie. "Was it Aisha's ex?"

"I'm not sure. She looked shocked when she saw him walk through the door."

"I wonder who he was." Rosie was worried about her friend. She'd been so caught up in the drama in her own life that she'd hardly had time to consider Aisha.

"It was strange. She jumped up from her seat, downed her glass of wine, and left with him." Chloe's eyes were blazing with the drama. Rosie loved her, but Chloe enjoyed the thrill of other people's drama a little too much.

"Have you heard anything from her since?" Rosie asked. She pulled out her phone, but there was nothing from Aisha.

"No, nothing. I'm sure she's fine. If we don't hear from her by tomorrow, we'll check in on her." Chloe agreed to check in on her in the morning on her way to opening the cafe.

The girls spent the evening speaking about business and local gossip. They were careful to keep the conversation away from relationships. Rosie was worried about Aisha; it was unusual for her to have anyone visit. Especially someone who had obviously upset her. Rosie was almost relieved when it was time to go home. The last few days had emotionally drained her.

"Thank you for dinner, Chloe!" Rosie hugged her before leaving. It was late. She really should go straight home, but something told her to check in on Aisha. The streets were dark and a thin layer of ice coated them. Rosie took each step carefully. She slipped a few times but reached out to steady herself on the closest wall. It was a slow walk to Aisha's house, but as soon as Rosie knocked on the door, she knew it was the right thing to do. She could hear someone sobbing from inside.

"Aisha, it's Rosie!" she called, not wanting to scare her. Although it was only nine o'clock, it was pitch black, as there was very little street lighting in Ives-On-Sea. It wasn't a time when a single female wanted to open the door to a stranger.

"Rosie?" Aisha opened the door. She stood there wringing her hands, her eyes wild with emotions.

"What's wrong?" Rosie pulled her friend in for a hug.

"It's a long story. I'm fine, I promise."

"You're obviously not fine."

"I'm not. Come in." Aisha moved aside to let Rosie into the cottage. Rosie immediately noticed the absence of the usual smell of something yummy cooking. Whenever Aisha wasn't in the sweet shop, she was at home trialling new recipes. Rosie followed Aisha into the kitchen, where a heavy oak table sat in the middle. "I'm so sorry, Rosie. This is the last thing you need after the weekend you've had."

"Oh Aisha. Don't you dare feel guilty! Sit down. I'll make us a drink. What do you want?" Rosie pulled her coat off and hung it over the back of one of the dining chairs.

"Can we have hot chocolate? My mum always made it for me when I was sad." Aisha sat on the chair and pulled her legs up to her chest. It shocked Rosie to see how vulnerable she looked.

"Of course. You talk while I make the drinks. Chloe said a man arrived at the pub wanting to speak to you?" Rosie prompted her as she went searching through the cupboards for mugs and hot chocolate powder.

"It was my brother-in-law." Aisha's voice

trembled, and she leant forward for a box of tissues.

"Your brother-in-law?" Rosie questioned.

"Yes. My husband's brother."

Rosie busied herself with the drinks, waiting for Aisha to continue her story.

"What did your brother-in-law say?"

"My husband... ex husband... is in hospital. The next forty-eight hours are critical." Aisha's eyes glazed over as she said the words out loud.

"Oh, Aisha." Rosie squeezed her hand. She didn't know what to say without knowing what had happened between Aisha and her husband.

"I still love him, Rosie. I shouldn't, but I do."

"What happened? You don't have to tell me."

"We wanted different things from life. I moved here, he moved to America. At least I thought he had." Aisha caught her breath. "Rosie, I never stopped loving him. I don't think I ever will stop loving him. He emailed me last week saying he was ill and missed me. Apparently his health then took a turn for the worst."

"Is he still in America?" Rosie was ready to pull out her phone and book a flight.

"No. I found out yesterday that he stayed in London. Apparently, he decided he couldn't move so far away from me. For almost two years, I've believed he got on that plane and left."

"Aisha, go see him. Tell him how you feel. I think you'll regret it if you don't." Usually, Rosie wasn't one for giving advice in circumstances like this. However, the past weekend had taught her how important it was to get closure. If Aisha didn't see her husband, then she might never get to speak to him again.

"I have to. Don't I?" Aisha's eyes sought hers, looking for reassurance.

"I'm afraid you do."

"What time is it?" Aisha was looking frantically around the room, but there was no clock. Rosie pulled out her phone. It was half-past-nine.

"He's leaving in thirty minutes!" She jumped up and raced up the stairs to her bedroom. Rosie helped her throw a few pairs of jeans, a couple of jumpers, and some underwear into a small suitcase.

"Where is he?" Rosie asked. She had already guessed they were talking about Aisha's brother-in-law.

"He said he'd wait in the pub for me until closing time. They're open until ten tonight."

Rosie grabbed her coat and helped Aisha to the pub with her suitcase. The pair of them slid over more times than they could count, but neither of them cared. All that mattered was that Aisha got there in time to travel back to London.

"He's there!" Aisha breathe a sigh of relief as they stepped into the pub. Sat at the bar was a young man, staring down at an empty glass in front of him.

"Let me know how it goes." Rosie pulled her in for a hug. She could only imagine what Aisha would go through over the next few days. It made her problems with Matt seem trivial. Life was too short to drag things out. She needed to speak to him and ask him what was going on. With a last squeeze, Rosie left Aisha and made her way home. She was too impatient to wait until she arrived home and so she pulled out her phone and scrolled down to Matt's number. Her finger hovered over the call button. Without allowing herself to overthink it, she clicked call. She had already allowed this to drag on for too long.

It rang once before Matt answered.

"Hello, Rosie?" His voice floated through the speaker.

"Hi, Matt." She wished it had rung a little longer. It might have given her more time to decide what to say. Instead, she was now making a fool of herself.

"Are you okay?" he asked.

"Yes. I'm just walking home. I had to pop in and see Aisha." Rosie shook her head and glanced up at the sky. Why was she bothering with small talk? The last few days had taught her how precious happiness and relationships were. She had to know the truth about what had happened with Matt and his ex. Then she could decide what to do next.

"Rosie, what's going on? I don't understand why you've been so funny with me this weekend."

Rosie took a deep breath. This was it, she had to tell him. "I wanted to surprise you on Friday by meeting you in London." She paused for a moment to allow him to confess anything.

"I would have loved that. Why didn't you?"

"I came to your office and saw you leaving

with Mimi. Just after you'd told me you were going into a meeting."

"Oh, Rosie." There was silence. Rosie could hear his breathing and so she knew he hadn't hung up. As the seconds ticked by, Rosie felt all of her hope disappear. He hadn't denied it. Why wasn't he denying it?

"Don't you have anything to say?" Rosie felt a lump in her throat. She had so badly wanted to believe he wouldn't do that to her.

"I know what it must have looked like, but I promise you I've had nothing more to do with Mimi since I met you. I admit, she's still finding it hard to understand that I've moved on. She wants the office to think we're still together. I wasn't lying when I said I had a meeting to go to. Mimi walked there with me. I promise you nothing is going on with her. We're very much over." Rosie wished he were standing in front of her.

"That's convenient for you." Rosie recoiled at her tone. She was trying to protect herself and push him away.

"Rosie, I don't know what I can say. I really like you and I promise things with Mimi are over. She's finding it difficult to accept, but I can promise you I've done nothing to encourage her. Why didn't you walk over on Friday? I could have explained all this to you." She heard Matt let out an exasperated sigh.

"It hurt me." The words came out as a whisper.

"I'm so sorry."

Rosie was silent as she unlocked the door to her flat. She didn't know what to say. Did she believe him?

"What can I say or do, Rosie?" Matt sounded desperate.

"I don't know, Matt. It's hard for me to trust right now."

"I know, and I'm so incredibly sorry for putting you in this position."

"I need time, Matt. I need to decide whether I trust what you're saying and decide if I can put this behind me. It's dredged up a lot of feelings for me."

"I'll take Friday off and drive down, then we can speak Friday evening?" Matt's voice wavered.

Rosie thought about it. She really wanted to see him, and yet a big part of her was dreading seeing him. With a deep breath, she remembered what she had just told Aisha. She had to ensure she had no regrets.

"I'll see you on Friday." Without giving him the chance to reply, Rosie put the phone down. She was finally home on her own. Rosie started running herself a bath as the emotions from the last few days hit her. Some time for herself was what she needed. Whatever happened, she would cling on to the happiness she had found in Ives-On-Sea.

CHAPTER THIRTY TWO

The sound of seagulls squawking outside her bedroom window woke Rosie on Monday morning. She considered keeping the shop shut. A day to herself sounded like a nice idea. However, with Christmas looming, Rosie had lots of last-minute tailor appointments. She'd scheduled her first one for ten o'clock, allowing herself a leisurely morning. She pulled back the curtains to reveal another dreary day. In the distance, she could see the formidable waves crashing against the beach. There was beauty in the dreariness. Rosie had tossed and turned most of the night as thoughts of Aisha plagued her. She felt stupid for worrying about Matt when her friend was going through something so awful. As she thought about her friend, a plan formed in Rosie's head. With the shop shut, she would have no income. It wasn't something Aisha should have to worry about. The Christmas school holidays had begun and so Rosie's Sunday girl, Lily, would be at home studying for her A-levels. She grabbed her phone and hoped she wouldn't be waking the poor girl up.

"Hello?" Came a groggy voice at the end of the phone.

"Lily, I'm sorry to call you so early. Do you know Aisha? She runs the sweet shop."

"Of course. I helped her with the Easter market."

"She's had to go away rather last minute and I'm worried about the shop. Do you have any time to spare?" Rosie didn't want to pressure the girl, as she knew she had exams to prepare for.

"Of course! I'll be able to take my books with me to study. I know it's Christmas tourist season, but it won't be so busy I can't study too."

"Lilly, you're a star. I've got some spare keys. I'll pop them round to you in the next twenty minutes. We'll also alter the opening hours."

Rosie put the phone down and rushed to get ready. Her leisurely morning had now become very busy. It was worth it, though. She could text Aisha and tell her the shop was in good hands.

Once Lily had settled in the sweet shop and had promised to use every spare second to study, Rosie made her way back to the dress shop with five minutes to spare before her first appointment.

Despite the turmoil of the last few days, Rosie felt herself instantly relax as she stepped into the shop. It was as if all the memories were hugging her and thanking her for giving them a place to exist.

Rosie flicked through her bookings book to see who her first appointment was. It was Audrey and Grace, the teenager who she had designed a bridesmaid dress for. Rosie was excited to see their reaction when she revealed the finished dress. This was her favourite part of the process, seeing someone's face light up at something she had made. It wasn't just a dress; it was a confidence boost. She made people feel good about themselves.

The bell above the door pinged as Audrey walked in, shortly followed by her daughter, Grace.

"Good morning!" called Rosie. She put all her worries to the back of her mind, wanting this to be a lovely experience for mother and daughter.

"Rosie, hello. We've been so excited!" Audrey was almost jumping up and down on the spot. Grace rolled her eyes from beside her. Underneath the broody teenage scowl, Rosie spotted the twinkle of excitement in her eyes.

"Audrey, why don't you take a seat while I help Grace into the dress?" Rosie led her towards one of the plush chairs just outside the changing area.

"Are you excited?" asked Rosie as she led Grace into the changing room.

"Yes, but don't tell mum." Grace chuckled.

"Your secrets are safe with me," promised Rosie. She slowly undid the zip on the dress bag to reveal the beautiful gown that she had painstakingly designed and stitched. It was truly beautiful. The pastel blue shimmered underneath the lighting as Rosie pulled the bag from around it. Her heart swelled as she heard Grace let out a small gasp at the sight.

"Do you like it?" she asked. Rosie already knew the answer just by looking at Grace's expression. Her eyes had glazed over and a dreamy smile had taken over her face. She was miles away from the sulky teenager who had trailed in behind her mother mere moments ago.

"It's perfect." Grace finally answered. She helped Grace put on the dress. The Bardot top hugged her shoulders, the cinched waist showed off her petite figure, and the petticoat underneath accentuated the style. She looked beautiful.

"Hold on a second." Rosie left her admiring herself in the mirror and went to grab one of the vintage hair clips from the display in the shop. She carefully styled Grace's hair into a French twist and finished it with the hair clip.

"Wow." Although Rosie had spent hours working on the dress, she couldn't believe how perfect it looked. Especially on Grace. As she walked out to show her mother, Rosie noticed how she stood taller. The smile was still firmly on her face. Audrey grabbed for a tissue almost as soon as Grace came into sight.

"Oh Grace, you look beautiful." The woman stood up to hug her daughter. Rosie felt privileged to be a part of such a special moment between the two. To some, it was just a dress, but Rosie knew how much more it could be.

"Rosie, I cannot thank you enough." Audrey dabbed at the tears running down her cheeks and turned to face Rosie.

"You're welcome. I'm so happy that you both like the dress."

"We love it!" Grace was beaming as she twirled and watched herself in the mirror.

"It's perfect. Grace, you look beautiful and confident."

The women left the shop with the dress wrapped up, ready for the Christmas Eve wedding. Rosie had gifted the hair clip to Grace and told her to enjoy every second of the day.

The rest of the day continued on the same note with appointment after appointment. Some were for minor things, such as a dress needing taking in a size. Others were bigger. Rosie's two o'clock appointment was a much bigger task, but it was one she would relish. Joyce, a ninety-year-old woman, had arrived with her granddaughter, who was dutifully carrying a dress bag. Rosie watched Joyce's face light up as she looked around the shop at all the styles she recognised.

"How can I help you?" Rosie asked once she had them sat down with a coffee in hand. She had used the delicate china set her mother had brought her to congratulate her on opening the shop.

"My husband and I are renewing our wedding

vows on Valentine's Day. I know you must be busy with Christmas coming up, but I wanted to give you enough time. My dress is here. It was originally my mother's. It's an original 1930s wedding dress. Over the years it's become a little tatty, and I was hoping together we could salvage it. I may also need to let it out a little. I've put on a little weight in the last seventy years." Joyce gave her orders. She was gentle but firm and Rosie admired her for it. Rosie was beside herself with excitement as she slipped on a pair of cotton gloves and pulled the original dress from its bag. It was a simple silk fitted dress, and it was breathtakingly gorgeous. The bodice was fine, but the skirt was not. It was moth eaten.

"I don't think we can just repair the skirt, as it will show. What we can do is repair it and then perhaps put a lace layer over the top. That way, you still keep the original dress beneath it." Rosie waited for Joyce to consider her suggestion.

"That sounds perfect, dear. Do you feel you can do the dress justice?" For the first time since she had stepped foot in the shop, Joyce looked nervous. Rosie thought about the question. A few months ago, she would have said no. However, her confidence was growing in leaps and bounds and she was sure she could work her magic on this beautiful dress.

"I do, Joyce. You're going to look just as stunning as you did seventy years ago." With a smile, Rosie took Joyce's measurements and booked her in to return just after Christmas to see the progress. As Rosie waved them off, she felt a little sad for herself. She would probably never get to celebrate her seventieth wedding anniversary. Did it matter, though? The time didn't matter. All that mattered was the person, and Joyce had clearly been lucky enough to find her person early in life.

CHAPTER THIRTY THREE

Rosie's phone buzzed on the bedside table. Groggily, she reached out for it and squinted at the bright light from the screen. It was Friday, and it was seven o'clock in the morning and Matt had just texted her to say he was leaving. She sent a message back, wishing him a safe journey. By the time Rosie hit the send button, she was wide awake. She pulled on her dressing gown and slid her phone into the pocket as she went to make herself a cup of coffee. As she poured the milk in, her phone buzzed from the pocket. It was Aisha.

"Hello?" Rosie answered. She was eager to speak to her friend. They'd only shared a few texts since Aisha had rushed off with her brother-in-law.

"Rosie! I'm so sorry, I've only just realised

how early it is. I've just left the hospital and thought I'd call you on my way back to the hotel. Hospitals are strange places. You completely lose track of time." Aisha's attention sounded as though it was miles away.

"Are you okay?" Rosie asked. It was a silly question given the circumstances, and yet it was still a question that needed to be asked.

"Yes, and no. Jay's woken up, but I've not been able to speak to him properly. We're not allowed in the room with him because he's in isolation. There's so many nurses, doctors, and medical equipment. Oh Rosie, it's awful." Aisha sobbed down the phone.

"Hey, I'm here." Rosie tried to soothe her. There was no point in telling her everything would be okay because it wouldn't be. Rosie could hear Aisha taking some deep breaths. "Do they know what's wrong with him?"

"He's contracted an unknown disease from a holiday he took. The doctors know nothing about it. He seems to be responding well to the treatment. They're hopeful."

"Are you hopeful?"

"I don't know, Rosie. When I'm home, we're going to need a lot of wine and an evening to talk. I've so much going around my head right now."

"There'll be time to process it all. Make sure you're looking after yourself."

"I will. Thank you for sorting the shop out. At least I have one less thing to worry about."

"It's fine. Lily and I will keep it open for as

long as possible."

"Thank you, Rosie. I better get some sleep before I head back to the hospital. I'll keep you updated. Thanks again for being such an amazing friend."

Rosie said her goodbyes and put the phone down. Despite Aisha's acclamation of her being a good friend, she couldn't help but feel she had been an awful friend. Since the day she moved to Ives-On-Sea, Rosie had been so wrapped up in her own life. She'd hardly thought about Aisha and how she might be feeling. All of her friends had their own problems and yet she had been so consumed by her own life that she hadn't taken the time to ask them how they were and to listen. Rosie promised herself that she would be a better friend.

By now, Rosie's coffee was cold and had grown a skin. She left the mug on the side and went to her wardrobe to dress for the day. Each day was becoming increasingly gloomy and rainy. Rosie pulled on a black knitted vest and tucked it into a pair of white waist-high flared linen trousers. The trousers had been her mother's, and the vest had been a bargain at one of the many boot sales Rosie frequented when she lived in London. Her hair was sticking in all directions from sleeping, so she pulled it into a quick side platt.

The day passed slowly. A few couples came into the shop. Many of them were tourists having a short getaway before the stresses of the festive season descended upon them. Rosie sold several items, including the fringed dress she had worn in London. She was sad to see it go, but she knew she was unlikely to wear it again. It was only right it found a new home with someone who would make new memories in it.

Matt kept texting her updates on his journey. The traffic was terrible, and he was taking a lot longer than usual, much to Rosie's relief. She was still unsure how she felt or how she should act around him. Aisha's situation had reminded her how fragile life was. She knew she and Matt had a connection and there was potential for a future between them. They had spoken a little throughout the week, but it was polite and asking each other about their day. Rosie hoped it wouldn't feel awkward when she saw him in person.

An hour before closing time, Matt texted to say he was just getting petrol before driving into Ives-On-Sea. He asked whether he should come straight to the shop or drop his bags off at his parents' house. Rosie considered her response. She wanted to tell him to drop his bags off, but she knew she was just trying to delay the inevitable. With a deep breath, Rosie told him to come straight to the shop. She crossed her fingers as she hit send. Who knew how the evening would end? Rosie certainly didn't.

All too soon, Matt walked through the door. He wasn't wearing a suit, instead he had dressed in black chinos with a navy jumper. Despite the lack of suit, he still looked as though he was ready to walk into a board meeting.

"Hi." Rosie greeted him. She blushed as his eyes met hers. It surprised Rosie to find herself feeling shy around him.

"Hello. How are you?" He immediately walked over to her and kissed her on the cheek. Despite his calm exterior, Rosie knew him enough to recognise how uncomfortable he was feeling. They both felt at odds with each other.

"I'm okay. How're you?"

"I'm good, thank you." It was awkward small talk, and Rosie hated it.

"Why don't I close early? It's not raining, so let's get a coffee and walk down to the beach."

"I'll just grab my coat from the car." Matt left Rosie to put her own coat on and lock up the shop. They were both grateful for a few seconds alone.

In silence, they ordered coffees from Chloe's cafe. Thankfully, Chloe was off today doing some Christmas shopping in town and so she wasn't there to ask questions. They left the warmth of the shop and made the descent down to the seafront.

"Where shall we start?" Matt was the first to break the silence.

"I'm not sure. It's been so difficult learning to trust you. Seeing you with your ex was painful. I just don't know what to think or how to feel."

Matt stood still and turned to face her. "Rosie, I promise you nothing is going on between me and Mimi. We've been over for ages, but she just won't accept it." Now he was standing in front of her.

Rosie could read his expression and his eyes. As she watched him, there was not a doubt in her mind that he was telling her the truth. He had the same vulnerability on his face as he had when he had spoken to her about his mother. Matt wasn't one to manipulate her emotions. He struggled enough with his own.

"I believe you." Rosie let out the breath she hadn't realised she'd been holding. Matt's face softened as a smile spread across it.

"Oh, Rosie. I'm so sorry you had to see it. I cannot tell you how much I wish I had spotted you. If I could go back in time." He slid his hand into hers, but neither of them made a move to continue walking.

"I'm sorry I didn't give you the chance to explain." Rosie was feeling a little silly for doubting him.

"Rosie, you don't have to justify your actions. You've been through so much. I know I need to earn your trust."

"Thank you." Rosie made the first move. She reached up on her tiptoes and pressed her lips to his.

"Shall we go back to yours instead of a beach walk?" Matt pulled his lips from hers. They were both breathless. The cold air was whipping around them and thunder rippled through the sky above.

"Let's go." Rosie grabbed a hold of his hand as they walked back to her flat.

CHAPTER THIRTY FOUR

"You're so beautiful." Matt whispered. He was lying next to her in bed, wrapping one of her curls around his finger.

"Thank you." Rosie smiled and closed her eyes. This time last week, her world had caved in on itself. She was trying not to think too far ahead and just enjoy the moment with Matt.

"I should go drop my cases off at my parents," he whispered, although he made no move to get out of bed.

"We really should get up and have dinner or else it'll be time to go back to bed. Why don't you stay here tonight?" It was dark outside, and Rosie's stomach was grumbling with hunger. She'd been too worried about seeing Matt to eat lunch. After their walk along the beach, they'd come straight back to Rosie's flat and hadn't left her bed since.

"Are you sure about me staying? I can just go to my parents' house after dinner."

"I want you to stay."

He pressed his lips to her forehead before pulling away with a huge smile on his face. "Okay. You go start dinner and I'll go grab my cases from downstairs."

Reluctantly, Rosie got out of bed and pulled on her pyjamas. She really needed to go food shopping and so they had limited options. They'd agreed they would rather scrape something together than go out. Neither of them wanted to share the other with anyone else. It was nights like this when a tiny part of Rosie missed London. There were many benefits to having hundreds of takeaway restaurants within a five-mile radius. Instead, here in Ives-On-Sea, they would have to make do with microwave jacket potatoes.

Matt left his suitcase in the bedroom and joined Rosie in the kitchen as she watched the potatoes turn in circles in the microwave.

"Asides from last Friday night, how was the dinner with your family?" Matt wandered over to her and wrapped his arms around her waist. She relaxed into his embrace as she thought back to last weekend.

"It was so nice. We got to meet my brother's boyfriend. They took us to this amazing speakeasy, and we had a few too many cocktails."

"That sounds lovely. Perhaps next time I can come with you?" His lips brushed her neck as he spoke, and Rosie couldn't help the shiver that went down her spine.

"Would you like to meet my family?" Rosie asked. She did her best to steady her voice.

"I would. Will I still meet them at Christmas?" The question hung in the air as Rosie considered it. She still wanted to spend Christmas with Matt, but was she ready for him to meet her family? Will knew about everything and she was sure he would play the protective big brother. However, she couldn't imagine not introducing him to them. They all meant so much to her it was only right they all met.

"Of course you will."

"I need to get presents for your family. Perhaps you can help me this weekend?"

"I'm afraid we're both working this weekend."

"I'm working?" he questioned.

"Yes. Aisha's had a bit of a family emergency, so we're juggling both the dress shop and her sweet shop. Lily's been helping all week, but she needs the weekend to study and have some time for herself."

"That's fine. Can I work the sweetshop? I promise I'll put money in the till for anything I eat." His eyes twinkled as he joked. Rosie suspected the sweet shop would have a very profitable weekend.

"We'll talk about it in the morning." Rosie reluctantly pulled herself from his embrace as the microwave pinged. It was nice to hear how eager he was to step in and help one of her friends. Even if his motivation came from a room filled with sweets.

Rosie dished up two jacket potatoes with cheese and beans while Matt opened a bottle of red wine. They sat at the small table in the kitchen and ate the simple dinner.

"I went to see my ex, Oliver, last Friday." Rosie blurted out. She had been meaning to tell Matt about it, but she hadn't meant to drop it into the conversation like that. Matt's face clouded over as he considered what she was about to say. "Don't worry, nothing happened." Rosie quickly reassured him. His face visibly relaxed as he took a large sip from his wineglass.

"What happened?" he asked.

"He's been asking me to talk to him face-to-face, so I thought I should, since I was in London with no plans. It was actually really nice to get some closure." Matt nodded his head, encouraging her to keep speaking. "He finally signed the divorce papers once he saw I had moved on with my life and how much happier I was. It was sad to see him. He was still clinging on to any hope that there might be something between us." Rosie sighed and took a sip from her own wineglass.

"And you didn't feel there was still anything between the two of you?" Matt's brow creased as he asked the question. Rosie reached forward and took a hold of his hand.

"There is absolutely nothing between us. I

don't think there had been for a while, even before Oliver cheated. There's still a part of me that cares about him, but I'm not in love with him."

"I'm glad you got your closure." Matt smiled and turned his palm over to intertwine his fingers with hers.

"So am I. I'll be a divorcee soon." Rosie cringed at the word. Never did she think she'd be divorced before thirty.

"There's something a little sexy about that." Matt teased.

"It's awful!"

"It's just life experience, Rosie. There's nothing awful about it."

"It was certainly an experience." Rosie chuckled darkly into the wineglass.

CHAPTER THIRTY FIVE

It was still dark in the bedroom when a strange buzzing woke Rosie. She pulled the covers off herself and felt the cold air hit her. The heating wasn't on yet, so it must have been the early hours of the morning. The buzzing was a phone vibrating. She searched the bedroom for her phone. Fear gripped her heart. What if there was something wrong with one of her parents? Who else would call her at this time?

"What's wrong?" Matt asked sleepily from the comfort of the bed.

"I think my phone's ringing."

They listened for a moment as the vibrations continued.

"I think it might be my phone. It's coming

from my heap of clothes over in the corner. Will you get it for me?"

Rosie walked over to where Matt had discarded his chinos in the corner of the room. She dug through his pockets and pulled his phone out. The screen was lit up with in incoming call. Instinctively, Rosie looked at who was calling.

"It's Mimi." She threw the phone onto the bed and left the room before her emotions could bubble over. He still hadn't removed the heart from beside her name.

Rosie heard Matt's footsteps follow her out of the bedroom.

"Rosie?" he called into the darkness.

"What?" she spat back at him, spinning around to face him in the pitch black.

"Please, don't let this ruin us."

"Your ex is calling you at three in the morning, Matt. What am I supposed to think?"

"I can't control when she calls me."

"Then block her number."

"I can't." She heard him sigh.

"I think you ought to stay somewhere else tonight."

"Rosie, please don't do this," he pleaded with her.

"What do you expect me to do, Matt? You're in contact with your ex. Last week I saw you leaving the office with her and now she's calling you in the early hours of the morning? I can't trust you."

"Don't say that." Matt looked down at the

phone in his hand as it started ringing again.

"Just leave, Matt. Then you can answer the phone." Rosie walked into the living room and turned the television on to act as a distraction whilst Matt repacked his suitcase. He didn't argue with her. Instead, he picked up his things and left without a goodbye.

Silence echoed throughout the flat as Rosie sat in the dark. A few hours ago, life felt perfect as she fell asleep in Matt's arms. Now everything was uncertain again. Was life trying to tell her not to jump into another relationship? Perhaps she just wasn't ready. Rosie let out a sigh. She shouldn't have made him leave like that. They should have spoken about it. She understood he couldn't stop his ex from calling him, but why couldn't he block her number? If he really wanted to ignore her, he could have a work phone that she could contact him on. Rosie forced herself to go back to bed. She had to get some more sleep before another long day in the shop. Sitting thinking everything over wouldn't change anything. Maybe she had to accept that she would never be able to trust anyone again.

The night passed slowly. Rosie tossed and turned with just a couple of hours of broken sleep in between. At six am, she gave up on sleep and jumped in the shower. She applied a thick layer of concealer and wandered down to the shop. It was still dark outside, but with the gentle glow of the lights, the shop felt comforting.

Rosie's phone bleeped from her pocket. It was

from Aisha, saying she had come home for the weekend. Rosie immediately texted her back, saying she was around if Aisha wanted to speak. A few minutes later, there was a knock on the door.

"I could have come to you!" Rosie exclaimed as she opened the door to let Aisha in.

"I felt like stretching my legs." Aisha followed Rosie into the shop.

"Let me make us a coffee." They walked through to the coffee machine and Rosie switched it on. The familiar hum filled the small room.

"You're up early." Aisha commented.

"Boy trouble." Rosie rolled her eyes.

"What happened?" Aisha unwound her scarf and sat down.

"No. Aisha, you're not here to listen to my problems. You've got enough going on in your life."

"Don't remind me." Aisha sunk back into the chair and took the cup of coffee Rosie offered her.

"What's happened? Why are you home?" Rosie took her own mug and sat down beside Aisha.

"They think his body is finally fighting the disease."

"Oh, Aisha, that's brilliant news!"

"It is, and it isn't. I love him, Rosie. I don't think I could leave him again."

"Have you spoken to him?"

"Not properly. He's still in isolation until they can guarantee the infection is out of his body. We've spoken on the phone on the other side of the window. He said he still loves me."

"That's good, isn't it?" Rosie could see the confusion on Aisha's face.

"I'm not sure. What if he's just saying it because he almost died?" A stray tear trickled down Aisha's cheek.

"Aisha, he didn't move away. He couldn't be so far away from you. That says a lot."

"But what am I going to do? I'm happy here in Ives-On-Sea. Am I ready to give all that up and go back to my old life?" Rosie understood what Aisha was saying. When she had visited Oliver in London, she had realised just how much her life had moved on. This village had stolen their hearts, but now they were being torn apart by love.

"I don't think you can go back, but perhaps you could move forward together."

"I like that idea."

"Don't get ahead of yourself, Aisha. There'll be plenty of time to talk about your future. Just enjoy being back with Jay." Rosie internally rolled her eyes at her words. Who was she to be giving out relationship advice?

"Thank you, Rosie. Thank you for everything you've done. It's been such a weight off of my mind to know the shop has been in safe hands."

"It's fine. Lilly did most of the work!"

"I must pop in and see her today. Neither of you need to worry about the shop. My cousin is going to come and stay for a couple of weeks in the lead up to Christmas and she'll look after the shop for me."

"If you're sure. I don't mind juggling the shops for a little longer." Truthfully, Rosie wanted an excuse to avoid Matt.

"No. You've done enough. It's why I'm home this weekend. I'm going to show my cousin the ropes, then I'll head back to the hospital Sunday night. Anyway, enough about me. What's going on with you? And don't say it doesn't matter. I need a distraction from my own life."

Rosie explained how she had spoken to Matt last night and they had made up. Only for his ex to call in the early hours of the morning.

"It sounds like he's hiding something." Aisha reluctantly admitted.

"But what? We have such a connection, but I'm not prepared to have three of us in this relationship. I'm going through a divorce, but I've never made Matt feel as though my ex-husband is part of our relationship."

"You need to give him an ultimatum. Either he tells you what he's hiding or it's over." Aisha made it sound so simple. Perhaps it really was that simple. If he wouldn't tell her what was going on, then she couldn't trust him. The decision whether to end the relationship would be made for her.

"Why does it have to be so difficult?"

"You're asking the wrong woman. If you find out, then please tell me."

"If it doesn't work out, then at least we have each other." Rosie leant forward to clink her mug with Aisha's. Both women knew heartbreak. It had made them stronger and yet here they were, walking right back into the fire.

"Life's for living. Which is why I need to leave, and you need to answer the door to a very handsome man with a few secrets." Aisha stood up and pointed to the door where Matt was standing, knocking.

"Wish me luck."

"Good luck!"

"If I don't see you before you leave on Sunday, good luck." Rosie walked over to the entrance and gave Aisha a quick hug before opening the door.

"Aisha, hello. I hope everything's okay." Matt's eyes were wide as he noticed Aisha's presence.

"Thank you, Matt." Aisha waved goodbye to Rosie and left.

"Is everything okay?" Matt asked, tilting his head in the direction Aisha had just left in.

"Yes. Her cousin is staying to help in the shop and she's come home for the weekend to show her around." Rosie stepped back into the shop, allowing Matt to follow her.

"That's good." He stood in the middle of the shop, not meeting her eyes.

"What do you want, Matt? Something is obviously going on and until you tell me what, I don't see a future for us." Rosie let out a breath. There, she'd taken Aisha's advice and said it.

"Rosie, I don't know what to do. There is something going on." Matt pulled at his hair as he took the seat where Aisha had sat mere minutes ago. Rosie felt her emotions closing in on her. He had just admitted there was something going on.

"Perhaps you should leave." Rosie kept her voice tight as she took the other seat. She didn't know how much longer her trembling legs could support her.

"No, Rosie. You don't understand."

"No, Matt, I don't understand because you've been lying to me."

"It's not my secret to tell."

"If we're going to have a relationship, there should be no secrets between us. Please, just leave." Rosie turned away from him and waited to hear his footsteps across the shop floor. However, he didn't move.

"Okay, I'll tell you. I have been spending time with Mimi, but not because there's anything going on between us. Just after we broke up, she found a lump and has been going for tests since. They suspect it's cancerous and I've been supporting her through it. Rosie, please believe me when I say I don't love her. I'm doing it because she has nobody else."

Rosie took a moment to comprehend what Matt had just said. He was trying to do his best and ensure his ex was okay. Rosie admired him for it. However, she didn't know whether she was ready for a relationship where she had to share him with his ex. It might have been selfish of her, but she'd been through too much heartbreak to be okay with the situation.

"That sounds like you've got a lot going on."

Rosie didn't know how else to respond. She couldn't cope with the situation and she couldn't pull him away from Mimi. Not when she so desperately needed the support.

"Don't say it like that, Rosie." Matt shrunk back into the chair and rubbed a hand over the stubble on his chin.

"Say it like what? I'm stating the truth." Rosie shrugged. She had been through too much to put her feelings second to anybody.

"You're implying I have too much on to make time for you, too."

"I'm not implying that. Matt, if I'm honest, I don't want any part of this. My trust is fragile as it is. I can't cope with you going back to your ex every week. I'm not asking you to choose between us because I know that's an impossible task. This is me deciding for you. This situation isn't right for me and I have to put myself first. I can't risk being hurt again. It ruined my entire life, and I'm not prepared to risk that again. Not for anyone." Rosie forced herself to remember the pain of leaving Oliver behind. She was happy here on her own. Nothing was worth going back to that pain. Rosie wouldn't allow anyone to ruin her new life she'd made for herself. Not even Matt.

"Rosie, please don't." Rosie watched the emotions play out on Matt's face. He might not always be very good at expressing his emotions, but he was awful at hiding them.

"I'm sorry, Matt. This isn't fair to any of us. I

really wish you and Mimi the best, but I cannot be a part of it. Perhaps it's a selfish decision, but the past year has taught me to put myself and my happiness first." It was slowly sinking in for Rosie that this was goodbye. Finally, she knew what was going on. Despite it not being his secret to tell, he had kept it from her. Matt had watched her struggle to trust him and yet he had protected his ex.

"I understand. I'm sorry, Rosie. If things were different, we could have been so happy together." He looked back one final time before leaving the shop. Rosie sat still in the silence. How had things changed so drastically from last night? Anger welled up inside of her as she thought about how unfair the situation was. They could have been so happy together. It was just the wrong time for both of them. Rosie wondered if there might be a chance for them in the future. However, before she could properly explore the thought, she stopped herself. There was already too much of a past between them for the possibility of a future.

CHAPTER THIRTY SIX

Rosie opened the shop late. It had taken her a little while to gain her composure and to reapply the concealer that had washed off in the barrage of tears. She felt like crying was all she did lately. Rosie had to remind herself that it was better to learn the truth now than wait until they had intertwined their lives. With only two weekends until Christmas, the shop was busy with people looking for presents. Some were locals, others had travelled from afar for a pre-Christmas break and a picturesque shopping experience. A man around Rosie's age came in looking for a vintage coat for his mother. Rosie helped him pick out a beautiful charcoal swing coat with a faux fur trim. When the coat had come in as part of a donation to the shop, Rosie had altered it and swapped the original fur for a faux trim. Throughout the day, Rosie used her expertise to find the perfect gifts for people. It was good; it kept her mind busy. There was no time to pine over Matt. Around lunchtime, there was a lull in customers as they all headed to the cafe for homemade hearty soups and toasted sandwiches. During those few spare minutes, Rosie texted Aisha to see if she fancied a girl's night. She immediately replied, saying she was looking forward to it. Her cousin was visiting a friend in town, so she would drop her off at the station and then come straight over. It was just the distraction Rosie needed.

Every time Rosie felt a wave of sadness crash over her, she reminded herself it was for the best. A few days of being sad was preferable to the inevitable soul-destroying heartbreak if she continued things with Matt and allowed herself to fall in love with him. It was far too complicated for her to risk her heart.

Eventually, the day passed and Rosie made her way back up to the flat and changed into some garish 80s lounge wear. The clashing colours were too horrific to display in the shop. However, there was something about it that Rosie loved. She knew it would never sell and yet she couldn't bring herself to throw it away.

"What the hell are you wearing?" Aisha asked as Rosie opened the door to her. The smell of fish and chips rose from the paper bag clutched in Aisha's hands.

"It's not that bad!" Rosie defended herself. She led the way to the kitchen to get some plates out.

"You're wearing a lime green shell suit!" Aisha was laughing now. Rosie rolled her eyes but couldn't stop joining in.

"It is awful, isn't it?" Rosie drew a deep breath to stop herself from laughing anymore.

"It is. You own a gorgeous vintage shop and you're wearing that."

"I couldn't throw it away. This horrific shell suit was once a part of someone's life."

"You're awful." Aisha was only teasing, but Rosie knew she had a point. She became far too attached to things and people.

"So, where's Matt? Something's obviously happened since you're having fish and chips with me rather than spending the night in bed with him." Aisha didn't hesitate to get to the point. Rosie had only just sat down with her plate of food.

"I took your advice and told him he had to tell me what was going on." Rosie sighed as she stared down at her plate of chips. A tiny part of her wished she hadn't asked. Perhaps then they would have been together this evening. She might have been in the dark about what was really going on, but would one more night together really have been so awful?

"And what did he say?"

"He's broken up with Mimi, but apparently he's been supporting her. Just after they broke up, she found a lump, so he's been going to appointments with her and standing by her."

"Oh." Aisha was speechless.

"I ended things." Rosie felt like a terrible person admitting it to Aisha. She had been selfish, expecting all of Matt's attention.

"Rosie, I can see the guilt written all over your face. Don't you dare feel guilty! It's a rubbish situation and not one you should have to involve yourself in. Matt should never have got close to you when he knew Mimi still needed him. If anyone is in the wrong here, it's Matt." Aisha's tone was stern and Rosie didn't dare argue with her, despite the guilt that was still gnawing away at her insides.

"No, he's not in the wrong, Aisha. He's being incredibly selfless and thoroughly admirable. I just can't stand by while he supports his ex. Not with my lack of trust. After everything I've been through with Oliver, I thought I'd finally found someone for me. What am I going to do now?"

"We're going to get a little bit drunk and you're going to have an awful hangover tomorrow."

"I'm not sure, Aisha." The last thing Rosie felt like was working on a busy Sunday with a hangover.

"Rosie, if I leave after this meal, what will you do?" Aisha's eyes bore into Rosie's. They both knew the answer, but Rosie didn't want to say it out loud. If Aisha left, she would cocoon herself in her duvet and throw a pity party for one. "Whatever route you choose, you'll feel awful tomorrow. Let's have some fun in the meantime." Aisha was right.

"Fine, but none of that cheap wine. If we're going to do this, we're doing it properly."

"Deal! We'll eat this and walk up to the pub. They'll sell us a few bottles to bring home."

Rosie never would have believed she could laugh so much the night of a break-up and yet here she was, her stomach hurt from laughing as Aisha recalled the story of her disastrous honeymoon. The evening was a break from both of their realities. They were both at a crossroads in their lives, neither of them knowing what would happen next.

CHAPTER THIRTY SEVEN

Waking up on Sunday morning was awful. Rosie's head was pounding, and the room was spinning. She left the curtains pulled and staggered to the coffee machine to force some caffeine into her body. As Rosie waited for it to heat up, she drank a glass of water and swallowed a couple of paracetamol tablets. Last night had been just what she needed. A chance to just be and to let go of her emotions for a few hours. For those few hours, she was carefree. It would take time to heal from Matt, but she'd be okay. At least she'd be okay once she had some coffee. After her third glass of wine, she had blocked and deleted Matt's number. It was the last thing she wanted to do, but she knew she had to. She couldn't risk calling him in a moment of weakness.

Deep down, Rosie had known from the start that it couldn't ever be anything serious with Matt. It was her own fault for allowing herself to start falling for him when she knew they had no future together.

Outside, the sun was rising above the sea, and the seagulls were squawking. Today, Rosie wasn't doing the usual market. Instead, she was pitching the bus at the Ives-On-Sea Christmas market, which was set up along the seafront. It wouldn't be the same without Aisha running the stall next to her, but she had to get back to her husband and didn't have time to organise herself. With her coffee poured into a travel mug, Rosie took a brisk walk down to the yard to collect the bus. Her breath lingered in the air as she walked through the empty streets. In the distance, Rosie could hear the chatter as people set up for the market. Ives-On-Sea was renowned for its Christmas market. People travelled from miles away and it would be Rosie's final big day of sales before the holidays, so she had to make it count.

Despite the chill, the day was a success. People were out in hordes, wrapped up in countless layers, all looking for unique Christmas presents for their loved ones. Rosie finally had a smile on her face as she watched her business thrive. Just as she was thinking about getting some lunch, a couple of familiar faces appeared with hot chocolates and bacon sandwiches.

"Mum!" Rosie cried. She ran to her and hugged her tightly.

"Hello, darling." Her mother hugged her back.

"I'm so happy to see you." It was true. Until that moment, Rosie hadn't realised how much she needed a hug from her mother.

"Oh darling. Whatever is the matter?" Rosie's mother had stepped back and saw the look on her face.

"It's a long story." Rosie let out a sigh.

"Then you better start before a customer interrupts us." Her mother wasn't allowing her to just shrug it off. Rosie took her drink and sandwich from her mother and told her about the problems she'd been having with Matt.

"Perhaps you should just focus on you right now." Rosie's father suggested once she'd finished telling her story.

"I think your father's right. You're happy here and you adore your shop. Focus on that right now. There's plenty of time for love and relationships." Her mother sent her a reassuring smile.

"Come on, let's get selling!" They wiped their hands on some wet wipes and all three threw themselves into the market. It was great fun with Christmas tunes blaring out from the speakers Milo had set up outside the Surf Shack. Her friends were all at the market. Milo and Craig were selling gift vouchers for thrill seekers. Meanwhile, Chloe had a stall selling Christmas cakes and mince pies. Rosie's father kept wandering over for samples.

The day was a success and as Rosie packed up the van, she realised over half the stock she'd brought with her had sold.

"I'm going to need to visit a few auctions after Christmas to restock." Rosie commented as she sat down. They had come to the pub to celebrate the day's success. Thankfully, the items she had bought in London had been delivered last week and so she had just enough stock to get her past Christmas.

"I'll come with you." Her mother smiled knowingly.

"No! The pair of you will buy the entire auction." Her dad sighed, knowing he had already lost the argument.

"When are you heading home?" Rosie had been so surprised to see them, she hadn't even asked how long they were staying.

"We're going to drive home tonight. Your father has to be at work tomorrow afternoon."

"Oh, I'm sorry I didn't realise you were leaving so soon." Rosie felt guilty for suggesting they go out for dinner. Her parents had only accepted because they thought she needed cheering up.

"Don't be silly. Besides, we came to talk to you about Christmas and we've been so busy that we've not had the chance to."

"What about Christmas?"

"We'd like to spend Christmas here. Well, not in the pub." Rosie's father explained, while her mother rolled her eyes at his terrible explanation.

"What your father means to say, dear, is that we're looking at renting a large cottage a few miles away. We thought you and your brother could come and stay with us. It'll be an escape for us all, but we'll still be in beautiful surroundings. That's why we drove down yesterday to look at a cottage to rent."

Rosie sighed wistfully at the thought of spending Christmas holed up with her family in a cottage nearby. It sounded idyllic.

"I'll bring the board games." Rosie joked.

"We'll make it fun." Rosie winced as her mother's tone turned to one of pity.

"It's fine, mum. I'm looking froward to spending time with you all. It'll also be nice to have a break from the shop and the orders. Have I told you about the wedding dress I'm working on?" Rosie steered the conversation on to Joyce's wedding dress.

Once their meals arrived, they ate quickly so her parents could begin the long journey home.

"We parked outside the shop, so we'll walk you home." Her dad opened the pub door and stood aside to allow Rosie and her mother to leave before him.

"Thank you, dad." Rosie walked in between her parents. It was pitch black outside, with the moon hidden beneath the cloud. As they turned the corner onto Rosie's street, Rosie could see the outline of her parents' car. She could just make out the silhouette of someone stood outside the shop. Even in the dark, and with some distance between them, Rosie knew who it was. It was Matt.

"Do you want us to stay?" Rosie's mother had noticed him too.

"No, it's fine, mum. You go home like planned.

I'll message you tomorrow. Let me know you're home safe."

"Be strong. Don't go back to him just because you're scared to be alone. You're good on your own, Rosie. You don't need anyone." Her mother engulfed her in a hug.

"Want me to have a chat with him?" Rosie's father joked. At least, she hoped he was joking.

"I'll be fine. I won't settle for just anything and he knows that now."

"Come on, you can't delay it any longer." Rosie's mother linked her arm through hers as they walked the short distance to the car.

Matt looked up as he saw them approaching. He gave a slight wave and Rosie motioned with her finger for him to give her a minute with her parents. Slowly, she said goodbye to them. She was putting off the inevitable conversation with Matt. Why had he returned?

CHAPTER THIRTY EIGHT

"What do you want?" Rosie asked. She had her back turned to Matt as she fumbled through her handbag for her keys to unlock the front door. It was too cold to stand out on the street and bicker with him.

"Rosie, be nice." He stepped behind her until she could feel his breath against her neck. Rosie closed her eyes and took a deep breath. This wasn't happening. It couldn't be happening.

"Matt, what are you doing here?" Rosie turned the key in the lock and stepped through the door to create some space between them. She couldn't think properly when he was so close to her.

"I can't walk away from you. From us. We work, Rosie. I don't want to just give up on this when we could be so happy together." His words resounded in Rosie's head. There was once a time when she would have melted under Matt's gaze as he said those things to her. Now she just wanted to run. To put as much distance between the two of them as possible.

"Matt, please don't do this," her voice was a whisper in the dark hallway.

"I'm yours, Rosie. Completely yours. Can we go upstairs and talk? I'd like to see your face." Matt shifted from one foot to the other. The small corridor that led to the stairs up to Rosie's flat was dark and enclosed.

"Okay, come on." With him stood in front of her, Rosie couldn't say no. The strong woman that she had resolved to be mere hours ago had disappeared at the sight of him. She led the way up to the flat and flicked on the light in the kitchen. Rosie shrugged off her coat and threw it over the back of a chair. Matt stood in the middle of the room, not knowing what to do with himself.

"Say something, Matt." Rosie prompted him. She walked over to the kettle and filled it up, needing something to keep her busy.

"When I left you the other night, I drove a few miles home and realised I couldn't give up on us. I know we haven't been together for very long, but you already mean so much to me, Rosie. You've brought me out of the shell I've been hiding under and made me realise what makes me happy. Maybe we won't work out, but I can't give up now. I'm falling in love with you, Rosie." The words lingered in the air as Rosie froze midway through getting the tea bags out of the cupboard. She hadn't expected him to say that.

"Rosie?" Matt questioned. Rosie was still stood frozen to the spot, oblivious to how much time had passed.

"What, Matt? What do you want me to say? Yes, I can see myself falling in love with you. But I won't let myself. I'm sorry, Matt, but I can't share you with your ex. I deserve more than that, and I won't risk my happiness." Rosie resumed her tea making to avoid having to turn round and look Matt in the eye. One look at him and she would forget all of her reasons not to be with him. They would only end up hurting each other more than they already had.

"Rosie, you don't understand. I don't want you to share me with anybody. I want to be yours. Completely yours. Come and sit down and let's talk properly." He walked over to her and took the mugs of tea, placed them on the table, and walked back to take her hands in his. With a squeeze of her hand, he led her over to the table. They were sitting opposite each other and Rosie couldn't ignore him any longer. She looked up into his eyes and felt her heart pound in her chest. Despite everything, she still felt those butterflies in her stomach every time she laid her eyes upon him.

"Matt, we've known each other for such a short time and already we've had so many problems. Perhaps we're just not meant to be." Rosie fought the urge to wrap her hands around her mug and stare down at the contents. She kept her eyes on Matt.

"Just because we've faced some struggles doesn't mean we shouldn't be together. Despite it all, we still feel something for each other." He shrugged his shoulders and broke eye contact, looking down at his mug.

"Matt, this is all completely irrelevant. You're still involved with your ex. I know it's no fault of yours, but it's not something I'm comfortable with. It's admirable that you want to support her, but the situation isn't for me." Rosie sighed. Standing up for herself and her feelings was surprisingly painful.

"Rosie, I'm not explaining this very well. I've told Mimi I can't support her through this. Honestly, I feel bad, but I don't think it's healthy for her to rely on me. I'd never get back together with her and I think she hopes I'll change my mind. I've not told you much about my relationship with Mimi because there's not much to tell. We were together for a very short amount of time and I quickly realised she wasn't for me. There was something very off about her. If I went out for drinks with friends, she'd coincidentally be at the same pub. Sometimes, I'm sure I'd never told her where I was going. I'm sure underneath it all she's a sweet girl, but she's not right for me. Mimi needs someone to care for her who has her best interests at heart, and that isn't me. It's your best interests that I'm thinking of. Does that make me a terrible person?" The question lingered in between them. Were they both awful people for prioritising a relationship over someone's health?

"Don't do that." Matt groaned.

"Do what?" Rosie blinked.

"Think. Just answer with your heart. Do you want to see where this relationship can go? Just us. Nobody else."

A smile crept across Rosie's face as she thought about it. Just the two of them,

"I said don't think!" Matt chuckled as he watched her emotions play out across her face.

"Yes. I want to be with you." It felt good saying it out loud.

"Good, because I want to be with you."

"Right. Well, that's sorted. Now what?" Rosie let out a nervous laughed. Had she really just agreed to a relationship with Matt?

"Stop asking questions and thinking! I've got permission to work from home until after Christmas, so I thought I'd stay down here. We can be together properly, then after Christmas we'll be sensible and figure out how this is going to work."

"Okay. No thinking. Just us." Rosie smiled across the table at Matt, whose face mirrored hers. Finally, they were together... again.

"We're going to be the gossip of Ives-On-Sea with the amount of times I come and go!"

"It's publicity for the shop. All the gossips pop in and usually buy something. We might have to keep this up as a marketing technique."

"Glad I could help."

"You know what else you could help with?"

Rosie stood up from the chair, abandoning her cup of tea.

"What's that?" Matt's eyes followed her across the room.

"The zip on my dress. They didn't design it to be taken off by the wearer." She winked at him as she walked out of the kitchen and to the bedroom. He followed closely behind.

CHAPTER THIRTY NINE

"What's this for?" Matt asked, holding up the tail end of a mink stole. Rosie winced as her eyes followed the item to the head, which was still intact. Matt let out a cry and dropped the item as he spotted the head at the same time as her. "What is that?" He pointed at the heap of fur now on the floor.

"It's a mink stole. Absolutely disgusting, but I come across quite a few of them." Rosie shrugged her shoulders and went to pick the fur up. She didn't agree with it, but she couldn't see the animal disregarded. It deserved respect, even in death.

"That's horrible. Do you sell them?" Matt hadn't taken his eyes off of her.

"No. They often come in bundles like this. I

have someone who buys them from me." Rosie had just taken delivery of two crates filled with vintage clothes.

"I can't imagine why anyone would want to wear a dead animal around their neck." Matt sighed and walked over to the counter where his cup of coffee sat. His phone lay next to it, vibrating.

"Is it her again?" Rosie asked. Ever since Matt had blocked Mimi's number, she'd been calling him from others. It was constant. Every time Matt blocked a new one, she would call on another.

"It is. You know what, anyone at work can contact me by email. I'm just going to turn this off." Matt switched the phone off and picked up his cup of coffee. Rosie placed the fur stole into a separate box and went over to her own mug.

"There's still so much to unpack!" she exclaimed, staring at the boxes which were scattered around the shop floor. On Saturday evening, after a few glasses of wine, Rosie and Aisha had done a little online shopping. It was quite a shock for Rosie when a lorry turned up on Wednesday morning. However, she couldn't feel too annoyed at her drunk self because she really needed the stock.

"It's fine. We have another couple of hours until your next appointment." Over the last couple of days, Matt had embraced working in the shop. During quiet periods, he would catch up on his own work while Rosie was frantically sewing away at Joyce's wedding dress. Rosie was so grateful to have Matt helping her in the busy lead-up to

Christmas. She hadn't imagined she'd be so busy. Yesterday morning she'd walked into the shop and was astounded at how empty the rows were. It was great for business, but not so great for her budding relationship with Matt. They'd hardly had more than a few minutes together since he had returned to Ives-On-Sea.

"Stop thinking!" Matt laughed. He knew from the frown on her face what was going through her mind. "It's okay. We're a team. We can relax over Christmas and enjoy each other's company. For now, I'm here to help you." Matt's work had realised how unhappy he was with their constant demands, and so they were being incredibly accommodating with him taking some time off.

"Thank you." Rosie put her mug down and wrapped her arms around Matt's waist. He pulled her against him. When she was in his embrace, she felt her mind quieten. All that mattered was him. All too soon, he let her go and suggested they got back to work.

The day passed in a blur of unboxing clothes and sketching new designs for customers. By the end of the day, Rosie's feet and hands hurt, and she felt exhausted.

"Shall we go to the pub for dinner?" Matt suggested. He stood staring at Rosie's bare fridge.

"Yes, please." Rosie sighed at the thought of sitting down while somebody cooked for them. "I'll just get changed and then we can go." Pen marks from sketching covered her clothes. Rosie quickly changed into a pair of vintage jeans and an old jumper, which was too big for her, so she rolled up the sleeves. She noticed her phone still lying on her bedside cabinet. Quickly, she picked it up to check it before they went out. There was a message from her mum asking if Matt had any dietary requirements for Christmas Day. Rosie had to laugh at how thorough her mother was being. She was excited to have her children and their partners together for the festive period. Quickly, Rosie sent a reply and then looked at the other messages she had missed that day. There was one from an unknown number that caught her eye. She clicked on it and gasped as she read the message.

'He's mine. I'll show you.'

It was clear who it was from. Mimi had obviously found her number. How? Rosie did not know.

"You ready?" Matt asked. He had poked his head around the bedroom door. Rosie jumped and automatically locked her phone. Should she tell him about the message? He was already so stressed about the situation.

"Yes! Sorry, mum texted asking if you have any dietary requirements for Christmas Day." She left her phone on the bedside cabinet and walked over to Matt. There was no need to tell him about a stupid message. Mimi would soon realise he wasn't going back to her.

"I'm excited about this Christmas lunch! Do

you want to give your mum my number?" Matt took her hand in his and led her out of the flat. Rosie's mother had a new question each day about Matt and so it made sense for her to just speak to him.

"What was Christmas like at yours?" Rosie asked as they walked up the hill to the pub. It was freezing, and the clouds above were threatening to unleash a torrential downpour.

"It was lonely. Really lonely." Matt sighed.

"I'm sorry." Rosie squeezed his hand.

"It was just the three of us. As a child, I would have to wait until after lunch to open my presents. There was no excitement on Christmas morning as I knew we had to get up, get dressed up in our smartest clothes, and take my father's mother to church."

"Your father's mother?" Rosie asked. His description of the woman who was his grandmother bewildered her.

"Yes. She was nothing like a grandmother. She firmly believed that children should be seen and not heard. We would sit in a draughty church for the Christmas Day service, then go back to hers, where my mother cooked dinner. They would send me out into the hallway to read a book." By now, they were at the pub and had chosen a table close to the fireplace to keep warm.

"I'll order. Then you can tell me more." Rosie grabbed a menu and walked up to the bar. She didn't need to ask Matt what he wanted. He always ordered the fish pie. As she waited to be served, Rosie glanced down at the menu to see what she fancied.

"Thank you." Matt smiled warmly up at her as she placed a pint of beer down in front of him. She had opted for a mulled wine for herself.

"You're welcome. I'm sorry your Christmas mornings were so awful." Rosie prompted him to continue his story.

"Once we were home, things improved. My mum knew how much I hated the morning, so she'd make a chocolate pudding in the afternoon and I'd get to open my presents. I appreciated her trying to make it nice for me. However, when school started again and everyone was excitedly comparing their Christmas mornings, I always felt a little left out." Matt's eyes had clouded over as he looked down at his drink.

"I'm sorry. I promise Christmas morning this year will be nothing like you experienced as a child. Despite my brother and I being adults, we'll be up at the crack of dawn in our matching pyjamas, ready to unwrap our presents."

"I'm excited to be a part of it. Thank you, Rosie. You've made me feel welcome in your family and that means a lot to me." Matt looked up and met her eyes. Rosie knew how tough it was for him to be so vulnerable and to open up to her. He was a different person to the man she had first met. The one who had been burying the grief of his mother's death.

"I think we're good for each other." Rosie smiled coyly at him. Their food came, interrupting their conversation. As Rosie took a bite of her lasagne, her mind wandered to the message she had received. It angered her that Mimi was still interfering in their lives, and yet a small part of her felt awful for taking Matt's support from her.

"You look deep in thought." Matt commented. He had been studying her face.

"Sorry, just lots to think about with the shop so close to Christmas."

"I've got a few Zoom meetings tomorrow morning, then I'll be down to help." He smiled at her and Rosie felt the butterflies in her stomach awaken.

"Thank you." They still had a couple of boxes to go through from today's delivery. Rosie's customer had arrived early for their appointment and so Matt had stashed the boxes in her kitchenette, meaning if she wanted a coffee, she had to go upstairs to the flat or along the road to Chloe's cafe.

They finished their meal in a comfortable silence, both considering what they had to do the following day. The walk home was awful as the wind whipped around them. She snuggled into Matt's side and hid her face from the gale force winds. When they got home, Rosie was grateful to curl up in bed with Matt beside her. She had missed having someone beside her. Since leaving Oliver, sleeping wasn't the same. Matt was asleep within seconds of his head hitting the pillow. Rosie, meanwhile, was feeling wide awake. Staring up at the ceiling and willing sleep to steal her away. The room lit up with the light from Rosie's phone. She picked it up to see another text from an unknown number.

'I hope you enjoyed your cosy dinner together. He'll be back in my arms by Christmas Day.'

A chill ran up Rosie's spine. How did Mimi know about their dinner? Rosie took a deep breath, trying to straighten her thoughts. Perhaps she had just got lucky and didn't really know about their dinner plans. Maybe Matt had mentioned it to someone from work. Yes, that was probably it. Rosie put her phone back down on the bedside table and closed her eyes. Should she tell Matt? It would only worry him and bring Mimi back into their lives, just as they had shut her out. No, telling him was a bad idea. Rosie forced herself to fall asleep, knowing the alternative was to toss and turn all night with worry.

CHAPTER FORTY

"Sorry, what did you just say?" Rosie asked. Matt had been speaking to her, but she hadn't been listening. Her mind had wandered off to the texts she received yesterday. She still hadn't told him about them.

"I asked if you want a coffee?" Matt was standing by the coffee machine in the kitchen. He had set his laptop up on the table, ready for his morning of meetings.

"Yes, please." Rosie attempted a smile. She wanted to pretend nothing had happened and that the messages hadn't shaken her. She was lying to herself. The text about them enjoying their dinner had upset her. Rosie would be looking over her shoulder for the rest of the day. Was Mimi really following them?

"One very strong coffee!" Matt handed her a coffee in a travel mug so she could take it down to the shop with her.

"Thank you." Rosie pushed all the worries to the back of her mind, placed the mug on the worktop, and stepped into his embrace. She inhaled his familiar scent and felt her body melt into his.

"As much as I would love to stay here cuddling you, I have a meeting in five minutes and I need to check the link works." Matt reluctantly pushed her away.

"Sorry." Rosie grabbed her coffee from the worktop. "Shall we do something nice on Sunday? I'm going to shut the shop and there's no market this week. I think we both need a break!"

"That sounds perfect. I think Chloe said something about a Christmas party at the pub on Saturday evening?" Matt had popped out earlier to buy some bread from Chloe's cafe to make some toast for his breakfast.

"Oh, I forgot about that! We don't have to go."

"No, I want to. It'll be fun." Matt sat down at his laptop and started typing.

"See you soon!" Rosie called, leaving him to his meetings.

*****

The rest of the week passed in a blur of vintage clothes and Matt's arms. Saturday was their busiest day, and Rosie was grateful to have Matt's help. Lots of tourists had descended on the shop on the last Saturday before Christmas. Rosie watched as clothes quickly found their new homes. She smiled as each piece left the shop bound for their next journey. All those memories going out into the world and continuing to make history. By Saturday evening, both she and Matt were exhausted, but they knew it was too late to cancel the Christmas party. Chloe had been organising it all week and Aisha was back for the weekend. It was a chance for the entire village to come together and celebrate. Ives-On-Sea had welcomed Rosie with open arms when she had arrived with a broken heart and a suitcase filled with vintage clothes. She owed it to everyone to turn up and show them her appreciation.

"Rosie!" Chloe squealed as they stepped through the door to the pub. Rosie braced herself as Chloe threw her arms around her.

"Hello to you, too." Rosie chuckled and hugged her back.

"She's already had a few wines." Aisha appeared from behind Chloe, rolling her eyes at her behaviour.

"Oh, you're already here!" Rosie unwrapped herself from Chloe's embrace and went to hug Aisha.

"How are you?" Rosie kept her voice low. The pub was noisy, but she didn't want to risk sharing Aisha's news with the residents of Ives-On-Sea.

"I'm really good. Things are going really well." Aisha smiled back at her. She was glowing with happiness.

"We'll talk properly later."

"You should probably save your boyfriend."

Aisha pointed over Rosie's shoulder to where Matt stood with Chloe clinging on to him.

"We could leave him and get a drink?" Rosie teased. Raising her voice so Matt could hear her.

"A drink! What a wonderful idea! Chloe, would you like a drink?" Matt used the opportunity to pull himself from her friend's embrace and marched over towards the bar before anyone could tell him what they wanted.

The night was lots of fun. Rosie had caught up with Aisha, who told her all about her plans to bring her husband to Ives-On-Sea after Christmas. He wanted to see what her life here was like. Aisha confessed that a part of her was hoping he'd fall in love with the Cornish village by the sea and want to move. Rosie had hugged her friend and wished her luck. She wanted to see her happy. They agreed to meet for lunch when Aisha was back so Rosie could meet her husband.

"Have you seen my phone?" Rosie asked once they were home from the pub. She had scrubbed off her make-up and thrown her hair up into a messy bun so it didn't tangle while she slept.

"No. When did you last have it?" Matt garbled his reply as he was brushing his teeth.

"I'm not sure." Rosie couldn't remember having her phone since the last text she had received.

"It'll turn up." Matt emerged from the bathroom. He slowly walked across the bedroom to her before pulling her against his naked chest. Rosie didn't think about her phone again.

*****

Sunday was wonderful. Despite waking up with a pounding head, Rosie climbed out of bed and popped down to Chloe's cafe for a takeaway breakfast. She noticed Chloe was nowhere to be seen. Rosie carried home two steaming boxes of sausages, eggs, and bacon. Matt was already awake and in the kitchen making coffee.

"That smells amazing!" He sighed as she walked into the room. Ignoring the beeping coffee machine, Matt walked over to give her a quick peck on the lips.

"I'm starving." Rosie exclaimed as she grabbed knives and forks and sat down at the table.

"What shall we do today?" Matt asked as he speared a sausage with his fork.

"Can we go to the cinema?" Rosie had been thinking about what they should do with their day. After being on her feet all week, she didn't want to walk anywhere. The cinema seemed like the best option.

"Of course. There's one about an hour's drive away." Matt beamed at her. Sometimes Rosie forgot Matt knew the area better than she did.

"Let's do that. We can watch a film then eat out somewhere."

"How can you already be thinking about food?" Matt groaned as he watched Rosie load up her fork with bacon and egg. Rosie rolled her eyes and continued to eat her breakfast.

The drive to the cinema was long, but it was a treat to have Matt to herself. As they drove, Rosie realised she hadn't had the chance to look for her phone. She wouldn't be able to use it in the cinema, so it didn't matter. It would be somewhere at home. She would look tonight.

They treated themselves to plush seats and ordered boxes of fresh, buttery, salty popcorn. There was a storm brewing outside, and it felt snug and cosy in the dark room. There were only a few other people inside the cinema. Most people were out doing some last minute frenzied Christmas shopping. Thankfully, Rosie had done all of hers online. Matt felt for her hand in the dark and they both lost themselves in the film. It was just the escape they needed after the past couple of weeks. Once the film finished, they had an early dinner at one of the nearby chain restaurants.

"That was lovely. Thank you." Rosie smiled sleepily as she sunk down into the heated seat. They were back in the car on their way home.

"Thank you. It was nice to get away from work and just relax. Actually, that reminds me, I need to speak to you about something." Rosie felt her calmness evaporate at Matt's words. She opened her eyes and sat up in her seat, ready for him to speak.

"I've been staying at yours ever since I came back, and I want you to tell me if I'm overstaying my welcome." Matt's tone was full of concern, whilst Rosie breathed a sigh of relief.

"Matt, don't be silly. I love having you around. Besides, it's only until Christmas then you have to go back to work." Rosie was dreading the day Matt had to go back to London.

"Perhaps. I'm seeing some benefits of staying in Ives-On-Sea." Matt gave her a cheeky smile and winked at her. Rosie decided not to push the subject and allowed them to lapse into silence. She would love nothing more than Matt moving nearby, but she wouldn't force him. Any decision he made had to be made on his own.

The journey home felt much longer than the journey there had been. It was already dark by the time they pulled up outside the shop. As they got in, Rosie switched on the lights inside the flat.

"Shall I put the kettle on?" Rosie called to Matt as he went to put his phone on charge.

"Yes, please!"

The kitchen light flickered a few times before it switched on. It always had been a little dodgy. Rosie put the kettle on and went to get two mugs out of the cupboard. However, it baffled her when she couldn't find her favourite one. She hadn't used it that morning. Rosie checked the dishwasher, but it was empty.

"You okay?" Matt asked. He had come to find her after hearing all the clattering around in the kitchen.

"I can't find my mug."

"Perhaps you left it down in the shop."

Rosie shrugged her shoulders and got out another mug. She never brought the mug down to the shop. It was a special one that her mother had given her and she always took care of it. She made their tea, and they went to sit in the living room.

"Oh, can you help me find my phone? I haven't checked it in a couple of days and I'm worried mum might have tried to contact me." Rosie started looking in all the usual places she left her phone. It wasn't there.

"Rosie, where have you put my laptop?" Matt called from the kitchen.

"I haven't touched it," she called back.

"It's gone." He walked into the bedroom where Rosie was on her knees checking to see whether her phone had slipped underneath the bed.

"I think my phone's gone, Matt. And my mug." Rosie sighed. She should have told him about the texts from Mimi.

"What's wrong?" he asked. Matt could see the concern etched across her face.

"I received some texts from an unknown number."

"Mimi."

"Do you think she's broken in?" Rosie felt a chill run up her spine. To think somebody had been in her home. "Matt, what if she's still here?"

"Rosie, I love your flat, but it's the size of a matchstick box. She can't still be here. What did these messages say?"

Rosie told Matt about both of the messages.

"It's okay." Matt pulled her into his embrace.

"I'm scared, Matt. This woman is obsessed with you and she's broken into my home and taken my things."

"Do you want to stay at the blue cottage tonight? I've never told Mimi about it, so I don't think she'd be able to find us there."

"I want to, but I don't want to risk leaving the shop. She's unhinged. No, I can't leave the shop. Who knows what she might do to it?" Rosie was shaking now.

"I'm going to call the police." Matt grabbed his phone and called the police to report a break in.

Ives-On-Sea was a sleepy town where nothing much happened, and so it was no surprise when five minutes later the police pulled up outside. They took statements from both Rosie and Matt about Mimi, the texts, and the break-in. The officers promised they would contact the police in London and ask someone to visit her property to see whether she was home. It was a relief to know that the police were taking it seriously.

"What about my phone? Could you track it to find her?" Rosie asked. She also really wanted her phone back.

"I'm afraid we don't have the resources available to us to do that. We'll be in touch once we've spoken to the police in London. Don't hesitate to call us again tonight if you feel you're in danger. Goodbye."

Rosie and Matt promised them they would call if they felt they were in any danger.

The police officers let themselves out as Rosie stood in the middle of the living room, still trying to process what had happened.

Do you want to use my phone to contact your family?" Matt asked.

"I don't know any of their numbers." Rosie felt a sob building in her chest.

"I have your mum's number. She's been texting me daily with Christmas related questions." Matt handed his phone to Rosie so she could message her mum and tell her she had lost her phone. She decided against telling her mum the whole story. It would only cause her mother to worry, and there was nothing she could do to help.

CHAPTER FORTY ONE

They had just climbed into bed when Matt's phone rang. The vibrations echoed throughout the room, and Rosie watched as the phone moved around on the bedside table. She had insisted on keeping the bedside light on because she couldn't sleep in the dark tonight. Every little shadow would terrify her until she convinced herself it was Mimi lurking in the corner.

"Who is it?" Rosie whispered.

"It's a friend from work," Matt replied as he swiped to answer. He had asked a friend to visit Mimi's address to see if she was in London.

Rosie held her breath as she listened to Matt's side of the conversation. It sounded as though Mimi hadn't been there. Rosie had to still her body to stop herself from shaking at the thought of her being out there. What if Mimi broke in during the night whilst they were sleeping?

"She wasn't there." Matt confirmed as he put the phone down. Rosie didn't know what to say. She could feel her emotions swirling around inside of her.

"It's okay. I'm here." Matt pulled her to him and kissed the top of her head.

"I'm scared." Rosie's body shook as she spoke. This flat was her safe space. Where she had healed from all the heartbreak. It was hers. And yet, Mimi thought it was okay to just let herself in. She might be ill, but Rosie no longer felt an ounce of sympathy towards her. The woman was dangerous, and the police had to find her. She was obsessed and Rosie didn't know what lengths she would go to get what she wanted.

"The police said they'll keep driving past throughout the night to ensure there's nobody around the shop or flat." Matt reminded her. It brought some comfort knowing the local police would keep an eye out for her. However, Mimi had already proven how savvy she was at breaking and entering. Rosie didn't know the woman and didn't know how far she would go to get what she wanted.

"Do you think she's dangerous?" she asked.

"I don't know. I'm sorry, Rosie. This is all my fault." Matt's arms tightened around her.

"How could you date a woman like this?"

"She's an excellent actress. We only dated for six months. When I heard my mother was ill, her real side started to show. She would check my phone whenever I'd been speaking to my mum. There was one time I was planning to visit my mum and the evening before she broke down telling me they had rushed her brother to hospital after an accident. With the way she's behaving now, I'm questioning everything. This is an awful thing to say, but I'm even questioning whether she's ill. I think she might be the world's best manipulator."

Rosie pulled back to look into Matt's eyes. She could see the guilt flooding out of him. He blamed himself for all of this.

"Matt, it's not your fault. You met the wrong woman who preyed on your own insecurities and manipulated you. Don't blame yourself for that. Look at how she's behaving now. She broke into my home! That's not normal behaviour." Rosie's voice had got louder and louder as her anger spilled over. How dare Mimi hurt him like this? How dare she think she had any claim over him? Six months was all they had dated for and yet she was acting as though he had walked away from a twenty-year marriage.

"I brought her into your life, Rosie. Of course it's my fault. I should have seen through her from the start. I was a different person when I met her. Oh, I was such an idiot. The first day I met her, she tripped, and I caught her. I'm wondering whether that really was an accident. She engineered our entire relationship. I missed seeing my mother for the last time because of her." Tears filled Matt's eyes and Rosie pulled him to her. His heart was breaking as his chest heaved with sobs.

"It's okay. Matt, it really wasn't your fault. You weren't to know she was manipulating you."

"I briefly told my mum about Mimi, and she hated everything I told her. Why couldn't I see what was right in front of me?"

"Hey. Stop it. It's okay. Your mum wanted what's best for you. Nobody would ever have been good enough in her eyes. Take some deep breaths." Rosie stepped back from him and took a hold of his hand, squeezing it in hers.

"Why don't you take some flowers to your mum's grave tomorrow and tell her everything you didn't get to say to her?" Rosie wanted to do everything she could to help Matt process his grief. He was intent on supporting her, but he was the one in need of someone to care for him.

"I can't leave you." His eyes were red and puffy as he looked at her.

"Matt, I'll be fine while the shop's open. I have tailoring customers booked throughout the day, so I'll never be alone. You need to do this for you."

"Are you sure?" his voice wavered. Rosie knew he was looking for an excuse. As much as he wanted to confront his emotions, it scared him.

"I'm sure. Come on, let's try to get some sleep." Despite being terrified of Mimi breaking in during the night, Rosie knew she had to be strong for Matt. He had been through so much in such a short amount of time.

They pulled the covers around them and Matt pulled Rosie against him, wrapping his arm around her waist. It felt as though it was them against the world. In the distance, Rosie could hear the sea crashing like thunder. It was an awful night, but they were wrapped up inside. A part of her pitied Mimi if she really was outside watching them. She'd never know what it was like to care for someone. To truly feel as though someone is the other half of you. To love someone. Rosie jumped. Had she really just thought of love?

CHAPTER
FORTY TWO

The morning after the break-in, the police called to say they had tracked Mimi's car, and she was back at her address in London. They would keep a close eye on her movements and would contact them if her car returned to Cornwall. Matt had made the journey to his parents' grave. He had come home with a tear-stained face, but promised Rosie he was okay. It was something he had to do, and it had helped him with his grief.

That evening, they held each other in bed, neither of them wanting to let go of the other. It felt like they were safe in their little bubble. Whilst ensconced in their duvet fortress, they could forget about everything that was happening around them.

"Would you come with me next time?" he

asked a shocked Rosie. "I'd like them to meet you. They can't be here, but it's the next best."

"Of course I will." Rosie promised him and squeezed his hand. In their short time together, so much had happened and their connection had strengthened.

"Thank you, Rosie. I think my mum would have loved you. She'd be over the moon to know how much time I'm spending in Ives-On-Sea."

Rosie held him tightly.

*****

The following day, Matt drove into the next town to do some Christmas shopping for Rosie and her family. As Rosie was closing the shop, she heard a car beep from outside. She looked up to see Matt's car outside with a Christmas tree strapped to the roof. Life had been so busy that Rosie had completely forgotten to buy a tree. When she left Oliver, she had left him with all of their Christmas decorations and so it seemed pointless this year to buy a tree when she had nothing to put on it.

"Surprise!" Matt called from outside the shop. Rosie giggled and grabbed a coat to go outside and help him.

"I wasn't going to bother with a tree!" She showered him in kisses, grateful to have him back by her side.

"I know, and that's why I got you one. I had a little snoop around your flat but couldn't find any decorations, so I've bought some. There's also a bag in the back of the car with decorations I've been collecting from the junk shop up the road."

"It's not junk!" Rosie cried, horrified at his description.

"Okay, the shop up the road that sells pre-owned items. Kind of like your shop, but for charity." He winked at her.

"Come on, let's get all this inside." Rosie could see bags of Christmas shopping in the car's boot.

Half an hour later, they both stood panting as they stared at the tree in the corner of Rosie's living room. Getting it up the stairs to her flat had been like reenacting a comedy.

"Why don't you make us a coffee while I sort through which bags are Christmas presents and which are decorations?" Rosie gave him a quick peck on the lips before disappearing into the kitchen to leave Matt to go through his bags. A small smile spread across her face as she waited for the machine to heat up. Without being prompted, he had thought of her and made the effort to surprise her. Rosie made the coffees, adding a dash of Irish cream to give them a Christmas makeover.

"Right, you can come back in!" Matt called.

"Here you go." Rosie passed a mug to Matt. He'd moved half the bags out of the room. Rosie decided against asking where he had moved them to or else she might be tempted to peek at the presents.

"There are lights in that bag, new decorations in that bag, and the tote bag has the second hand decorations." Matt sat down on the sofa with his coffee. Rosie immediately went for the bag with the second hand decorations.

Rosie gasped at the bag's contents. There was a range of vintage Christmas tree decorations. A collection of wooden decorations drew Rosie to them. The colours faded from years of use. There was a Santa Claus with a faded red suit, a skier, and even a little wooded Christmas pudding. Rosie's mind wandered to all the trees that these decorations had been on. All the Christmas Days they had witnessed. It put a smile on her face to think that all of those hopefully happy memories were now sitting in her living room about to adorn her tree.

"Do you like them?" asked Matt. He was sitting watching Rosie go through the bag.

"I love them! Thank you so much." Rosie left the decorations and sat down next to him, resting her head against his shoulder.

"I'm glad. I can't change what's happening around us, Rosie, but I want to do everything I can to put a smile on your face this Christmas. You deserve it." Matt put down his mug and leant forward to grab a bag that was next to him. "I've also got you a new phone. It's a bit of an upgrade from the old one. This one has a much better camera and won't take ten years to go online."

"Hey! Don't be so mean about my old phone. Thank you."

"I thought I could help you create an online

presence for the shop in the new year."

"Oh, Matt. Thank you." Rosie threw her arms around his neck and nuzzled her face into his.

"Come on, we ought to get decorating." Matt gave her a quick kiss before pushing her away so they could decorate the tree.

"Let's go. Remind me later and I'll pay you back for the phone." Rosie took a big swig from her alcohol infused coffee.

"Rosie, you are not paying me back. It's my ex-girlfriend that stole your mobile. The least I can do it replace it for you."

They wrapped the tree in the twinkling lights Matt had bought. He'd misjudged how many lights they would need, and so the top was a little sparse. Together, they hung the assortment of decorations on the tree.

"It's perfect." Rosie stepped back to look at the tree. It was a mishmash of old and new - the perfect representation of the two of them.

"I've never decorated a tree before." Matt commented as he stepped back to take in their hard work.

"Never?" Rosie's jaw had dropped open at the confession.

"No. My mother always insisted on decorating ours because my father wanted it to be perfect. When I moved out, I didn't see the point of having a tree." He shrugged his shoulders, brushing it off.

"Congratulations on your first tree." Rosie

tucked herself into his side.

CHAPTER FORTY THREE

As Christmas Eve approached, Rosie's mother's messages became more and more frantic. She wanted to make the holiday amazing for everyone. It was the first time her brother was bringing a boyfriend to a family occasion and her mother knew about the problems with Matt's ex. Her parents were arriving a couple of days before Christmas Eve to decorate the cottage and to do a food shop. Rosie had suggested her mother do an online food shop, but her mother had gasped in horror at the thought. She wanted to choose her own food and ensure it met her high standards.

Rosie woke the morning of Christmas Eve to Matt standing in the bedroom doorway, holding a tray filled with coffee and pastries.

"I was going to do a cooked breakfast but as I got the eggs out of the fridge, your mum texted me asking if I like gammon because she's cooking one for tonight. We're going to do nothing but eat over the next few days, aren't we?" Rosie stifled a giggle. Her mother had quickly added Matt to the Christmas WhatsApp group and bombarded him with messages. It must have been quite a shock for Matt after having grown up in such a conservative household. Meanwhile, Will had taken the sensible approach and had refused to give their mother Niall's number.

"I hope you're hungry." Rosie pulled back the duvet so he could climb in beside her. It was lovely to be together with nowhere to be and nothing to do. They hadn't had many moments like this.

"The pastries are from Chloe's." Matt commented. Rosie picked up a croissant and bit into the flaky pastry. It was heavenly.

"Is she open already?"

"No, she was in the back baking. She tried shouting out that she was closed, but I can be quite persistent when I want to be. Once she realised it was me, she let me in and let me pick from the freshly baked goods."

Rosie rolled her eyes. Her friends were enamoured by Matt and would do anything for him.

"Thank you. They're delicious."

"What's the plan for today?" Matt picked up a pastry and leaned back against the pillows.

"Mum's expecting us around three. Until

then, we have no plans." Rosie sighed contentedly.

"So we could stay in bed until three?" Matt grabbed another pastry from the tray.

"Do not get pastry crumbs over the bed!"

*****

"We need to leave!" Matt called from the doorway. They were going to be late, but Rosie was still doing some last-minute packing.

"I'm coming!" Rosie called back. It was a lie. She was still flicking through her wardrobe, trying to decide what to bring. Although her family spent most of Christmas in their pyjamas, Rosie wanted a few nice outfits just in case. Normally, Rosie would have meticulously planned. However, she'd been so preoccupied with the shop and Mimi that she hadn't had time to think about anything else.

"Rosie, your mum's texting me, asking us where we are." Matt had left his spot by the front door and had found her. He let out a frustrated sigh as he spotted her in the middle of the room with clothes surrounding her.

"How many outfits have you packed?" he asked.

"Three." Rosie replied. She didn't take her eyes off of a pair of emerald green velvet flared trousers. They were beautiful, but she couldn't think of when she would wear them.

"Rosie, we're coming home on Boxing Day. You will not need more than three outfits."

"Okay. I'll bring four. Let me just grab a jumper to go with these trousers." Rosie took a black cashmere jumper from a drawer and placed it in her suitcase beside the flared trousers. Before she could even consider adding anything more, Matt swooped in and swiftly closed her suitcase.

"Now you're ready." He picked up the suitcase and walked to the door. Rosie had a last glance around the flat. She hoped it would be okay and Mimi wouldn't do anything stupid while they were away.

"Don't worry." Matt called from the hallway. For someone who was only just learning to express his own emotions, he was great at knowing how she was feeling.

"Worrying is my default setting." Rosie joined him in the hallway and picked up her handbag.

"Ready?" Matt asked. He had a hold of both of their suitcases so Rosie could easily lock the door behind them. They had added an extra lock to the door in an attempt to deter Mimi. Rosie only hoped it would work. It was pouring down outside, with thunder rumbling in the distance. Thankfully, the cottage was only a short drive away. Soon they would be snuggled up in front of a roaring fire with Rosie's mother pouring them various drinks and offering them snacks.

The cottage was in the middle of nowhere. It was a gorgeous red brick building with a sage green door in the middle, with a huge handmade wreath hanging from it. Before Rosie and Matt could even climb out of the car, Rosie's mother had swung open the door and was waving at them.

"Quick, before you get soaked!" she called. They grabbed their suitcases from the boot and ran through the rain to the front door. As they stepped inside, the overwhelming smell of cinnamon hit them. It was toasty inside and Rosie could hear the crackle from the fire.

"Mum, this is Matt. Matt, this is my mother, Lisa." Rosie introduced them. Matt beamed at her mother and enveloped her in a hug. Rosie could see her mother had already fallen for his charm.

"Let me get you both a drink. Your father, brother, and Niall are in the living room. Go say hello and then go get changed." It wasn't until Rosie's mother mentioned getting changed that Rosie noticed just what she was wearing. Christmas themed pyjamas.

"Mum, please tell me we're not all wearing matching pyjamas." Rosie was cringing. Meanwhile, Matt was stifling a giggle. This was a million miles away from the formal Christmas he was used to.

"Oh, come on. It's the first time I've had both you, your brother, and your boyfriends together. Please indulge me this Christmas."

"Fine, but my hot chocolate better have a good glug of Irish cream!" Rosie called as she pulled Matt in the direction of her brother's voice.

The fire was roaring in the living room, and the television was playing *The Grinch*. Rosie's father, brother, and Niall were sitting watching, all dressed in their matching pyjamas.

"Will, why didn't you stand up to mum?" Rosie whinged. She had been looking forward to wearing a beautiful red silk wrap dress. The dress had been in Rosie's recent auction purchase. Wrapped in tissue paper at the bottom of a box, it felt like fate when Rosie found it so close to Christmas. Instead, she'd be wearing polyester tartan pyjamas.

"Come on, it's fun." Will laughed and got up to hug her. Rosie hugged everyone and introduced them to Matt.

Once introductions were over, Rosie and Matt went to unpack and change. Their room was in the eaves with exposed floorboards, white-washed walls, and pastel soft furnishings. In the corner was a small writing desk with a tiny potted pine tree on top of it. The tree had a few of Rosie's childhood decorations on it. Her mother had done everything she could to make this Christmas special. No doubt she remembered last Christmas when Rosie spent the day in bed refusing to speak to anyone. It was just after she had discovered Oliver's affair and she felt her whole life had come crashing down around her. There had been no point in celebrating Christmas. This year was different. She had a lost Christmas to make up for.

"Those pyjamas clash with your hair." Matt laughed as she pulled the red top over her head.

"Mum definitely didn't consider me when she was buying these." Rosie huffed and pulled her hair back into a bun so there was less hair to clash with the hideous red of the pyjamas.

"I wondered why your mother messaged me asking for my sizes. I assumed it was for a Christmas presents or a Christmas jumper. Not once did I consider we might all be sitting in matching pyjamas watching mindless television."

"Did you just call *The Grinch* mindless television?" All thoughts of pyjamas had left Rosie's mind.

"It is." Matt rolled his eyes.

"Take it back. That's my favourite Christmas film. What's yours?"

"*White Christmas.*"

"Of course."

"What do you mean, 'of course'?" Matt had a glint in his eye as he stepped towards her.

"I'm just saying we have very different tastes. When I first met you, I thought they had sewn you into your suits."

"Sewn in!" he scoffed. "I just like to make the effort."

"I prefer you in nothing." Rosie winked at him. She had completely thrown him and he'd lost his retort.

"I'd like to say the same, but I just cannot get over these pyjamas." By now, he was standing in front of her with just millimetres between their bodies.

"I love you." The words slipped out before Rosie could stop herself. She hadn't meant to tell him yet, and she certainly hadn't meant to tell him now when tensions were running high. Matt dropped his hands from her face and took a step back. Rosie felt her heart hammer in her chest at his reaction. Rather than tell her he loved her, he had stepped back from her.

"Your drinks are ready!" Rosie's mother called from the bottom of the stairs.

"Thanks, mum. We'll be right down." Rosie called back. She was grateful for the interruption.

"Wait." Matt caught her hand as she tried to walk past him to the door.

"Matt, don't. Just forget I said anything." Rosie's cheeks were ablaze with the humiliation of rejection. She just wanted to forget it ever happened and drown her sorrows in Irish cream hot chocolates.

"No, Rosie. You don't understand. I was just taken aback. Mimi is the only other person to have said that to me and frankly, I don't believe she ever loved me. She might have an infatuation with me, but there's no love there. Oh, I'm making such a mess of this. I'm talking about my ex when I'm trying to tell you I love you." It was out of character for Matt to be floundering. He always knew just what to say. However, Rosie hadn't even noticed. All she heard was that he had said it back to her. He loved her.

*****

Christmas Eve had been wonderful. Well,

Rosie's mother might not have agreed. The dinner burnt as they didn't know how to use the oven and when her father plugged in his record player, the electrics blew and they had to hunt for the fuse box using the torches on their phones. None of it had mattered to Rosie. She was still in a little bubble of happiness from Matt confessing his love for her. Those three words had made her Christmas Eve, and nothing could spoil that. Once they had restored the electrics, thrown the burnt food in the bin, and the frozen pizzas were in the oven, they settled down to watch *White Christmas*. It was a lovely film, but Rosie still couldn't understand how it was Matt's favourite.

Before going to bed, Rosie fetched the bag of presents from their room and positioned them around the tree. The clothes she ordered from auctions often came with accessories bundled up in vintage newspapers. Some were really old, others dated back to the nineties. Rosie would unwrap them and store the paper both for wrapping items from the shop and for presents. Her presents were all wrapped in the newspaper with red silk bows tied around them. Her Christmas shopping had been easy, as most of her presents were from the shop. There were a few presents from Matt at the bottom of the bag. He had wrapped them in tartan Christmas paper with matching tags and ribbons. Rosie hid her smirk. It was very Matt.

"Ready for bed?" Matt asked as she finished positioning the last present under the tree. It looked pretty for everyone to wake up to the following morning.

"Yes. Let's go." She slid her hand into Matt's as he led her towards their bedroom for the night.

CHAPTER FORTY FOUR

A loud banging on their door woke them on Christmas morning. Rosie groaned and pulled a pillow over her face to ignore her mother.

"It's seven in the morning, mother!" Rosie shouted. She'd given up with the pillow and her mother was now singing Christmas carols on the other side of the door.

"I know. I'm just too excited to sleep. Your father and I have been up since five peeling vegetables."

"We'll be down in ten minutes." Rosie called back. She knew there was no point in trying to argue.

"Why is your mum so excited about Christmas?" Matt asked. He'd been hiding his own head under the duvet.

"I was in a terrible state last year. I think mum's remembering that and she wants to make this year special because of it. Both me and Will are happy so I think all of her Christmases have come at once.

"I'm sorry last Christmas was difficult for you."

"It's okay. I'm grateful for it. I wouldn't be the person I am today without having gone through it." As Rosie said the words out loud, she realised how much she believed it. The pain was awful, and she felt as though she would never be happy again. Yet, a year later, she was grateful for the pain and the experience. She had grown from it and now had her shop and Matt.

"Good. This time last year, I was driving up to see my mum. I had lunch with her and then left. Looking back, I feel awful. I should have stayed and spent time with her. She had always tried to make Christmas special for me without upsetting my father or his mother."

"Matt, don't beat yourself up over this. You can't change the past. I'm sure your mother knew how much you loved her. From what I've heard, she was quite popular in the community, so I'm sure she wasn't alone."

"Thank you." Matt bent forward to kiss her, but a knock on the door interrupted them.

"Mum says if you're not downstairs in the next two minutes, she's getting dad to take this door off its hinges." Will called through the closed door.

Rosie groaned and threw the covers off of her. "We're coming!" she shouted.

"We'll be home soon. Just the two of us." Matt reminded her.

"Come on then. Let's get this day over with. I warn you, mum's going to fill us with so much food and drink we won't fit back in your car."

Matt laughed, thinking she was joking.

They walked into the kitchen in their matching pyjamas to be greeted by a table filled with food.

"Merry Christmas!" Rosie's father greeted them with hugs and glasses of Buck's fizz. Matt looked dubiously at the bubbling orange glass of alcohol. A playlist of instrumental Christmas tunes played in the background as Rosie's mother placed further plates of food on the already heaving table.

"Merry Christmas!" Will leant across the table to clink glasses with Rosie and Matt.

"Merry Christmas. Sorry about this, Niall. Mum's not normally this over the top." Rosie smiled over at an overwhelmed looking Niall.

They filled their plates for breakfast. Rosie piled her plate with scrambled eggs, smoked salmon, and a hash brown. There was so much food.

"What are we going to do with the leftovers?" Will asked as he picked up his third cinnamon swirl.

"There's a soup kitchen down the road. They are open on Christmas Day. Perhaps we could run the breakfast leftovers there?" Matt suggested.

"Sure. We'll help you." Will gestured to himself and Niall.

"Thanks. I'll drive since I've not had anything to drink." Matt gestured to his untouched glass of Buck's fizz.

"Rosie, will you stay and help me prepare lunch?" Her mother's eyes pleaded with her.

"Of course. Then I'll help with the lunch run to the soup kitchen." Rosie joked. She really hoped her mother hadn't gone overboard with Christmas dinner.

They all helped load Matt's car, and he drove off with Will and Niall.

"Come on, let's have a coffee before we think about the next meal." Rosie's father suggested. They made their way back into the cottage and sat around the farmhouse table in the kitchen.

"He's lovely," her mother commented, referring to Matt.

"He is." Rosie smiled dreamily.

"I can't tell you how happy it makes me to see you smile again." Her mother reached out to squeeze her hand.

"Thank you, mum. You really didn't have to do all of this. It's nice just being together."

"I know. I'm sorry I've gone over the top. You should see the desserts. There's an extra fridge out in the garage! We'll keep one and send the rest to the soup kitchen. At least some good has come from it."

The three of them sat in silence as they sipped their coffee. The sound of the fire crackling in the living room drifted through the open doors. It was the cosy Christmas Day that Rosie had been pining for.

An hour later, the boys returned, and they all settled down to open their presents. Rosie had gifted Matt a vintage suit, which she had found in the shop. It was a pale blue 1920s suit. As Rosie had unwrapped it from the tissue paper encasing it, she knew it had to be Matt's. His face lit up at the sight. Matt had got Rosie a few gifts. One was a vintage biscuit tin filled with old buttons. He had also bought her tickets to the opera in London.

"I've got cover in the shop for that weekend. I thought we could treat it as a weekend away." It was perfect. He'd even thought to check the dates with Lily.

Once they had exchanged gifts, they watched a couple of Christmas films before it was time to consider the dinner.

"I'll check on the potatoes. Rosie, would you go to the fridge in the garage and choose a dessert?" The soup kitchen had asked them to drop the remaining food over early the following morning. They would have lots of people returning on Boxing Day. Not only were they feeding the homeless this Christmas, but they had also opened their doors to those who couldn't afford Christmas dinner. Rosie's mother had dissolved into tears. She was so grateful the food wouldn't go to waste.

"What does everyone fancy?" Rosie asked, stretching as she got up from the sofa. Matt had disappeared into the bathroom a few minutes ago.

"Anything." Came the unhelpful comment from her brother.

"Just choose something we'll all enjoy." Her father smiled at her before following her mother into the kitchen.

Rosie rolled her eyes and went in search of a dessert to please everyone. As she undid the door from the utility room to the garage, Rosie shivered as the icy air hit her. She wrapped her arms around herself in a vain attempt to stay warm. The fire in the living room had been roaring away, as they ignored the storm outside. Rosie took a deep breath and went in search of a light switch. Her fingers felt along the dark wall until she found the switch. She flicked it, but nothing happened.

"Here, use the light on my phone." Rosie jumped at the sound of the voice. She hadn't heard Matt follow her.

"Thanks." Rosie took the phone and shone the light into the room. On the far wall was a fridge.

"I've had a voicemail from Mimi." Matt's voice was strained. Rosie rolled her eyes.

"Of course you have. It's Christmas Day. Have they brought her surgery forward?" Rosie cringed at the spiteful words as they tumbled out of her mouth. "I'm sorry, Matt. I didn't mean that. I'm just so angry. Today was supposed to be perfect and yet here she is interfering." Matt pulled her into his embrace and placed a soft kiss on the top of her head.

"I'm sorry, Rosie. I know she's an awful person, but that doesn't mean I wish her any harm."

"Oh, Matt. You're such a caring person and that's why I like you so much. I never want you to change that about yourself. What did the call say?"

"What she was saying made little sense and I couldn't hear much because of the wind in the background. Then she sent me a picture of herself stood at the top of a cliff. I think she's trying to kill herself."

Rosie's hand flew to her mouth.

"Do you still have the photo?" Rosie controlled her shaking hands as she gave Matt his phone back. He unlocked it and brought up the picture Mimi had sent him. Rosie squinted. The picture was of Mimi standing at the edge of a cliff, the sea below her. "I recognise that costal path. We went for a walk there. Do you remember?"

"I do. I should go to her." Matt's voice was strained.

"You're a good person, Matt. You should go to her, but I'm not letting you go alone. Drop me off so she doesn't see me arrive with you. I'm also calling the police on the way. Who knows what she might do?"

"What about Christmas Day? Your parents?"

"I'll explain. You go get the car keys and our coats, and I'll meet you in the car."

Rosie's mum was in the kitchen, turning the roast potatoes.

"Excellent timing. I've just put the kettle on

to make the gravy. You can stir it. Did you pick a dessert?" Her mother noticed her empty hands.

"Wait mum, before you get carried away. Matt's had a text from Mimi. She's threatening to kill herself." Rosie watched as her mum's eyes bulged at the news.

"What are you going to do?" Her mum sat down. Rosie wanted nothing more than to take the seat opposite and pour her heart out to her mother, but there wasn't the time.

"Matt's going to talk to her. I'll go with him, but stay out of sight. I'm also going to call the police."

"Do you want me and your father to come?" Her mother was already standing up and taking off her apron.

"No, mum. Please, just enjoy Christmas Day. We'll be back before you know it. Plate us up some dinner and leave it in the oven to stay warm."

"Be careful." Rosie gave her mum a quick hug before running out of the house to join Matt.

CHAPTER
FORTY FIVE

"Left here!" Rosie shouted. They were almost at the entrance to the car park. Rosie had called the police, who told them they would be there as soon as possible. The officer had advised them not to approach Mimi. Rosie had explained her fixation on Matt and the police felt it would be best to wait for them to accompany them.

"I can pull in here and walk the rest of the way. What will you do?" Matt pulled the car onto a grass verge and turned off the engine.

"I'll follow you at a distance and try to hide. Don't get too close to her, Matt. We're not waiting for the police?"

"I know Mimi well enough to know that she'll do something stupid at the first sight of the police."

Rosie threw herself into Matt's open arms. He was right. His embrace didn't ease her nerves. It only reminded her of how much she had to lose.

"Maybe we should just wait for the police, anyway?" Rosie suggested. It was a selfish suggestion. She didn't want Matt being the one to talk to Mimi.

"Rosie, any sign of the police and she'll jump." Matt released her and stepped back. His face was unreadable.

"Okay. Let's do this." Rosie watched as he walked away. She wanted to run after him, pull him back to the car and tell him to never think of Mimi again. However, she knew he couldn't do that. Rosie knew that if he didn't try, he would never forgive himself.

After waiting a couple of minutes, Rosie followed Matt. On any other day, she would have marvelled at the beauty of the seascape below her. Today, however, her attention was solely on putting one foot in front of the other, as quietly as possible. She knew that in a few meters she would turn a corner and then she would be able to see Mimi and Matt. The path was only a few feet wide, with a sheer drop to the left. Wind whipped around her, blowing her hair across her face. Rosie wished she'd thought to tie her hair back. Here she was, standing on a clifftop on Christmas Day, dressed in ridiculous pyjamas with her coat over them. In that moment, Rosie knew how deeply she felt about Matt. She would do anything for him, and she would do whatever she could to keep him. With a deep breath, she took those last few steps.

Her breath caught in her throat at the sight in front of her. Matt was standing only a few paces from Mimi. The woman's hair whipped around her face in a tangled mess from the fierce breeze. Her eyes were puffy and red from crying. Rosie thought back to the confident and beautiful Mimi who she had seen in London. The woman opposite her was worlds apart. She looked unwell. Her eyes were ablaze with emotions as her arms flew to emphasise what she was saying. She was merely a step away from the edge of the cliff. Rosie had to get closer. The wind was howling and she couldn't hear what was being said.

Carefully, Rosie edged closer to the cliff's edge. There was little to hide behind on top of the bleak cliff. She only hoped that Mimi was so focused on Matt that she wouldn't spot the figure inching towards her.

"Mimi, you don't have to do this! We can get you help." Matt was almost shouting to be heard above the wind.

"I don't need help. I need you!" Mimi called back. Her voice cracked as she spoke. In that short moment, Rosie felt sorry for her. This poor woman was so unwell and heartbroken that she felt the only solution was to end her life. Tears pooled in Rosie's eyes. She swiped angrily at them and forced herself to keep watching the scene in front of her.

"Let's focus on getting you well. You

shouldn't be up here in this cold. Not when you're so ill." Matt's eyes mirrored Rosie's.

"I'm not ill. I don't have cancer. We can be together, Matt. Just the two of us." Mimi's words echoed in Rosie's ears. She had lied. She didn't have cancer. Rosie wanted to lunge forward and pull Matt back. The woman had lied about being ill. What other lengths would she go to? The pity Rosie had felt mere seconds ago had changed to anger. How dare this woman try to manipulate Matt in this way?

"You lied about having a life-threatening illness?" Matt's voice shook. How low would this woman stoop to have Matt to herself? Fear bubbled up inside of Rosie. If she couldn't have him in life, would she try to have him in death? The sea felt like it was rising as Rosie struggled to stay up on her feet. She couldn't let her feelings envelop her. Matt needed her.

"Matt!" Rosie called, revealing herself. She couldn't stand and listen to anymore. "Step away from her!" Mimi lunged towards Matt as soon as she spotted Rosie. Her fingers sunk into his arm and he staggered, briefly losing his balance.

"You brought her?" Mimi roared above the wind.

"Rosie, I thought you were going to keep your distance?" Matt's eyes looked pained.

"She's crazy, Matt. Just walk away before she does something stupid." Rosie's eyes didn't leave Mimi's grip on Matt's arm.

"He's mine. I'll show you." The words echoed

the message Rosie had received.

"Let go of me, Mimi." Matt tried to shake her from him.

"No." she cried, tugging him towards the cliff edge.

"The police are here, Mimi. Let go of Matt and step away from him."

"The police?" Mimi screeched. She dropped her hold on Matt, her face froze. Rosie watched as her eyes glazed over with fear. Every thought she was having played out across her face, and Rosie knew exactly what she was about to do.

Time seemed to stop as Mimi turned to Matt. "I love you," she whispered, before turning towards the sea. Matt must have realised what she was doing, because he lunged forward and caught her just in time. They both tumbled backwards onto the grass below. He pinned her floundering arms to her sides and held her down until the police reached them.

"Are you okay?" An officer asked Rosie. She had frozen as the scene played out in front of her. She had recognised the look on Mimi's face as she realised her entire life had come crashing down around her. There was nothing for her to keep fighting for. Rosie had felt that way when she walked out of the home she shared with Oliver. However, she hadn't allowed those emotions to consume her. Instead, she had embraced herself and rebuilt her life. It was sad to see Mimi struggling, but she could never forgive her for what she had put them through today. Rosie hoped they would never see her again.

"Yes. Sorry, I'm just in shock." Her voice quivered and her body shook as the cold seeped into her bones.

"Come, there's an ambulance back on the road." The officer tried to take her arm. However, the touch jolted Rosie back to the present.

"Sorry, I'm fine. Just in shock." She didn't want to leave Matt. The other officers had handcuffed Mimi for her own safety. Meanwhile, Matt was just finding his feet again.

"Are you okay?" His eyes found her and he immediately went to her.

"That was horrible." Tears fell from Rosie's eyes.

"I know, but it's over now. Hopefully, they can get Mimi the help she needs."

*****

Once the police had taken their statements and established that Mimi was mentally unwell, they left them to drive back to Rosie's family. Mimi was being taken to a secure hospital to be assessed before they decided on her future. The police assured them they wouldn't release her until she was well. Both Rosie and Matt breathed a sigh of relief at the news. They remained silent for the journey back. Neither of them knowing what to say.

"I'm so sorry." Matt apologised for what must have been the hundredth time as he finished telling everyone what had happened. They were now ensconced in the cosy holiday cottage with Rosie's family surrounding them.

"Matt, it's okay. You weren't to know Mimi was going to turn so crazy." Rosie's mother hugged him.

"Thank you. I appreciate how nice you're being, considering I put your daughter in danger. I really didn't know what she was truly capable of."

"Matt, it's not your fault. Anyway, now Niall can be the perfect son-in-law." Will joked.

"Rosie, do you want to go home?" Her mother was staring at her, trying to see underneath the mask. Rosie was trying so hard to be okay, but underneath the facade, she was crumbling.

"I'm not sure. The police said she won't be going anywhere for a while, so I suppose there's no point in going home." Truthfully, Rosie didn't know how she felt.

"I'm going to put the kettle on." Her mother announced. Rosie had to stifle a giggle. After everything they had gone through, her mother was going to put the kettle on.

"I'm not sure a cup of tea is going to fix this." Her father commented. He was rolling his eyes at her mother's antics.

"I'm not making tea. I thought we could all have hot chocolate with a dash of Irish cream." At the mention of an alcoholic hot chocolate, Rosie's father jumped up from his own seat and went to help her mother in the kitchen.

"Are you sure you're okay?" Matt asked. He had moved up on the sofa so Rosie could nestle into his side. Her brother and his boyfriend had turned their attention to the film on the television to give them some privacy.

"Honestly? No, I'm not okay. Are you okay?"

"No, I'm not. I feel so guilty for bringing Mimi into your life."

"Matt, please don't feel guilty. You dated the girl for six months. You weren't to know she was going to do this. I was so scared of losing you." Their faces were just a breath apart. Neither of them wanted to move from the other.

"I love you." Rosie whispered.

"I love you, too." Matt replied. A smile broke out on both of their faces. They were okay, and they were together.

CHAPTER
FORTY SIX

It took a while for the events of Christmas Day to feel like a distant nightmare. They had made the best of their remaining time with Rosie's family, but nobody felt as though they could relax. Rosie's mother had tried to convince her to return home with them, but Rosie knew she had to return to normal life soon, or else she might never want to. Slowly, she was settling back into the flat. It still felt strange knowing how unwell Mimi had been and that she had broken into Rosie's home.

The shop was closed in the lull between Christmas and New Year, and they had spent most of the days holed up inside the flat together. Today was New Year's Eve, and they had decided to go to the party at the pub. Neither of them felt like it, but they knew they had to. It was time they saw people again. Rosie's phone hadn't stopped ringing with calls from her friends checking to see if they were okay. Even Sofia had heard about what had happened and had sent a polite message wishing her well. She had texted them all to let them know they were fine, but she didn't feel like talking yet.

Rosie focused on choosing an outfit for the evening to keep her mind off the nerves which were furiously bubbling away in the pit of her stomach. The businesses of Ives-On-Sea liked to support each other. Which was why the pub had set an 80s dress code. Everybody had come to Rosie looking for gaudy 80s outfits, the kind that were usually very difficult to sell. The party was being catered by the pub, but dessert would be a selection of Chloe's delicious cakes, some topped with sweets from Aisha's shop. They would adorn the inside of the pub with decorations from the charity shop. It was lovely to see everyone coming together, supporting each other, and having fun.

Although Rosie loved 80s fashion, most of the colours clashed wonderfully with her hair. She had put aside a pale blue shell suit for Matt.

"Have you decided what you're wearing?" Matt asked. He had been sending a couple of work emails before logging off for the evening.

"I think I might wear these dark green leggings with a black leotard and black leg warmers." Rosie had carefully chosen items from the shop in muted colours.

"Sounds perfect. Will you be embracing your curls?"

"I've even got a green bow for my hair."

"What am I wearing?" Matt asked. He was frowning, worried about what Rosie had chosen for him. Rosie laughed and went to fetch the shell suit from her wardrobe.

"That's truly horrific." Matt gasped as she showed it to him. For a man that lived in suits, an 80s shell suit was his worst nightmare.

"It's wonderful." Rosie giggled.

With some 80s pop music playing in the background, they both got ready for the evening. Rosie completed her look with some green eyeshadow and allowed her curls to express their wild side. She pinned the green velvet bow at a jaunty angle on her head and looked at herself in the mirror. She looked ridiculous, but she loved it.

"What do you think?" Rosie turned around to show Matt. As soon as she saw him, she dissolved into a fit of giggles. The shell suit was a couple of sizes too big for him and he had rolled up the sleeves on the jacket.

"How do you get to look amazing while I look like an idiot?" He rolled his eyes and stepped towards her.

"Are you ready to party?" Rosie stepped into his embrace. A carefree evening was just what they needed.

"I'm more than ready to drink enough to forget what I'm wearing."

"You're such a drama queen. It's an original 80s shell suit, appreciate the history and stop whinging." Rosie was only joking, but Matt's face turned serious.

"Rosie, before we leave, there's something I want to speak to you about." He guided her to the edge of the bed and gestured for them both to sit down.

"What's wrong?" Rosie asked. She was fearful of what Matt was about to say. The last few days together had been wonderful, but she knew it was all about to end. He'd soon be going back to London, and she'd be alone in Ives-On-Sea, afraid of her own shadow.

"I've just emailed work telling them I'm not going back." The crease in his brow was prominent and his eyes were distant. He had put his walls up, protecting himself from the conversation they were about to have.

"You're not going back to work or you're not going back to London?" Rosie had to know exactly what he was saying.

"I'm not going back to work or London. I want to stay here in Ives-On-Sea. I'd like to stay here with you, but I understand if that's too much too soon."

Rosie blinked as she processed everything Matt had just said. How long had he been planning this?

"You want to stay here? With me?"

"Yes, please. I can go back to my parents' house, or even the blue cottage, but I'd rather stay with you."

"I'd love you to stay with me." The words flew out of Rosie's mouth before she even had the chance to consider the matter.

"Thank you. I have to clear out my London apartment soon but I thought perhaps we could go together? See your family while we're there."

"That would be lovely." It flattered Rosie that he had considered her in his plans. It would also be nice to get a glimpse of what Matt's life in London looked like before it was all boxed up.

"Then it's all set. I'm moving back." There was lots to discuss, and Matt would need to consider what he would do for a job. It could all wait until tomorrow. Tonight was a night of celebrating and toasting to their future.

CHAPTER FORTY SEVEN

The new year brought with it lots of changes. A few days into the new year, Matt and Rosie travelled down to London to pack up Matt's flat. It had shocked Rosie to discover how modern and minimalist Matt's flat was. He had told her he wanted everything to be brand new, with no memories attached. The exact opposite of Rosie's taste. Since meeting her, he had embraced his memories and the past. It no longer seemed so scary. They had boxed up some items to take back to Rosie's, and they had sent the rest back to his parents' home for them to sort through in the future. Matt was selling his flat in London. He was going to use the proceeds to update his parents' home and let it out, alongside the blue cottage.

Despite his tumultuous upbringing, he didn't feel ready to sell the home he grew up in. He was planning on doing some freelance work and hoped it would be enough to live on. The future was unsure, but they were going to do their best to be happy together.

With the shop open again, Rosie was busy. Today she was making the final touches to Joyce's dress, ready for her Valentine's Day vow renewal. The bodice had needed a few touch-ups. Meanwhile, Rosie had transformed the skirt into something truly beautiful. As promised, Rosie had kept the original skirt. She had sourced some original 1930s lace to layer the skirt with. Whilst the original skirt was slim fitting, Rosie had cut the lace in an A-line to flatter Joyce. It was truly stunning and Rosie felt she had done the dress justice. Joyce was due any moment for her last fitting and if all was well, she would take the dress home with her.

Rosie had laid out drinks and snacks. She wanted this to be a truly magical moment for Joyce and her family. It would be a memory they would treasure forever.

"Hello, dear." Joyce greeted her with a peck on the cheek as she walked through the shop's door. The woman was glowing with excitement.

"Joyce, hello. How are you?" Rosie ushered everyone into the shop.

"Stressed. Things are so much more complicated these days. My first wedding wasn't half as difficult as this renewal." Joyce sighed. Despite her complaints, the smile hadn't left her face.

"I'm sorry to hear that. Hopefully, seeing your dress will relieve some of the stress." The pressure was on for Rosie to have got everything right.

"Yes, come on then. I'm not getting any younger."

Rosie showed Joyce's daughters and granddaughters over to some seats where the drinks and snacks were. She told them to help themselves and then whisked Joyce off to get changed.

Rosie had left the dress zipped up in a bag in the changing room.

"Are you happy with it?" Joyce asked. For the first time, Rosie could see some trepidation on the woman's face.

"It's beautiful. I'm sure you're going to love it." Rosie was honest.

"Come on then. Let's see it." Joyce clasped her hands together and Rosie unzipped the bag. She heard a gasp emerge from Joyce as she pulled the dress from its bag.

"Oh. It's even more beautiful than it was when I got married in it." Tears filled the woman's eyes.

"You're happy with it?"

"It's beyond anything I could have imagined."

Rosie helped Joyce into the dress. It fitted perfectly. As Joyce turned to see herself in the mirror, Rosie saw her face light up at her reflection.

"I feel seventy years younger. Thank you, Rosie. Nothing else matters. I cannot wait to stand beside my Ron in this dress and tell him how much I still love him."

Rosie had to wipe a tear from her own eyes. It was beautiful to see a love so pure after all these years. They went outside to show Joyce's family the dress. By the time they had finished, there was not a dry eye in the shop. It excited Rosie to know that Joyce would get to relive one of the most special days of her life.

"Have a lovely time, Joyce. Pop in for a cup of tea and show me the pictures soon." Rosie hugged everybody goodbye and waved them off. Hours of work and research had gone into Joyce's dress, but it was so worth it. To know that Joyce would walk back down the aisle to the love of her life wearing her original wedding dress filled Rosie's heart with joy. She was an old romantic at heart.

"How did the dress fitting go?" Matt asked as he walked through the shop door. He had spent the morning meeting with a builder at his parents' home. It worried Rosie that it was too soon for him to be changing the home he grew up in. However, he promised her he was ready. They were both moving forward with their lives and leaving their pain in the past.

"It was perfect." Rosie smiled dreamily.

"I love you, Rosie." Matt wrapped his arms around her and swung her round.

"I love you." She beamed back at him. Everything she had been through the last couple of years was worth it. Without the pain and upheaval, she wouldn't be here standing in her shop with Matt by her side.

The End

The Cornish Vintage Jewellery Shop

CHAPTER ONE

The door wouldn't open. Belle braced her shoulder against it and pushed with all her strength. Hinges groaned, and the door inched open. The bottom scraped against the floor and a high-pitched screech resounded around the shop. Belle breathed in and a musty smell assaulted her senses. She screwed up her nose and left the door ajar to allow the salty sea air to filter in. She took another step into the shop, ignoring the echoes of memories surrounding her.

"How does it look?" her father, Louis, asked.

"It looks like nobody's stepped inside for ten years," Belle replied. She flipped the camera on her phone so Louis could see for himself.

"It's how we left it," Louis said. His French accent thickened, and he cleared his throat.

"Just with a few inches of dust," Belle said, trying to lighten the mood.

"Yes, well, that can be cleaned. When's the builder coming?"

Belle checked her watch. "He's late. Should have been here five minutes ago."

"That's Cornish time for you."

"It's like that in France, too."

Louis let out a harrumph. "I have to leave for an auction. I'll speak to you tonight about what the builder says. Au revoir, ma chérie."

Belle said her goodbyes and hung up. The shop was eerily quiet. Outside, the sun shone brightly in the sky as eager tourists milled around with cups of takeaway coffee. Seagulls lurked at every corner, waiting to swoop down and steal flaky pasties from unsuspecting hands. The water was a hive of activity as skippers bustled around on boats, readying them for their daily outings. It was like the calm before the storm as the little harbour prepared for the daily influx of visitors.

The builder was now ten minutes late and the stuffy air inside the shop felt as though it was becoming thicker with every breath. Belle opened the windows and winced as a chunk of paint came away. It had been ten years since she was last inside the shop. She'd been fourteen years old and life had looked very different. Then everything changed after that phone call. Belle could remember the day as though it were yesterday. She'd finished school and walked to her father's antique shop on the harbour. It was a dismal November day, and the weather was horrendous. Belle was soaked through from the rain and windswept from the gale-force winds. Her father had ushered her into the backroom before she could drip on any of his priceless antiques.

She had sat in his office, warming her hands by

the electric heater, when the phone trilled. She knew better than to answer and waited for him. Belle had watched his face turn ashen as he listened.

"Hello?" a male voice with a Cornish twang called from the doorway, pulling Belle from her memories.

Belle jumped and turned to see a pair of green eyes staring at her. The light caught them as they glistened a deep Colombian emerald shade of green.

"Can I help you?" she asked. Her mouth was dry, and it was an effort to get the words out. His sandy hair stuck out in all directions from underneath his baseball cap. He wore a tatty t-shirt which was almost see-through in the bright sunlight and highlighted his toned body. Belle tore her gaze away.

"I'm Nick, your builder," he introduced himself and pointed to the door in an unsaid question.

"You're late," Belle said, motioning for him to come in.

"Sorry. My alarm didn't go off. You know how it is."

Belle frowned. She didn't know. "Does it happen often?"

"More than it should." He winked.

"Brilliant," she sarcastically bit back. "I'm Belle." She held out her hand.

"I was expecting you to be more French," he said and shook her hand. His grasp was firm.

"French?" She glanced down at their hands. He still had her hand clasped in his. At her look, he let go, and Belle took a step back.

"Your email address was French."

"Oh, of course. I've just moved back from France."

"That's a relief. I was worried you'd only speak French."

"My emails were in English." Belle's thoughts were becoming muddled and with it, she was moving away from the tangled emotions that had crept up on her.

"You could have been using a translator." Nick shrugged and looked around the shop.

"I don't speak French."

"Really?"

"Really."

"Nor do I. All I know is Voulez-vous coucher—"

"I think we all know that one," Belle interrupted. A blush rose on her cheeks and she cleared her throat. "Shall we have a look around? I'm only looking for a quote at the moment."

"You won't get anyone else. It's the busiest time of the year. Everyone's getting their building work finished before the season starts. Lucky for you, I'm free."

"Why are you free when everyone else is busy?" Belle raised her eyebrow. His business card had been pinned to the Padstow-on-Sea's community noticeboard. She'd expected a middle-aged man with experience to turn up, not a muscular, Cornish, Ken doll.

"I've just started. You're my first customer. Congratulations." He smiled. His face lit up and a cheeky glint danced in his eyes.

"You've just started?" she enunciated each word. However good-looking he was, it was his experience she was interested in.

"Yep. Lucky you, eh? Right, let's have a look around." He rubbed his hands together before he pulled a pencil from behind his ear and a tatty notepad from the back pocket of his jeans. It was falling apart. "I'll take some notes on my phone instead."

Belle went to take a deep breath but stopped as she saw the dust particles floating through the air. "There's nobody else available," she muttered under her breath and followed him through to the office.

Nick wandered around and made notes.

"So, what's the verdict?" she asked.

"It's structurally sound," he said, nodding as he looked up towards the ceiling.

"I know that. I had a survey." Belle's father had insisted on having a structural survey before he signed the shop over to her.

"What do you want doing?" His gaze bore into hers and a flush rushed across Belle's cheeks.

"The place needs re-plastering and then decorating. The kitchen and bathroom look as though they'd be fine after a good scrub. I'll need some new shelves and cabinets. The office needs painting. It's got all the safes in there and I want to keep them."

Nick raised his eyebrows at her. "What kind of shop are you opening?"

"Vintage jewellery."

He let out a low whistle. "You should probably get those safes serviced."

"Is that a thing?" Belle's brow furrowed. Something else to add to her endless list of things to do.

"No idea. Should be though. Maybe it's a service I should offer." He winked at her again, and Belle ignored the way it made her stomach flutter.

She decided not to point out the pitfalls in his plan. "The shop needs a complete refit," she said, drawing his attention back to the matter at hand. "The shelving is all dated and damp. I think it's best if we rip it out and replace it."

"Sounds good. What did you want to replace it with?"

Belle pulled out her phone and brought up her Pinterest app, which was filled with interior inspiration. She didn't know exactly what she wanted, although she had gathered a handful of pictures.

"I could use reclaimed wood to make the shelving units and whitewash them to give them the shabby-chic-meets-nautical style you're going for," Nick said. He held Belle's phone and was studying the picture.

Belle blinked. "You can do that?"

"Woodwork is my speciality. There's not enough demand for it around here, so I've diversified into building work." He handed her back the phone.

"Sounds smart," Belle commented.

"What about security?" asked Nick.

"I've got the safes out the back and I'll look into some CCTV."

"I've got a friend who can do that and he can install a panic button under the till. I'll give him a call."

"Nick, I'm not sure I can afford it."

"He owes me a favour."

"I couldn't ask that."

"I'll sort it," he promised. "So, when do you want me to start?"

"Shouldn't you send me a quote first?" Belle raised her brows.

"I can, but you want to snap me up before someone else does." He smirked, and the edges of Belle's lips quirked upwards. She stifled the smile before he could see it.

"I suppose you've got me backed into a corner, but I expect a first-customer discount."

"Sounds fair."

"So, when can you start?"

"Tomorrow?"

"Don't you need to get permits for skip hire and stuff like that?" Belle didn't know much about building work, but she suspected the quaint town of Padstow-on-Sea wouldn't appreciate a skip filled with rotting wood on their picturesque seafront.

"I'll fill my van and take it to the skip at the yard."

"Tomorrow sounds good," Belle agreed.

"Perfect. We'll get you open before the end of the season. The winter months can be tough."

"Thanks."

"See you tomorrow, Belle." He waved and Belle's stare fixed on him as he left, already missing how he made her smile.

Alone, Belle glanced around the shop. She should start clearing things to make it easier for Nick in the morning, but being here sent a chill down her spine. It was an empty shell of the once bustling Louis's Emporium. Her father's antiques had left Cornwall with them, packed into the back of a hire van. After the death of Belle's mother, Cornwall lost its charm and Louis took Belle home to France. They hadn't been back since.

The shop's beating heart had stopped that day and never started again. Once settled in France, Louis started buying and selling antiques, and Belle spent her spare time working with him. She'd never really settled into their new life. Her poor grasp of the language kept her on the outskirts of the community and her father's successful business afforded a tutor for her, which meant outside of their bubble she had very little contact with children her age. Despite it all, Belle was never lonely. How could she be when she was always surrounded by antiques and the memories they held?

Unable to bear the emptiness any longer, Belle grabbed her keys and locked up. Outside, the sun was high in the sky and the sound of chatter drowned out the gentle crashing of the sea. Belle wound her way through the crowds of tourists to The Little Coffee Shop by the Sea on the opposite side of the harbour. The exterior was painted black with its name in gold swirls above the door. A little brass bell rang out as the door opened. Inside, the dark interior was complemented by the big windows and their sea view. Rich coffee beans and sweet cakes filled the air, and Belle's stomach rumbled. She'd been too nervous to have any breakfast.

"Can I help you?" asked the woman behind the counter. Her hair framed her face in an explosion of corkscrew curls as dark as a starless night in winter. She wore silver rings on both hands, each with intricate detailing on the bands.

"Could I have a cappuccino and a slice of that chocolate cake, please? To take away." Belle pointed to the decadent dark chocolate sponge cake, covered in a tempered ganache with fresh, vibrant berries piled atop. She deserved an indulgent treat after stepping back into the shop after ten years.

"Good choice. I'm Jada, by the way. Owner of this delightful coffee shop and baker of these delicious desserts."

"Lovely to meet you, Jada." Belle smiled timidly at the woman.

"This is usually the part where you'd introduce yourself." Jada shot her a wink.

"Sorry, I'm out of practice meeting new people." Not that she'd ever been in practice. Her experience with meeting new people was limited to auctions where they all had a passion in common. "I'm Belle. I've taken over the old antique shop." She glossed over the fact it had once been her father's.

"Lovely to meet you, Belle. It'll be nice to have another young female business owner around. Give me a shout if you need anything."

"Thanks, Jada. I doubt I'll be able to stay away from your café for very long." Belle's eyes lingered on the other goodies on display as Jada made her cappuccino.

"I've recently bought a recipe book from an amazing patisserie chef, Carrie Mackenzie, and I need someone to try my creations."

"I'm your girl." Belle relaxed in the woman's presence.

"Perfect. See you soon, Belle." Jada handed her the coffee and a large slice of cake nestled inside a takeaway box.

"Bye," Belle called. "I'm sure you'll be seeing a lot of me."

It was a short walk home, although it was made longer by the tourists milling around and stopping to take pictures down the quaint cobbled streets. Belle had to move someone off her doorstep. Her little cottage had no front garden and tourists could come straight up to her door. She breathed a sigh of relief once she'd closed the door behind her. The cottage was the one place Belle truly felt at home.

She'd grown up there with her parents, and it was where her happiest memories lived. Belle set her coffee down on the worktop and got some cutlery for her cake. The forks were all small and Belle suspected they were meant for children. Over the last ten years, Louis had rented out the cottage and an array of other people's belongings had been left behind. Belle was thankful for it since her budget hadn't stretched to furnishing somewhere. She'd made a few changes to make it feel like home. Belle had found a nautical blue and white striped rug in a charity shop, which she'd put down on the bare wood floors in her bedroom. The existing furniture was sparse, so she'd ended up with a jumble of cheap charity shop finds and expensive antiques. As a moving-in gift, her father had sent her a catalogue for an auction and told her to let him know what she needed. Belle had wanted to circle everything but had settled for an antique oak console table, a Georgian writing bureau, and an antique Rococo walnut bed frame. Her father had bought it all and had it shipped straight to her. He'd also picked up an old chair with worn blue upholstery, a collection of mismatched plant pots, and a hatstand. It was an odd collection, yet somehow, Belle had thrown it all together, and it worked.

At the back of the cottage was a small courtyard. It was a combination of weed-choked flower beds around the perimeter and an overgrown hedge. With a little time and effort, it could be pretty. For now, Belle was happy to have some outside space to herself. She sat on the bench and put her coffee beside her. The cake was rich and delicious as she sat with the sun shining on her. In the silence, she allowed her mind to wander over the day. Going into the shop had stirred up a plethora of emotions and memories that Belle would rather have forgotten about. Nick's appearance had silenced her mind and she couldn't help the way he'd made her smile. She was looking forward to working with him. Despite his infuriating cheeky charm, he would be the perfect distraction to her past.

Belle pulled her phone out to find an email from Nick. She was pleasantly surprised by his quote. He'd included a five per cent discount for being his first customer. The email ended with a jaunty 'see you tomorrow' followed by a thumbs-up emoji. She smiled and emailed back, reminding him to be on time.

Thank you for reading!

If you have time to leave a review on Amazon or Goodreads I would be incredibly grateful.

You can follow me on Amazon,
Twitter, or Instagram.
Sign up to my newsletter at
www.elizabethhollandauthor.com

Afterword

Thank you for escaping to Ives-On-Sea with me. Whilst Ives-On-Sea is based on many picturesque Cornish villages, it is fictional. Rosie's new home is a patchwork of Cornish villages I've visited.

I hope you enjoyed your stay in Cornwall

xxx

A Merry Christmas at the Castle

With Christmas fast approaching, Eve Merry loses her job and her boyfriend on the same day. She needs a miracle to put her life back on track. With nothing to lose, Eve jumps on the train to Scotland. However, she soon realises cooking in a castle is demanding - especially when the chef has lied on her CV! With a brooding Scotsman to contend with, this Christmas seems like it's going to be one to forget.

Turn the page to read the first chapter…

CHAPTER ONE

"Eve, I need to talk to you," Carlo's voice called from the other side of the restaurant.

Eve rolled her eyes. She'd just walked through the door. A glance at her watch told her she wasn't due to start work for another half an hour, and already her manager wanted to speak to her.

"I'll be right there," she called back. Eve dropped her bags on the closest table, careful to avoid the small fake pine trees wrapped in cheap tinsel. It was Carlo's budget attempt at making the backstreet Italian restaurant look Christmassy. After sweeping her hair back into a low bun, Eve walked through the kitchen to Carlo's office. When she applied for the job at Carlo's Calzones, Eve had expected the role to involve cooking. Instead, she was a glorified waitress who stepped in when the chef was ill. Three years studying Food Science at Reading University and this was all she'd amounted to.

"Morning, Eve." Eric, the chef, called to her as

she walked past. He had swapped his chef's hat for a red velvet Father Christmas one. Eve stopped herself from rolling her eyes again.

The kitchen was already hot and stuffy, despite it only being ten in the morning. *I Wish it Could be Christmas Everyday* blared out from the radio and Eve fought the urge to throw it out of the front door and into the Thames. Since the first of December, Eric had tuned the radio into Christmas FM and festive tunes had echoed around the kitchen.

"Morning, Eric." Eve waved but didn't stop to talk.

"Eve, come in." Carlo was sitting behind his desk in the office.

There was no seat for her and so Eve stood in front of the desk, clasping her hands in front of her as she waited for Carlo to speak. It wasn't unusual for him to call staff into the office. He had a very particular way of running the restaurant and liked everyone to know he was in charge. Even if that meant he did very little himself.

"I'm afraid I have to let you go." He took a drag from the vape he held in his hand. Eve winced as the sickly sweetness filled the air. She'd told him repeatedly that he shouldn't be vaping inside the premises.

"Let me go?" she gasped out.

"Yes. The last couple of years have been financially challenging and I've had to make cuts." He shrugged, refusing to meet her eye.

"It's three weeks before Christmas and you're

firing me?" Eve raised her voice. She'd worked for Carlo since graduating from university five years ago.

"I'm sorry, Eve."

Without uttering another word, Eve stalked out of the office, back into the restaurant, and picked up her bags. This time she swung them at the stupid faux Christmas tree, knocking it onto the ground. She walked out of the restaurant and onto the icy street. Eve bit her lip to stop tears forming in her eyes. It would do no good to cry. She went to pull her phone from her pocket, wanting to call her boyfriend. His comforting voice would help. Her fingers wrapped around the phone just as it started vibrating. It was Rihanna, her neighbour and best friend.

"Hi Rhi," Eve answered. She took in a deep breath of the icy London air to stop her voice from wobbling.

"Michael's moving his stuff out of your flat."

The words echoed around Eve's brain as she tried to make sense of them. Moving his stuff out of the flat? The flat they shared together? Rhi must have been wrong. Michael would be at work by now. Eve had waved him off earlier that morning, kissing him goodbye, and wishing him a good day.

"I'm coming," she replied and put the phone down before Rhi could say anything more. It would all be a silly mistake and they'd laugh about it over a glass of wine and a takeaway tonight. The sickening feeling in her stomach knew the truth.

The tube journey back to her flat in Stratford felt never-ending. Eve stared out the window, watching as they passed each station. Her mind was threatening to cave in, but she was forcing herself to keep going. Just a few more steps to her building. She took the lift to the fifth floor, where the door to her flat was wide open.

"Michael?" she called. Her legs shook as she slowly entered the almost-empty flat.

"Eve, what are you doing here?" Michael whirled around to face her. His eyes were open wide.

"What are you doing?" Eve asked, ignoring his question.

"I thought it would be easier this way." He shrugged.

"What would be easier?" she asked.

"Leaving you."

Eve stood open-mouthed, not knowing what to say.

"I think it's best if I go." He pointed towards the door and Eve nodded, unable to get any words out. Without a goodbye or a last hug, Michael walked out of the door.

"Eve?" Rhi was standing in the doorway peering in at the desolate flat. Most of the furniture had been Michael's.

"He's gone." Eve felt a sob rising in her throat.

"Oh, Eve. I'm so sorry." Her friend walked over and wrapped her arms around her.

"I lost my job, too." Eve needed to tell someone.

"Come back to mine. I'll make you a cup of tea."

Eve allowed herself to be guided into Rhi's flat across the hallway. She propped herself up against the kitchen cupboards whilst Rhi bustled around making tea.

"What happened?" Rhi asked.

"Carlo's struggling financially, so he had to let me go." Eve's voice sounded detached.

"What an ass." Rhi handed Eve a strong mug of tea and they made their way into the living room. "Hold on a minute. I saw something on Facebook this morning." Rhi grabbed her laptop from the coffee table and pulled up her internet history. "Here. Look!" She flung the laptop into Eve's lap.

Eve squinted at the screen, trying to read the tiny writing. It was an advert for a private chef.

"I'm not a chef." Eve went to hand the laptop back, but Rhi wouldn't accept it.

"No, but you can cook. We just need to tweak your CV."

Eve didn't have the energy to argue, and so, an hour later, Rhi had 'polished' Eve's CV for her and emailed it off with a cover letter.

"I can't believe you sent it." Eve shook her head and took a sip of the coffee she'd made while Rhi was drafting the letter.

"It's only two weeks' work. Do you want to spend Christmas alone? Or you could get this job and spend a wonderful Christmas up in the Scottish Highlands."

"The Scottish Highlands?" screeched Eve.

"Yes, didn't you read the advert?" Rhi chuckled.

"Rhi, I didn't think you were serious when you first showed it to me!"

"Oh." At least Rhi had the good nature to look a little guilty before a huge grin spread across her face. "You're going to Scotland!"

"I haven't got the job!" Eve argued.

"Oh, but you will. Your CV is very impressive."

"What do you mean?" Eve narrowed her eyes. She should have read it before she allowed Rhi to hit send.

"I embellished your role at Carlo's." Rhi shrugged.

"Rhi, what do you mean you embellished my role at Carlo's?" Eve spoke slowly, enunciating each word.

"I just tweaked your role at Carlo's slightly and possibly didn't mention that his restaurant is a backstreet Italian." Rhi shrugged and poured a handful of skittles into her mouth.

"Rhi," Eve grumbled. "Tell me exactly what you put on my CV."

"I said you were the head chef at an up-and-coming London restaurant which specialised in adding a modern twist to classic cuisine."

"Oh, Rhi." Eve hid her face in her hands. "Maybe we should email them and retract my application." Eve reached for the laptop.

"Absolutely not. I will not allow you to spend

the festive period sitting in that flat feeling sorry for yourself."

"I'm okay. If I'm honest, I'm more upset about losing my job than losing Michael." Eve had been thinking while Rhi was lying on her job application. She and Michael had been drifting apart for a while now, but neither of them had wanted to confront it.

"I never thought you two suited each other," confessed Rhi.

"I know. It was just easy with him."

"Anyway, enough about Michael. We should go shopping. It's going to be freezing in Scotland at this time of year."

"I've not even got the job yet. Besides, I can't afford to go shopping. I've got no income and I'll have to cover Michael's half of the rent." Reality was dawning on Eve and she wanted to bury her head in the ground. Maybe escaping to Scotland was a good idea.

"Give your notice on the flat and move in with me. I've got a spare bedroom." Rhi's tone made it clear this was an instruction and not a suggestion.

"That would be perfect. Thank you, Rhi." As much as Eve treasured her independence and having her own space, she could hardly afford her half of the rent, let alone Michael's.

"Shall we email the agents now to let them know?" Rhi grabbed for the laptop again, and Eve agreed before she could change her mind and allow her pride to resurface.

"Oh look, you've got an email." Rhi had just

hit send on the email to the letting agent. "It's from the job we applied to."

"Rhi, I think we should email them and retract my application. My CV is a lie and I can't cook for someone. My cooking isn't good enough."

"I think it might be too late to retract it," Rhi whispered, squinting at the screen.

"What do you mean?" Eve asked. It surprised her to find excitement bubbling away in the pit of her stomach.

"They want you to call them to arrange your transport. Oh my gosh, you got the job!"

Eve stared blankly at the screen in front of her. This morning she'd woken up ready for another day at work. With Christmas three weeks away, she had planned to nip out to the shops between lunch and dinner service to buy Michael's Christmas present. At least she hadn't wasted her money on a pointless gift. She glanced at the clock on Rhi's laptop. It was midday. Usually, she'd be flitting from table-to-table taking orders and bringing food out to hungry patrons. Instead, she was single and sitting in Rhi's flat, contemplating taking a job in the Scottish Highlands.

"Life can change in a matter of minutes," Eve muttered. She was still staring at the screen.

"Exactly. Do something a little crazy and accept this job. Eve, you're an amazing cook. It's just two weeks cooking for a posh family."

"Rhi, I can't do this. I've only ever cooked for friends and family. You can hardly call making a few pizzas and pasta dishes at Carlo's cooking."

"Come on, Eve! Your food is amazing. Besides, what's the worst that could happen?"

"I could make a mess of it and be forever blacklisted in the food industry."

"You're so dramatic. You'll be cooking for a family over Christmas. It'll just be lots of roast dinners and various cold meats."

"But I've lied, Rhi! Well, you've lied for me. They'll realise I can't cook and throw me out."

"But you can cook! Eve, remember last Christmas when my oven broke? Michael was away visiting his family so you were spending Christmas Day alone. Without a second thought, you took all my ingredients and told me to enjoy the morning with my parents and you'd bring lunch over at midday. We all loved your food, Eve. I'm not just saying this because you're my best friend. You're an amazing cook and I know you can do this!"

Eve thought about it. She was no stranger to throwing together last-minute meals, but that didn't mean they were restaurant quality. But perhaps Rhi had a point. What was the worst that could happen? After all, she was already unemployed. Without allowing herself another second to think, Eve grabbed her mobile from the table and dialled the number of the agency that was arranging the job.

"Hello, *Peace, Joy and Love Catering Company*. How may I help you?" The sound of a bored voice floated down the phone.

"Hello, It's Eve Merry. I applied for a role and I just received an email asking me to contact you to arrange transport."

"Oh, yes. Let me just pull up the information." The woman's tone remained flat. Eve could hardly believe she was making such an enormous change so close to Christmas, and yet this woman was acting as though it was nothing. "Here we go. The client has offered to pay for transport, so we can book you on a train on Friday. It'll be an overnight journey. You'll arrive Saturday lunchtime, staff will settle you in, and then you'll start work on Monday."

Eve reached out for a pen and paper. Thankfully, Rhi's job as a freelance writer meant there was an abundance of notepads and pens scattered throughout her flat. The conversation only lasted ten minutes and by the time Eve put the phone down, they had booked her on the Caledonian Sleeper to Fort William. Once she disembarked in Fort William, a driver would meet her and take her to The McLeod's Castle. She had almost choked on air at the mention of a castle. However, her nerves settled when the woman told her there would only be a party of seven in residence. Eve had covered Eric a handful of times so a party of seven should be easy.

Eve took a deep breath as she put the phone down. "I'm leaving on Friday," she whispered.

"Oh, my!" gasped Rhi.

"I can't believe I've said yes to this."

"I can. Carlo's Calzones was never enough for you, Eve. This is just the beginning for you.

Perhaps this agency will keep you on. You could spend summer sailing around St-Tropez cooking on a luxury yacht!"

They were getting carried away, but Eve wondered whether it would be a possibility. She was single and unemployed, there was absolutely nothing stopping her from travelling the world and cooking. At eighteen, when she started university, Eve had big plans to cook on every continent. However, life had got a little too real when she graduated and had to find a job. It was a field where experience was everything and Eve had spent three years studying, when it seemed everybody else in the industry had spent three years working. It had felt like an answer to all her problems when Carlo offered her the job of waitressing and asked if she would be open to being trained up as cover for when Eric was off.

"Are you listening to me?" Rhi interrupted her thoughts.

"Sorry. What were you saying?"

"We need to pack!" Rhi stood up, grabbing Eve's keys from the coffee table.

"Rhi, it's only Monday." Eve laughed. She'd be in the kitchen for the entirety of her stay, so she wouldn't need to bring much with her. The agency had told her chef whites would be available for her at the property. She would work each day, but with breaks outside of mealtimes, so Eve only needed a few pairs of jeans and jumpers.

Rhi stood with her arms crossed and her

steely gaze focused on Eve. "I'm not taking no for an answer."

Reluctantly, Eve followed Rhi back into her flat. She was shocked to discover Michael had even taken the chest of drawers, leaving all of her clothes on the mattress. He had bought the bed frame and so there was just a mattress left in the middle of the floor.

"He must have been planning this for ages," Rhi commented, looking around at the sparse flat.

"I know." Eve gulped. She'd been happily trundling on with life. Meanwhile, Michael was planning to leave. It was an eye-opener for her. She'd got too comfortable, and it was time for a change. Twenty-six was far too young to settle.

"Come on, let's move your stuff into my spare room. There's no point in delaying." Rhi grabbed Eve's suitcase and started piling her clothes into it. It didn't take long and the entirety of Eve's clothes fit in one case. She spent most of her life in chef whites or her waitressing uniform and had little time for clothes.

"I might have to lend you a few pieces," commented Rhi. It horrified her to see just how little Eve owned. Eve cringed at the idea. Their tastes were very different. Rhi was confident and had enviable curves. Eve was the polar opposite. She decided not to argue. So long as everything fit inside her suitcase, she didn't mind what Rhi put inside it. She glanced in the only mirror Michael had left behind and realised she didn't look like someone whose boyfriend had dumped them on the same day they'd lost their job. Instead, she looked like she was excited about the future. There was a sparkle back in her eyes. Food had saved her once before. It could do it again.

"Do you not own any makeup?" The horrified voice of Rhi echoed in the bathroom. Eve laughed and rolled her eyes. She owed a lot to her friend. Without her, she'd be sitting on the rug in the living room eating a gallon of ice cream, and contemplating how to pay the rent.

Printed in Great Britain
by Amazon

42983819R00223